SPIDER WOMAN

In the dark, Doc Savage had captured a woman.

One hand reached for the woman's throat. With the thumb of the other, he attempted to locate her earlobe, which would enable his fingers to find the nerve center by which he could render her unconscious.

But she was a clawing wildcat in his arms, and so he thought the trouble he was having was due to her frantic flouncing. Then, as the blackness before his eyes overtook his brain, he realized the surprising truth.

The mystery woman had no left earlobe!

Then her teeth were at his own ear, and there was a hissing that made him think of an angry cat, and the gas entered his nose, his lungs, everything.

Savage's last hollow thought was: *If this is the Red Widow, God have mercy on my soul.*

Coming soon:

THE WHISTLING WRAITH

Read the special preview in the back of this book and an Afterword written by Will Murray.

The New Adventures of Doc Savage
Ask your bookseller for the books you have missed.

ESCAPE FROM LOKI by Philip José Farmer
PYTHON ISLE
WHITE EYES
THE FRIGHTENED FISH
THE JADE OGRE
FLIGHT INTO FEAR

(*Don't miss another original Doc Savage adventure*, THE WHISTLING WRAITH, *coming in July 1993*)

FLIGHT
INTO FEAR

by Kenneth Robeson

BANTAM BOOKS
NEW YORK · TORONTO · LONDON · SYDNEY · AUCKLAND

FLIGHT INTO FEAR

A Bantam Spectra Book / March 1993

*Doc Savage is a registered trademark of Condé Nast
Publications, Inc. Registered in U.S. Patent and Trademark
Office and elsewhere.*

Interior art by Joe DeVito.

ISBN 0-553-29552-7

Published simultaneously in the United States and Canada

*Bantam Books are published by Bantam Books, a division of Bantam
Doubleday Dell Publishing Group, Inc. Its trademark, consisting of the
words "Bantam Books" and the portrayal of a rooster, is Registered in
U.S. Patent and Trademark Office and in other countries. Marca
Registrada. Bantam Books, 666 Fifth Avenue, New York, New York
10103.*

PRINTED IN THE UNITED STATES OF AMERICA

OPM   0 9 8 7 6 5 4 3 2 1

DOC

Unique among men is Doc Savage, man of amazing abilities, and of but one goal in life—to do good. His bronzed features, his flake-gold eyes, are symbols of power and mercy. There is strength unknown in the mighty thews of his body, and knowledge unfathomable in the brain of this remarkable man. Where others are experts in one line, he is a superman in many. Doc—Clark Savage, Jr.—was raised from infancy for his work of going from one end of the world to the other, righting wrongs, helping the underdog, and liberating the innocent.

HAM

Ham Brooks, whose mind, whetted by careful legal training, was clever enough to save a whole division in the war, was not able to overcome the weighty evidence piled up against him in a case of stealing hams from the commissary. Monk still reminds Ham of that incident, which is about the only thing that can upset the impeccable, waspish Theodore Marley Brooks, and his great legal mind. Ham's wit is as sharp as the point of the sword cane he invariably carries.

MONK

Monk, whose looks are described by his nickname, is Andrew
Blodgett Mayfair. He's the world's foremost chemist, super-
seded only by Doc, whose knowledge is greater than any of his
companions. Monk has a fortune in his own name: could make a
dozen fortunes by sticking to his profession. But as an aide of
Doc, he too gives his life so that innocent victims may not suffer,
and would rather fight than eat.

RENNY

Renny, or Colonel John Renwick, is a giant of a man who towers four inches over six feet. He weighs fully two hundred and fifty. His face is severe, his mouth thin and grim, and compressed tightly as though he is just finishing a disapproving *"tsk! tsk!"* sound. Altogether, his features have a puritanical look.

But despite his odd looks, Renny is noted for his engineering accomplishments. His favorite act is to slam his great fists—bony monstrosities—through the solid panel of a heavy door. It is his boast that there is no wooden panel which he cannot destroy with his huge hamlike hands.

LONG TOM

Long Tom—Thomas J. Roberts—known as the wizard of the juice—is the electrical expert of Doc Savage's band of intrepid fighters. Small in stature, his brain holds an enormous amount of learning. It is he who furnishes the electrical equipment and radio devices that have done much to further the success of Doc Savage's triumphs over his enemies—men who wish to further their own ends at the expense and suffering of mankind.

JOHNNY

Johnny—William Harper Littlejohn, one of the world's greatest ar-
chaeologists—is the man who assists *Doc Savage* when knowledge
of ancient countries and ruins is an absolute essential to the success
of any expedition undertaken. Johnny is frail-looking, but underneath
his gaunt appearance burns a strength and fire unbelievable—a
strength equal to that of the strongest man. No hardship is too much
for Johnny to endure: his long, lanky frame is capable of assimilat-
ing much punishment.

PAT

Patricia Savage, better known as Pat, is the beautiful and talented cousin of Doc Savage, and is well known to the bronze man's aides, having accompanied them on several of their trips.

Trying to keep Pat from coming along on these expeditions and subjecting herself to dangers that might result in her death has long been Doc's aim—but all to no avail. For Pat, like the other members of Doc's little band, is instilled with the love of adventure.

Contents

I

DEATH SENTENCE

By a piece of luck he found a tool for the ambush. His toe kicked against it in the gloomy street. Instinctively knowing it would do, he stopped and picked it up. It was a perfect thing for dealing with the trouble-making possibilities of an armed woman. An iron scrap two feet long and an inch through. Heavy. An iron rod pitted with rust, foul with soil.

Perhaps it had just fallen off a truck; off a junk truck or off one of the endless truckloads of debris from the tenements they were still demolishing to make room for more of the great, simple buildings they were perpetually constructing for the U.N. The tall, pure-looking buildings of pale stone and bluish glass for the United Nations, which he feared might be only premature containers for dreams— although he sincerely hoped they wouldn't be.

He put himself in ambush for her at once. There was a fork in the path, a Y of tunnel in thick shrubbery, darkness. It was very dark now. There was no moon, a fact whose irony was not lost on him. All they had told him when he had set out on the long trail that had brought him to this point was that it was very important and it involved some person or thing they called Moonwinx.

The right-hand fork would be altogether the more inviting to a woman, he decided. It had a flower border. It was drenched with the odor of fall-blooming asters and mums.

Everything in his experience told him that women invariably choose the inviting things, so he took his ambush on the right-hand fork. Not that his experience with women was great. To the contrary.

Women never fail to surprise me, he thought ruefully. *Never.*

Cold air touched his face. He had a handsome, regular face. But he was not wearing it now. The face he wore was wide and brutal, and as unlike his own as could be imagined. It was a devil face. Huge, almost repulsive. The air seemed clammy from the breath of all the people in the great city and faintly rancid from the odors of dinners cooked hours before. The air had a chill, dead-animal quality remindful of the atmosphere hanging over a corpse.

He grimaced and buried his chin against the turned-up collar of his neat lightweight topcoat. He smelled deeply of the crisp new store-bought aroma of the dark cloth. He drew this newness into his lungs, savoring it. There were no new things in the terrible places he had spent the recent past. It was not as tasteful a style as he would have preferred. His mission did not permit him to indulge in good taste spectacular, and attract the wrong kind of attention. Hence the plain style of dress.

The topcoat helped him to look like a dressed-up laborer sauntering in Central Park. A youngish laborer with a stupid face and an overabundance of muscular strength. Not a spectacular type and not worth remembering. A dim-witted and brutal sort of fellow out for a night stroll. That was all.

He listened to the woman's shoes tapping the path, approaching.

He waited for her to turn into the right-hand path.

She turned left.

Left!

For a moment, he did not believe it. The *tap-tapping* of the woman's shoes went down the left-hand path. He had the impression of suddenly standing there in a world that was incomprehensible. The club hung useless in his hands; abruptly, it seemed to weigh as much as another man. It was of no use at all, the bludgeon was.

He lay the iron bludgeon on the grass. One did not hurry about New York City carrying such an object. Especially this close to midnight.

The loose feeling in his hands told him they were trembling slightly. He was surprised at the severity of his case of nerves. But this entire affair had been in the pipeline for too long. To have it exposed at this late hour could be fatal.

He began to run. He could hear her *tap-tapping* walk carrying her along at a surprising rate. He must get ahead of her again.

He found a place ridiculously soon. It was almost as good as the first ambush spot. He crouched in the leaves and waited, regretting the loss of the cast-aside bludgeon. He never carried weapons. It was a personal fetish not to do so. He sometimes had cause to regret this choice. If she carried a knife, or worse, a pistol, a length of iron pipe could be a handy thing, possibly a lifesaver—if his aim was true.

Presently, he had to make his stomach butterflies calm. *Am I this afraid of her?* he wondered.

Why not? She is a goblin, a devil in skirts. She is a virtueless, depraved, heartless, poisonous, unprincipled vampire. She destroys live bodies and spits into living souls.

His mud-colored eyes, like the comparison microscopes the ballistics people use, caught her approaching figure and checked it to be sure she was the one. No mistake there. She was the blonde who had been following him for almost two hours. He could tell by her walk. He had yet to see her face. She had become his shadow. She must be very efficient, to be given a job like this one. If she failed to find him again, it would go hard on her. They would not forgive her readily. They never do.

He watched her cross a place where a streetlamp made the moon-lost night a bit lighter. He could see now that she wore gloves; this pleased him. The gloves covered her fingernails. Women had a disconcerting way with fingernails in a man's eyes. He could see some sort of beads flash at her throat.

There was a lot of bounce in her figure. She had dyed her hair. She dangled a hat, a turban thing, in her hand as she walked. He could see that her hair was a garish reddish-blond mess, like a shepherd dog astride her shoulders. The real color of her hair was a raven black. He could take oath to that. If only he could see her face clearly.

He was appalled by the confident lack of haste with which she walked. She had trailed him into the park. She had lost him. But she was not excited about it, obviously.

Her self-sureness was horrifying. It was as if he was sure to be the victim, not she. He fought the feeling, drove it back, as she came to him.

She called, "Banner!"

He almost laughed. She had called him by the name she should have. It meant danger. Yet, had she used his right name, it would have meant that the months of preparation had been for naught. That his carefully crafted imposture had been penetrated. And death. It would certainly have meant his death. But if she did not know who he truly was, she might not be intent upon harming him. As Banner, his reputation was fierce. But the whole world knew who Doc Savage was.

Steeling himself, he let her approach.

As soon as she was within range, he got her throat in his strong hands.

She gave vent to a thick scream that sought volume and achieved only a kind of tangled ugliness.

It raked his nerves. He was not in the habit of manhandling women. He was not, in fact, accustomed to their nearness in any way, shape, or form. His life's work precluded such entanglements. He changed his hold, his fingers questing along the shiny beads banding her neck, seeking a certain cluster of nerves, intent upon squeezing the consciousness out of her wildly animated form.

His brain experienced a sudden explosion. Angry red sparks danced before his retinas. Her infernal handbag! She had whipped it around on the end of its strap and whacked him on the head. There must be a gun inside to make it so skull-jarring. It would be a gun, he knew. Never overlook a woman's handbag in a struggle, he reflected grimly.

His head bellowed at him. He had lost his place among the beads.

She brought a hand to her throat and clawed. A lot of good that would do her, he thought. She couldn't tear loose; there was no judo expert good enough to rip free of his expert hold. He had learned it many, many years ago, while pursuing his medical studies. All he had to do was locate the lobe of her left ear, and work his fingers toward the nerve center. . . .

The trouble was, he could not find it. In the absolute darkness, this frightened him almost as much as not being able to discern her features in the murk.

He was puzzled and surprised to realize she was crushing her beads. The shiny baubles that had looked so cheap; squeezing them until they burst. He thought he heard glass crush.

And now his nostrils filled with the reek of marrubium that came—violently minty—from the crushed beads.

The sudden odor of marrubium shocked him. It was like a nail driven with one blow into his skull between the eyes. For this perfume, this marrubium, was a sensory password. It was used as the sign of a friend. It was a membership token. It was one of the ways by which a member of the Moonwinx team identified a fellow worker.

His thinking screamed: *She can't be one of us! She's a she-spider born with the name Anna Gryahznyi. I can't be mistaken. I've spent too many hours listening to the recordings of her fiendish interrogation sessions, and her shrieking, devillike questions. And I've heard her sentence me to death.*

Yet the odor of marrubium was supposed to be the sign of a friend.

He thought: *But I just heard her voice. It was Anna Gryahznyi's voice. I know Anna Gryahznyi's voice as well as I know my cousin's. Just as I know that Anna Gryahznyi is as deadly as a black widow spider.*

He hesitated, uncertain whether or not to release her throat and hear her out.

While he hesitated, she gripped his wrists and jerked

his large hands off her throat. Uncertainty made him momentarily unresisting, despite his great strength.

She said, "You stupid devil-faced oaf!"

He was shocked terribly—her voice sounded completely American.

She fell back a step from him. Her hands fluttered, settled in front of her throat. The helpless-damsel posture was bizarre under the circumstances.

"Don't curse, Anna," he admonished.

"You brutal, murdering son of a—"

"Anna Gryahznyi," he cut in, irony twisting his tone. "Imagine Anna Gryahznyi cussing with that accent."

"What accent?" she asked, momentarily startled out of her rage.

"Walnut Street, in Kansas City, I believe," he said. And instantly regretted it. Banner would not have such encyclopedic recall of accents. Banner was an oaf.

"I'm not Anna Gryahznyi," she said sharply, the slip going past. "My accent is my own damn business."

Now he thought: *She may not be Anna, after all. Really, I can't tell. I might have imagined the sound of her voice when she called Banner's name.*

But it was hardly conceivable that he would fail to know her, know the one enemy whom he had so intensively studied because she had been personally selected as his executioner.

She asked, "Who is Anna Gryahznyi?"

"You are," he said quickly. He tried to sound convincing. It was an effort. He could feel his heart climbing his throat with every beat. The ground under his feet felt rubbery. He realized the feeling was in his knees.

"You're crazy," she snapped. "You're a damn crazier crazy man than they said you would be. The hell with you."

"Don't curse," he said wearily.

"Why not?" she said blankly.

"Anna Gryahznyi never curses. It does not become you," he stated.

"Oh, hell!" she said. "You're really nuts, aren't you?"

He sucked in his wind. It was like kicks in the belly, this elemental fury coming out of her. Thunder from the lips of Anna Gryahznyi, that faceless female fiend.

But she had used the right name, which happened not to be his. Or was that imagination too?

"What name did you call me?" he asked abruptly.

"You want to hear it again, you ugly brute?" she said. "Well, I'll be goddamned glad to—"

He leaned down for her purse, which had gotten loose from her in the scuffle. She stopped swearing, jumped for it too. But he got to it first. The purse was heavy in his hands.

She swore at him again, too hoarsely to be intelligible. It might have been Russian, not English. He could speak the former as well as the latter, but the muttered imprecation was simply too unintelligible for comprehension.

He opened her purse. The thing that made it so heavy was a gun, all right. It lay in his hand in the murk. He did not look down at it. He felt his mouth drying. He could tell it was an Oostahf model such as *they* would give an agent to carry, unimaginative as they were.

He thought: *She doesn't know I'm Doc Savage. She thinks I'm Banner. Banner would not hesitate to shoot her, and whoever she is, she has to know that. If she suspects I'm Doc Savage, this bluff won't work.*

His hands jacked back the gun-slide. A cartridge flew out of the ejector; another went into the chamber as the slide snapped shut, making a noise like a steel beast closing its jaws.

"No! No! Oh, please don't!" she wailed, her eyes going wide with seemingly genuine terror.

He pointed the muzzle of the Soviet-made pistol in her direction, his finger barely grazing the cold steel of the trigger. He did not want a mishap. He put enough coldness in his stare to communicate otherwise. He hoped it would show through the tinted contact lenses that masked his flake-gold eyes.

"My name?" he said tightly.

"Banner! You're Banner!" she bleated, seeming to shrink in her own skin, much like a trussed prisoner before a firing squad. He hated to subject her to this mental torture. Or any woman, for that matter. Even Anna Gryahznyi, who, it was said, broke the souls of her victims to extract the information she needed and then shattered their bodies for the sheer enjoyment of it.

"And your name?" he prompted.

"It won't mean anything to you," she gasped. "Baker. It's Eva Baker. You never heard of me."

Her voice had terror on it like hairs of frost.

Into him came a hideous playfulness of a sort he had never felt before.

"So I'm Banner, a crazy man," he said carefully. "And you are a stranger. What was that name? Baker? Eva Baker?"

She was wordless. She stood there grotesquely, hands shielding her face, as if she feared a bullet that would disfigure more than one that would kill.

"Well?" he said patiently.

As if sensing he would not fire, she lowered quivering hands. Her eyes had a wet, glassy hugeness. In the gloom, their color was impossible to read.

"You were full enough of hard words a minute ago," he prompted.

He watched her pale face struggle and still remain absolutely immobile. It was a shape, and nothing more. He wished he had a flashlight.

Presently, she began to break words off the cold mass inside her, a few at a time, and push them out. They were stiff, lifeless sounds. He had to bend forward to catch them.

"I carry it as a gag," she said breathlessly.

"Carry what?" he asked.

"That gun." She pointed toward the Oostahf. "You decided to kill me when you recognized its make, didn't you. Isn't that right?"

"Yes," he lied, "I suppose that is true."

"Listen to me, Banner." Her words were rushing out now, fright hushing and garbling them. "The gun is a gag. A conversation piece. A New York City cop gave it to me. The cops took it away from one of their diplomats because he had no permit to carry it. That's the same gun. You remember reading about it in the newspapers, don't you . . . Oh, damn! That's right—where you've been, you don't see the newspapers, do you?"

He straightened. He gave up straining to catch her voice. And he was thinking: *If she is Anna Gryahznyi, she would want me to hear as little of her voice as possible, to keep me from being sure.*

"I can't hear you very clearly," he said. "It doesn't make much difference anyway. Anna Gryahznyi could explain anything. She's a very good explainer, is Anna Gryahznyi."

"I don't know any Anna Gryahznyi," she said, stubbornness creeping into her voice and giving it clarity.

"All right," he said, letting the hammer down slowly with a thumb. He had taken the bluff as far as he cared to.

"Don't you believe anything I say?"

"No."

"Look, you've got to listen, Banner. I was just doing my job. They told me to follow you. I was to make sure nothing happened to you. If anyone else was following you, I was to call Dryden. And Dryden would rush agents to protect you. Those were the only instructions Dryden gave me and—"

His astonishment must have come out of him as a grunt. At least, some sound from him stopped her. He prayed it wasn't that old trilling habit of his, which he had long ago suppressed. He was often oblivious to it, on those increasingly rare occasions when surprise dragged it from his vocal cords like a lost fragment of his strange childhood.

"Who did you say you work for?" he demanded.

"Dryden," she said. "But you don't know Dryden, either, do you?"

He got the surprise quelled in his voice and said, "Why didn't you tell me that before?"

It was her turn to express surprise. "You mean you know Dryden?" she asked.

"Yes."

"Whew!" Life came back into her voice. "Whew! Thank goodness. I don't know when I was so scared. Point that gun somewhere else, will you?"

"You're not out of the woods yet," he warned.

"I'm not dead, anyway." Her nerve was coming back. "What are you going to do with me, besides stand there like we're both posing for the cover of one of those cheap true-crime magazines?"

"I'm going to show you to Dryden," he said flatly, thinking that if he could steer her toward a streetlamp, he would finally get to see her face.

"Fine. If you don't mind, I'm going behind that bush and repair my makeup. I'll bet you've ruined it with those big uncouth paws of yours." She held out her hand for the purse. He shook his head and kept it. She shrugged and said, "Okay . . . but I assume you are gentleman enough to allow me to repair my hose." She pointed toward her right leg. The nylon was a dim serpent of sags and folds, having become undone from its anchorage.

Doc Savage did not want her out of his sight, but he knew he could not pilot her very far through the streets of the city in such a state without attracting undue and potentially harmful attention.

Reluctantly, he nodded agreement.

She started into the bushes, paused, and called back, "You know something, Banner? These goshawful stories I've been hearing about you—I think I'll believe a little of it the next time."

He did not say anything and did not interfere with her as she disappeared into a spreading lilac bush.

He stood, attentive to the rustling, trying to keep an eye on the bushes while not prying on her personal business, and simultaneously staying alert for passersby. As a result, he performed all three chores poorly.

In about three minutes, he realized what he would find when he looked for her behind the now-still lilac bush. He looked anyway. She was gone.

He plunged into the bushes, shoving aside dimly fragrant clumps of branches. He could not find her anywhere in the shrubbery.

He tried to make himself leave at a decorous but brisk pace. But he could not keep it down to a walk. Soon he was hurrying along in a wild, devil-ridden way, as if on a carpet of sticky spider silk.

II

WAR TALK

When Breckenridge stepped out of his hotel room, the door of the room across the corridor was open, as it always was. Three Special Security men stepped from this door at once. Breckenridge, of course, knew them by sight. He bent his neck slightly by way of greeting, but did not smile. The Special Security men were dressed as conservatively and inconspicuously as possible, except for the one who wore a yellow necktie. And the yellow tie had a purpose; it meant he was the one to deal with.

They were a nuisance to Breckenridge, of course. But they were a nuisance the way wearing clothes in hot weather can be a nuisance. Breckenridge had accustomed himself to them. They were not as much a nuisance as one day being unexpectedly dead.

To the yellow necktie, Breckenridge said, "I will use a car and driver for a couple of hours."

"Yes, sir." The man started to turn back into the room.

"Just a second," Breckenridge said. "Here is the schedule: Wilcox is speaking tonight at the Waldorf. I will pick him up there. The two of us will then go to a hotel and receive a caller. I believe you know what hotel. I will then drop Wilcox off at the Waldorf and return here."

"Yes, sir."

"At the hotel meeting," said Breckenridge, "it might be better if the bodyguard withdrew."

The yellow necktie nodded. His face had little expression. The man had been assigned to guard Breckenridge for several weeks, and he had shown extreme facial expression only once, to Breckenridge's recollection. That was when the man had looked at a herd of holstein cows grazing in a meadow in Maryland, and there had been such an expression of longing on his face that Breckenridge had felt one of his rare pangs of sorrow. The man really wanted to be a farmer.

"Beg pardon, sir," the would-be farmer said.

"Yes?"

"Is the hotel meeting with a man named Banner?"

Breckenridge nodded, and he was thinking: *Savage would not like this. Savage would not care for too many people knowing he is in town, even as "Banner." Officially, he's out of the country, and has been for as long as Banner has been in Scandinavia.*

Tight-voiced, he said, "Yes, with Banner."

"In that case," said the rural-minded yellow necktie, "it will not be possible to withdraw the bodyguard. Sorry. My orders, sir."

"Well, in that case . . ." Breckenridge said.

"Will you wait a moment, sir?"

The man went back into the room. Breckenridge saw he was picking up a walkie-talkie and summoning their cars.

"By the way," Breckenridge said when the man returned. "Anything about this chap Banner—even his existence—is top secret."

"Yes, sir. I understand."

Walking to the elevators, Breckenridge settled in his mind the matter of who had talked too much about Banner. It was Wilcox. It had to be Wilcox, for the simple reason that Breckenridge knew it had not been himself.

He felt a small anxiety about Wilcox. Any talk at all about "Banner" was too much at this time. Any whisper. Any at all. Wilcox should know that.

The Cadillac was waiting in front. Breckenridge got in, enjoying the feel of its luxurious appointments, yet understanding that it was not built for comfort. It was armored. The Special Security men got in two other machines. One would drive ahead, one to the rear.

Breckenridge switched on the rear-seat loudspeaker, which was hooked into the VHF radio by which the three cars maintained perpetual contact. The Special Security men used VHF radio almost as much as they used their voices. Breckenridge himself was a gadget man, an electronics experimenter, a radio ham, and he found the practical application of such gizmos fascinating. He listened to the cross-talk chatter with detached pleasure.

After a short wait in front of the Waldorf, Dwight Wilcox came out and got in. Breckenridge and Wilcox exchanged quick hellos; their smiles possessed a wary wanta-be-pals diffidence, like the meeting barks of puppies. And in both men a slight embarrassment followed, for they did not quite know how to deal with having known quite a bit about each other for years, yet never having met.

Then Wilcox giggled. The giggle was a repulsive little sound; it made Breckenridge uncomfortable. He said, "How goes it?" and offered his silver cigarette case. "Smoke?"

Breckenridge accepted a cigarette and set it alight. Wilcox followed suit.

Wilcox carried a leather dispatch folder, and delicately, with two fingers, he held it out before himself, then let it fall to the floor. He remarked, "I take it you do not have our occupational disease, ulcers."

Breckenridge took this to mean Wilcox himself had an ulcer, was not permitted by his doctor to smoke. He did not feel at ease with Wilcox. Yet Wilcox was a very good man. Wilcox was like that dispatch case he had dropped. The dispatch folder was Mexican, its leather hand-tooled by Aztec Indians; it was delicately fashioned and intricately designed and yet as tough as hell for service, and that was the way Wilcox was, or had been in the old days. Wilcox still was on the extraordinary side, judging from what

Breckenridge had heard. Yes, the dispatch case was Wilcox, Breckenridge thought, and Wilcox was the case.

Wilcox must be a little drunk, he decided.

"How was the banquet tonight, sir?" Breckenridge asked.

"Oh, glorious," Wilcox said. "The usual thing, I mean. The usual half a broiled chicken."

"Big crowd?"

"Mob. Between six and seven hundred."

"Egad," Breckenridge said. "Hardware people, I believe I was told."

Wilcox gave that awful giggle again. "Sheep or goats, that's the question. That's what's bothering them. And you know what they thought I was? The pen-sorting attendant—the guy who knew what was sheep and what was goat." Wilcox dropped his cigarette. It exploded a shower of sparks on his braided, full-dress trousers. He swatted at the sparks foolishly. Breckenridge helped him swat, recovered the cigarette, handed it to Wilcox. Breckenridge did not enjoy the reek of champagne on the man's breath. Wilcox muttered, "Thanks. Tell me, Peter, are we sheep or goats? Which? Does it ever bother you?"

Breckenridge settled back and said, "Not the least."

"Is there going to be a war? They wanted to know that, Peter," Wilcox said.

Breckenridge, feeling his discomfort grow, said nothing.

"The hardware gentlemen think there is going to be a war," Wilcox continued. "They think there will be a hell of a war, with no steel to make lawn mowers or golf club handles or pots and pans. They think things will be tough in their line."

"It's a cold, damp evening. Fall is coming on," Breckenridge said deliberately.

"That's not all that's coming on." Wilcox waved his cigarette. He peered into Breckenridge's face. "How about that? How about that now? You and I know, don't we?"

Breckenridge felt tension in his legs. He said, "Let's find a more harmless subject."

Wilcox kept his face close, saying, "Now that's exactly what I told them tonight in my little speech. Listen to this excerpt, old boy: 'Security is not the same as peace of mind and freedom from worry, gentlemen. The first does not bring the last two, necessarily. The man, the woman, the child, even the nation which is most secure often suffers the most nerve-wracking worries and fears. The lamentations of catastrophe are the acid with which we are inclined to burn away the soft gum of self-satisfaction. We have become, as an American nation, a people who steep ourselves in the frightening bubble-world of psychoanalysis. Every quirk of national human nature becomes terrifying. Better we should interest ourselves in raising rabbits—our troubles would multiply no more rapidly.' "

"It must have been a good speech, sir," said Breckenridge politely.

"State Department malarkey, Peter. You know that."

And Wilcox giggled again.

Breckenridge winced. He wondered when Wilcox had picked up the giggle. He found himself hoping it was only a champagne giggle; a thing like that could do a man harm. Especially a diplomat in Wilcox's position.

"We could tell them, couldn't we, Peter?" Wilcox said loudly. "About Moonwinx?"

"Shush, man," said Breckenridge.

"Don't shush us, Peter." Alcoholic stubbornness flared in Wilcox. "Don't shush at destiny, old boy. We are destiny, you know. You and I, and Dryden, of course." Wilcox brandished his hands before Breckenridge's nose. "Look at these two hands. With them, would you think the clay of destiny is molded? It is, you know. It is these hands that will cause the man in the moon to wink for the first time in history."

The driver could hear them. It was not good for the man to hear even such obviously alcoholic ravings. The driver was doubtless all right, but it was never good for stuff like this to be overheard. Breckenridge did not even like to hear it himself.

So Breckenridge put a hand on Wilcox's thigh. He dug

his fingers into it; he dug them in until it seemed to him that his fingertips could feel the hard bone in the man's leg. He got some satisfaction out of being cruel. He did not say anything.

Wilcox gasped, tore the fingers loose from his leg. He slid to the other side of the seat and glared at Breckenridge. "Hell!" he said, and did not say any more.

Presently Breckenridge said, "We had better stop someplace for coffee, sir." He let the suggestion sound like what was meant: It would be best if they got Wilcox sober.

Wilcox giggled again.

"Where," Breckenridge asked, "did you pick up that horrendous noise?"

Wilcox threw the giggle at him once more. "I stole it. I stole it tonight from a gilded sow who sat at my left elbow and ordered champagne cocktails steadily whenever she was not talking about the artist Thomas Hart Benton. You know what I think of artist Thomas Hart Benton? The guy scares me, Peter. Did you ever see those murals he did in the Missouri State Capitol in Jefferson City? The guy doesn't paint with a brush. He uses a meat-ax. I think that dame got a giggle like that from looking at Benton's work."

They got out at Grand Central Station. One Special Security car curbed ahead of them and another behind.

They went into the Oyster Bar. Breckenridge spoke privately to the bartender. A Special Security man stood at his elbow, listened, looked puzzled. When their waiter came, he brought a tall glass of reddish fluid. At Breckenridge's insistence, Wilcox drank the stuff.

There was quite a tense interlude while the red potion from the glass took effect on Wilcox. Wilcox hurried into the men's room. A Special Security man followed hurriedly. He came out, spoke to his men. Two of the latter moved quickly to spots where they could stop Breckenridge from flight, in case Wilcox had been poisoned. Breckenridge was sourly amused; he knew Wilcox was in the men's room vomiting alcohol out of his system. He knew also that he stood very little chance of getting out of the room alive during these few moments. He thought of Wilcox and his damned giggle, and was pleased with himself.

Wilcox was pale and his eyes were leaking slightly when he came back. "What in God's name was that stuff?" He grimaced, added, "That was a drizzly trick, friend."

Brecke..ridge, sugaring his coffee, laughed. "You really could be assassinated without too much trouble, couldn't you?"

Wilcox sat down. "Why did you do it? A tribute to this man, Savage?"

"You were lit up like a lighthouse."

"You think Savage would have minded?"

"I think," said Breckenridge with some feeling, "that you would have minded—very much—what Savage would have done to you if you tried to talk to him when you were tight. He's gone to extraordinary lengths to help set up Moonwinx, and on faith alone. We're about to brief him on what it's all leading up to, and here you are, tight as a drumhead. It wouldn't surprise me if he up and walked away. He's no frock-coated diplomat or salaried agent. Savage is free-lance. He doesn't need us. We need him."

Sobriety came to Wilcox. He put salt on the back of his hand and flipped it into his mouth. He drank coffee. "This fellow Savage impresses you, doesn't he?"

"That he does," Breckenridge agreed. "It was Savage who tricked that stiff-necked Soviet diplomat, Zardnov, into personally carrying back proof positive that the U.S.S.R. has atomic bombs. He was stood up before a Red firing squad accomplishing it, too.* Nearly lost his life doing his government that slight little favor. And don't think the Kremlin has forgotten. The agent who assassinates Doc Savage is set for life."

Wilcox grunted. "Ivan is not exactly free with his rubles, either." Wilcox beckoned the waiter. "I think I had better eat something. Like a raw hamburger. I'm becoming 'anxious to meet this bird Banner.' "

The Red Spider.

"You won't be disappointed, if what I hear is true."

Wilcox looked up, said, "That's right. You've never met him, have you?"

"I look forward to the pleasure," Breckenridge said with studied sincerity.

"Know what he looks like?" Wilcox asked. "As Banner, I mean."

Breckenridge leaned back, and something he was thinking made him smile thinly. "A big bruiser. An unusual face, a very brutal face. They say he is one of the most violent soldiers of fortune ever to roughneck through Scandinavia. Of course, that is the persona we selected for this assignment. I don't expect you will meet the true Doc Savage until this project is over—assuming all parties survive." He caught himself, and added, "Assuming the world survives."

Wilcox matched the other man's thin smile and asked, "What does his soul look like, I wonder?"

"I would not know how to examine it, but I fancy its color would be bronze." Breckenridge did not look amused. "He is sometimes called the Man of Bronze, although I understand it embarrasses him no end."

"Ask a cuckoo question and you get a cuckoo answer," Wilcox said. "Oh well, I guess I can take it this Banner is a tough buzzard."

"I prefer to think of Savage as unusually capable."

Wilcox finished his coffee. He looked at Breckenridge and said, "This bright boy had better be as capable as you claim, is all I can say."

"He is. Dryden recommended him," Breckenridge said curtly.

"I mean technically," snapped Wilcox. "There is more to this than cracking skulls and squeezing throats. This man Savage had better be the electronics whiz kid he's made out to be."

"He is." Breckenridge threw money on the table for their check. Breckenridge was angry with himself now. He stood up. He said, "Let's get out of here before I take the veil off some of my opinions of your State Department, Wilcox."

They stalked out, showing their displeasure with each other. The Special Security men handled themselves with much better control. There was no commotion, almost nothing to indicate anything more than some men leaving the restaurant and going to the street. Except for Breckenridge and Wilcox, it would be hard to imagine that any of the men even knew each other. But their efficiency was great. When a pedestrian attempted to shove past in front of Breckenridge, a normal act on a busy New York City sidewalk, the pedestrian was suddenly but gently collided with, found his arms held as if to restrain him from falling, found himself apologized to profusely—until Breckenridge and Wilcox were clear.

Breckenridge thought with bitter amusement: *How we do get around, we little tin saviors of civilization.*

III

UNWELCOME WELCOME

They had cabled him the name of a hotel in code before he left Norway. The Cory Hotel.

For some reason he had visualized that the hotel would be a large, clean-looking hostelry with gentleness its predominant air. That was the kind of a hotel it was, too, he saw. Big, clean, gentle-looking. And new-looking. It had been weeks, he reflected, since he had seen a brand-new hotel. There were none in Europe. He had not supposed one was to be found anywhere.

He crossed over and went in and the place wasn't new at all. It was an old fleabag they were refurbishing. The lobby was a mess. He took an instant dislike to the desk clerk for no other reason than that the fellow looked sloppy.

The Cory Hotel happened to be located in the theatrical district, a couple of blocks from Times Square, which meant it was a beehive of activity most of the night. It had three different street exits, and another one direct to the subway. There was no better place in the city to come and go unnoticed. It was for this asset that Dryden had chosen it, he realized. It did not mollify him one whit. He had been away from the comforts of civilization too long.

"I'm looking for a man named Dryden," he told the clerk in an impatient tone.

From the results, he might have just kicked a hive holding hornets that were pretending to be only houseflies.

Two men came to him, one to his left, the other to his right. One hurried over from the tobacco counter, the other had been seated in the lobby as if he were a guest. The clerk walked off, looking anxious to be out of it.

The two men eyed Doc Savage.

"Beg pardon, sir," one greeted him woodenly. "Who did you wish to see?"

He had short-cut brown hair. He was very thin and wiry, and his oval face was that of a department store salesman. Doc Savage realized the fellow had the kind of a face that was easy to forget immediately. There was nothing worth remembering about his clothing, either. The other man was shorter and had close-cut black hair, and his long face was neither handsome nor homely. His suit was gray, whereas the other wore a brown suit. Otherwise he was just as easily forgotten as his companion. By their carefully unnoticeable appearance, if nothing else, Doc Savage would have known what they were. They were called Special Security men and they were assigned to Dryden.

"I'm William Jones," Doc told them. "And I have an appointment with Arthur Dryden."

The two young men remained expressionless. "That so?" one said. They looked past him at each other. One jerked his head.

They entered an elevator and rode to the fourteenth

floor. Here they passed a man who wore overalls and a garish yellow necktie. He was taking the contents from a wastebasket and putting the stuff in a soiled canvas-sided cart. When they had passed him, he suddenly hurried after them.

"Who is this guy?" he demanded.

"I dunno," said one of Doc's escorts. "I think maybe he's the hotshot they're expecting."

"Has he said what his name is?"

"William Jones."

The man grinned. "I suppose you lads searched him?"

"Naw."

The man shrugged and went back to his wastepaper, saying, "Today we live daringly, don't we?"

At the far end of the corridor they entered a large room which smelled slightly of warm radiator paint. The wide windows offered a view of the U.N. buildings and three rusty steamers in the river beyond.

"You wait in the next room here, Mr. William Jones," said one of Doc Savage's guides.

"We'll try to find Dryden for you," said the other quickly.

Doc Savage was ushered through a door into a smaller room and the door closed, leaving him there alone. There was a faint noise of laughter outside and the bronze man went to a small window, finding it barred. He turned and looked at the crack of light at the bottom of the door; from the shadow outlines there, he concluded the two escorts were waiting for him to find out they had locked the door. He heard another suppressed snicker.

Doc shrugged indifferently. He produced the woman's purse from where he had been carrying it tucked inside his trouser waistband.

The room had two articles of furniture—a divan and a chair, both very massive, both bolted to the floor. Doc spread the contents of the purse on the chair seat.

He gave each item a careful inspection as he took it from the purse. There was an imitation silver compact, a brass lipstick which stuck out a red tongue at him when twisted, a clip of cartridges for the automatic, some silver and paper money, a ticket stub from the newsreel theater where Doc had spent part of the afternoon, a leather black-jack, a book of matches from a restaurant where Doc had his dinner. He counted the money. There was sixty-seven dollars and fourteen cents.

There came subdued sounds of telephoning in the other room.

The driver's license in a plastic cover bore the name: EVA BAKER. The description on it generally fitted the blonde who had shadowed him into the park. Doc thought it would also fit most average-sized blondes. The thought made him feel chilly.

Doc replaced everything in the purse. He passed a hand over his face, saw sweat on the hand. It was not very warm in the room. He wondered if his face was pale. He thought it would be, under the feature-warping rubber fillers and makeup.

He opened the one other door in the room, finding a bathroom. The shower had no curtain or curtain bar. The mirror over the washbowl consisted of a sheet of stainless steel bolted to the wall. He reflected that they had fixed it so a man would have a hell of a time committing suicide in this bathroom.

He also thought the stainless-steel mirror deceptive. It made his artificial countenance look ugly, coppery, and no more frightening than a spike nail.

He soaped and washed his hands thoroughly. But he could still detect the minty scent of marrubium on them.

The door opened hurriedly.

"You may wait in the outer room if you wish, Mr. Jones," said the brown-suited man. He looked agitated, was excessively polite.

"Very well," Doc told him.

"I'm afraid the spring-lock had the connecting door locked there for a few moments before we noticed, Mr. Jones. I'm very sorry."

"That's all right," Doc told him.

"Is there anything we can get you, Mr. Jones?" The man was perspiring slightly.

"Yes, there is," Doc said flatly. "You can dig up Dryden."

"Yes, sir. We're trying," said brown-suit. "We're doing our best. We have contacted Mr. Breckenridge, and he is hurrying here."

"Breckenridge?"

"Yes. He said he'd be right over."

"Who is Breckenridge?" Doc Savage demanded.

"Why, he's Mr. Dryden's chief assistant." The man wiped his hands on a handkerchief. His eyes were very apprehensive. "Mr. Dryden is chief of the Special Security section, and Mr. Breckenridge is his executive officer. I'm sure Mr. Breckenridge will be here at once."

Doc Savage's heavily dyed eyebrows lifted. "What is the matter with Dryden? Cold feet?"

"How's that?"

"Skip it," Doc said. "I'll wait around for a while. I don't mind. Much."

Doc washed his hands a second time. The marrubium scent was still there, although not as strong.

When the bronze man went into the outer room, no one else was there. However, low, angry voices were conferring in the corridor. He palmed the knob, eased the door open a crack, and eavesdropped.

He heard gray-suit say: "How the hell were we to know who he was? That's what I want to know."

"Yeah. Nobody tells us nothing," complained brown-suit.

The third party in the palaver was the man who had been emptying wastepaper. "I tried to warn you guys to get on your toes when you went through here with him," he said.

"Don't tell us you knew who he was!" said brown-suit skeptically.

"No. But I do know it was damn sloppy business to bring a stranger up here without even making him identify himself. I do know that. Why, you didn't even search him. Hell, he could have had his pockets full of bombs."

"Nuts!" said gray-suit.

"And locking him up in the hold-room!"

Brown-suit said in a pained voice, "We couldn't very well give him the run of the joint, could we?"

"Yeah, but locking up *that* guy! Oh, mother!"

"If you ask me, I don't believe he even noticed we had him locked up for a while," brown-suit said. He didn't sound very convinced.

"Wanta bet?" said wastepaper. "Your carelessness got all our necks in a noose, that's what it did. And another thing: Did you have to tell Breckenridge over the phone that we had him locked up? Why not just say the guy was waiting here?"

"I guess I didn't think."

"That's right. You didn't. And now we all get a peeling." The speaker took on a note of hope. "However, maybe Breckenridge wasn't as mad as you thought. It's hard to tell over the telephone."

"Hah!" said brown-suit. "I think he split a gut just before he hung up."

IV

MOONWINX

"This is embarrassing," said Breckenridge, waddling across the carpet to Doc Savage, hand extended.

"I imagine it is," Doc said dryly.

"I'm Breckenridge. Peter Breckenridge. I wish to God I had been here when you arrived."

While his hand was being shaken heartily, Doc saw that Breckenridge was a short, muscular, and dark young man. Under heavy talcum powder his beard was speckled blue-black, and his nose was flattened and puggy. His eyes were shiny with suppressed rage.

"It's a hell of a note, the kind of a reception you got," Breckenridge added. "I apologize for our whole outfit, Savage."

"You seem to know who I am," Doc said with vague unhappiness. His brittle, mud-hued eyes indicated the Special Security men, who stood about with the tense air of stabled race horses, just beyond earshot.

Breckenridge waved a thick, hairy hand dramatically. "My God, as soon as they described you, I knew," he said. "It's lucky these guys here had sense enough to know where to telephone me." He glanced at gray-suit, brown-suit, and the wastepaper man. His eyes were alert and unkind. He lifted his voice. "Not that that excuses them much. We'll take this up later. Get outta here!"

The three left hurriedly.

"College talent," said Breckenridge. "Still wet behind their diplomas." He gave his pants a hitch, and waved at a chair. "Well, these things happen. Won't you sit down, Savage?"

"That's the second time you called me by that name," Doc pointed out. "I seem to remember a phrase from the last war that fits this occasion: Loose lips sink ships."

Breckenridge fingered his collar uncomfortably.

"My apologies," he said, red-faced.

Reluctantly, Doc took a chair. "I expected to see Dryden," Doc said firmly.

"I'm Dryden's whipping-boy. I can take care of you."

"Where's Dryden?"

Breckenridge scratched his crab-apple nose.

"To tell the truth, Savage—I mean Banner—we didn't know exactly when to expect you. Not the exact hour, is what I mean. We knew you were coming, of course. As a matter of fact, we had been alerted you were in the country. We knew the exact hour you walked off that British overseas plane in Quebec. We had an agent up there to watch you and look after you. Sort of unbeknownst to you, if you get what I mean. She reported your arrival. But after that, damn her soul, not a word. So we were kind of hazy on your exact whereabouts."

"You assigned an agent to pick up my trail in Quebec?" Doc demanded, his voice sharp.

"That's correct, sir," Breckenridge replied, his voice suddenly crisp and formal. "Protective surveillance, you understand."

Interest flickered in Doc Savage's eyes. "A woman?"

Breckenridge shifted his feet. "Well, yes, sir. A woman."

"A blonde?"

Breckenridge acquired a taken-aback expression. "Huh? You mean you spotted her?"

Doc Savage released a pent-up breath with infinite slowness. So the woman who had followed him into the park was really not Anna Gryahznyi! He could not recall when he had been relieved of so great a fright. Being under a Soviet death sentence was a new experience for him.

Breckenridge whacked his knee with a fist. "Egad! That's why she hasn't reported in, evidently. What did you do with her, anyway? I'm given to understand you're not exactly a ladies' man."

Doc ignored the comment. "This blond agent of yours—was her name Eva Baker?" he asked.

"Sure. A nice kid."

Doc Savage felt as if he had just learned he had not really swallowed strychnine after all.

"She's all right, isn't she?" Breckenridge demanded.

"The last I saw of her," Doc told him, "she tore off through Central Park after I had relieved her of her pistol."

Breckenridge grunted. "That may be why she hasn't called in. I hope she doesn't up and resign."

Breckenridge looked at his hands and his lips moved as if in prayer. Doc decided he was swearing to himself.

Doc resolved not to say anything just now about mistaking the female Special Security agent for Anna Gryahznyi. It was warm and secure and safe in the hotel room. In such peaceful surroundings, it would be difficult to explain the terror that chance park encounter had instilled in him. In his lifetime of adventuring, many people had tried to kill him in the heat of combat—or even because they feared he would interfere with their evil designs. But he had never been stalked by a professional executioner before. It had been this way for three months now, and even wearing the face of another man could not dispel the coldness that had settled in his inner being.

"Oh well," Breckenridge was saying casually, "she was warned not to take chances with you."

The man in charge of the wastepaper entered the room and jerked his head at Breckenridge. He and Breckenridge conferred in whispers by the door. Doc saw Breckenridge's fists suddenly clench. Breckenridge snarled, "He picked a fine time to get the shakes!"

That was all Doc overheard. He wondered if they were discussing his seizure of terror over Anna Gryahznyi. He doubted they knew about that. The subject under discussion must be Dryden, he concluded.

"You never did say where Dryden is," Doc reminded, when the conference ended and Breckenridge returned.

"I just learned Dryden is—er—tied up for a while," Breckenridge said. His face was turgid with rage. "We'll have to postpone our conference until tomorrow," he added quickly. "I assume you'll take a hotel room under the name of Banner. You've come too far to fall out of character at this late date."

"I expect to settle our business tonight," Doc told him with pointed directness.

Breckenridge shook his head distractedly. "Impossible. The briefing alone will take several hours. Even if Dryden was in shape—" He caught himself, went on, "Uh—even if Dryden could join us, we couldn't wind it up tonight."

"What I have in mind won't take long," stated Doc.

Alarm suddenly made Breckenridge look as if he had been struck on the head.

He blurted, "Has somebody told you about Moonwinx?"

"No," said Doc, impatiently. "I have no idea what

Moonwinx is, other than nursery-rhyme hints about making the man in the moon wink. No one has let slip a clue as to the nature of the job you people want me to do."

"Then how in hell do you know how long it will take to go over everything?" Breckenridge demanded.

Doc stretched his legs out.

"It won't take me long to resign," he said flatly.

Breckenridge stood over him. "What?" he exploded. "Resign?" He clapped a hand to his head. "Egad, what are you talking about?"

"I'm quitting," said Doc Savage.

"No! But we've been months setting this up. The Banner identity. Norway. Sweden. Russia. You can't back out now."

"Can, and will," Doc said simply.

"You're the only man alive who can pull off this damn job they've handed us!"

"Am I really that essential?" Doc asked dryly.

"You bet your hat!"

"Poppycock," said Doc.

"You can't quit without notice," Breckenridge said angrily. "Leave a million-dollar secret operation hanging over the precipice like this! Where's your patriotism, man? This is for your country!"

Now Doc was angry himself. "For years, you State Department people have been dumping your stinkeroos on me." He jumped up. "I can see you're all set with another one right now. It has started out badly, as far as I am concerned. There are too many mouths yapping, too much loose talk."

"You're not walking out on us," Breckenridge said helplessly.

"That's the general idea."

"But you don't even know what we want you to do!" Breckenridge said quickly.

"Makes no difference. Use your head. Too many people know about me. Get yourself another boy and save yourself the bother of looking for my missing corpse."

The door opened. Gray-suit looked in to see what the

shouting was all about. "Get out!" Breckenridge shouted. "No, wait. Order the car up right away." He turned and said dramatically to Doc Savage, "If I take you to him, you'll talk to Dryden? You'll do that, won't you?" His voice was pleading.

"I'll agree to that much," Doc said. "But I'm not kidding about the rest of it."

There was a large green limousine waiting when they got downstairs. It went into motion with the quietness of a Diesel locomotive, so the bronze man knew it was armored. He did not mind the secure feeling the armored sides and thick bulletproof glass gave him. Anna Gryahznyi could be anywhere.

Breckenridge groaned unexpectedly.

"Egad, Savage, I never thought I'd blow my top when I finally met you," he said fervently. "I'm sorry. I really am."

"I hadn't planned for it to come to this," Doc told him quietly.

"Savage"—Breckenridge leaned across the seat toward him—"when Dryden decided to bring you in, I was as excited as a kid. I've been one of your profound admirers."

Doc looked at him, the beginnings of suspicion in his eyes.

"Thank you," Doc said aridly. He was in no mood to be buttered up.

"Look, I'm sincere," the other assured him. "You know how I feel right now? Like an alley cat that has been yowling at a tiger."

Like white gnats, small flakes of snow began to whizz around in the headlights. Doc was surprised. It had not seemed cold enough to snow.

"I crossed your back-trail in Prague last summer," Breckenridge continued in a smooth, ingratiating voice. "I tell you, I was impressed. Oh, I had heard stuff. But you know how it is in my game. Most of what you hear you don't believe. But I was impressed, believe me. Exactly the right people are scared stiff of you."

Except Anna Gryahznyi, Doc reflected bitterly. He gave Breckenridge a thoughtful look.

"Were you the Breckenridge who captured that Werner fellow, the scientist who slipped out of England after the Fuchs case, in Prague?"

Breckenridge nodded. The glow that came into his eyes was composed of sheer pride.

"That was good work," Doc said simply. "No doubt a great many innocent lives were saved. Werner was an expert in germ warfare and made no bones about the fact that his loyalty was to money, not nations."

"Thanks," said Breckenridge. "Sometimes the hard work pays off. It really does."

"It does," Doc agreed, and realized the conversation was being steered in an amiable direction, the better to put him off his guard.

The car stopped before a candy-striped awning supported on brass poles. The doorman's brass buttons gleamed in the light. "Yes, sir!" His cheeks were like polished apples. "Yes, sir!" He opened the door of the limousine.

Doc emerged first, and noticed the cartoonish moon done in bluish-white neon tubing that dominated one curtained street-level window. There was a humorous face inside the neon moon, consisting of a grinning mouth and two round eyes. The left eye continually winked as a circuit switched back and forth between a squiggly tube and a straight one.

Arching over this was more neon tubing. It spelled out a name:

MOONWINX

Doc turned to Breckenridge, his rough-hewn features twisting in disbelief.

"A nightclub?"

Breckenridge grinned sloppily. "You didn't think we made up the name, did you?" He waved Doc on. "Maybe Dryden will buy us both a drink," he added. "That is, if he's in here. I understand he's been paddling from one joint to another so fast it's hard to keep track of him." He paused, and said, "Oh, I forgot. You're not much of a drinker, are you?"

"Not much," Doc agreed.

The walked inside, into an atmosphere of shining shirtfronts, bare shoulders, mink wraps, perfume, noise.

The hat-check girl said languidly, "Check, mister?"

An obviously inebriated man was leaning on the check girl's counter. He turned and peered owlishy at them. "Joint's got bes' li'l ole check girl in town," he said blurrily. He came over and clapped them both on the shoulders. "Joint's got bes' li'l ole check girl in town," he repeated.

In a whisper—his lips hardly moved—he added, "Dryden's inside. Higher than a boiled owl." His voice was clear as silver.

He went back to pestering the check girl.

Breckenridge beckoned to Doc Savage.

"I was afraid of this," he said wearily.

Doc looked around, was conscious of a feeling of relief. Normally, he disliked the carnival air of places such as this one. But it had a sincere quality wholly absent from similar scenes he had witnessed in the last few weeks. Nobody had the desperate air of having to cram a lifetime of glee-making into one night because tomorrow there would be Siberia, or worse.

"Hello there, bulldog-face," a tipsy girl said to Doc.

The bronze man was momentarily taken aback, then remembered he was wearing the mask of Banner. Weeks of practice reasserted themselves and he gave the girl a very Banner reply.

"Bow-wow." He felt foolish, but the asinine comment did its work. The tipsy girl stumbled away, tittering.

Doc's attention returned to the crowd. "I don't see Dryden," he remarked quietly.

The deep bluish light in the room was soft with the sound of voices. Above their heads, above a fragile-looking blue netting, there was a glittering ball of light dancing back and forth, following the tight-clad figures of two men and a woman who were hurtling about on a trapeze arrangement. Suddenly the woman shot out into space, turning over and over, hurtling downward at them.

Breckenridge gasped in alarm. Before they could duck, another aerialist—a man—swished out of darkness on a trapeze, caught her, flipped her twice in the air, caught her again.

"Egad!" said Breckenridge. It was evidently an expression he was addicted to. Doc found this impossibly affected.

"Uh-oh, there's Dryden," Breckenridge muttered.

Doc searched the sea of patrons, asked, "Where?"

"Savage"—Breckenridge put a hand on his arm—"about those rumors you may have heard that Dryden is hitting the bottle."

"What rumors are those?" asked Doc, genuinely alarmed. He had gone behind the Iron Curtain on Dryden's assurances.

"They're exaggerated," Breckenridge said quickly.

"How exaggerated?" Doc wanted to know, his anger returning.

Breckenridge was keeping a friendly grip on Doc's arm. Doc shook it off. He was in no mood for psychology.

"I'd better explain it a bit more," Breckenridge said. "You see, Dryden went into Russia himself about a year and a half ago to personally set up an espionage unit. He failed. Frankly, he made a mess of it. It was the first real flop he'd ever had, I think. Dryden had never been a drinking man. Well, when he came back, they had to carry him off the plane. He was pouring down four to five quarts of vodka a day. But later he went to Hot Springs to take the cure. This is the first time since; I guess with M-hour getting close . . ."

"M-hour?" Doc asked. All these cryptic cloak-and-dagger references were beginning to rankle him.

"Moonwinx," whispered Breckenridge.

"The Russians must have done a job on Dryden," Doc said.

Breckenridge looked thoughtful. "I bet it would be interesting to know what did happen to him. . . . Well, anyway, Dryden's been off the stuff. But tonight, tonight is a special occasion. We were all cutting loose, just a little, for tonight. You may have noticed."

"Not my idea of diversion," Doc said, gazing about with a lack of appreciation. He watched the lady trapeze artist fly through the air again. He had to restrain an impulse to duck.

They pushed through the mill of revelers and stopped between two tables, Doc getting several looks due to his size and unlovely physiognomy.

"Dryden has changed a little, don't you think?" Breckenridge asked.

"I don't see him," Doc snapped, peering through the thick, smoky haze of cigars and cigarettes.

"He's right over there!" Breckenridge said. He pointed out a man with pouches under his eyes and lifeless white hair.

Doc's eyes narrowed in surprise. He had been searching the crowd for a wiry whip of a man. A lean man, delicately yet boldly outlined—everlasting.

"He *has* changed," Doc said with discernible disapproval.

"Come on," urged Breckenridge. "Let's join him."

The face that Arthur Dryden lifted to them was the color of milk with a little green ink in it. His jowls sagged, without having enough weight to warrant their sagging; they seemed to sag merely because they did not have the spirit to do otherwise. One hand clutched a long black cigarette holder. The other fingered an earlobe absently.

"Hello there, you homely apparition," he said when they drew near. He peered at Doc. The cigarette in his holder was bent almost double.

"Dryden," Doc said without emotion.

Dryden, still peering at Doc Savage, rubbed his hands over his eyes. "Say, you look almost real." He reached up to poke Doc's coat-front with an extended finger. "By all that's holy, are you real?"

Suddenly, Dryden sprang to his feet and gave out a yelp of surprise that caused the room to frown at him.

"Am I glad to see you arrive all in one piece!" he cried. He threw one arm across Doc's broad shoulders, pushed him at the others at the table. "Folks," he announced boisterously, "meet my pal. He's the world's greatest—"

"Shush," said Breckenridge loudly. "Not so loud."

Dryden peeked around Doc at Breckenridge. "Oh, it's you," he said with distaste.

Of the several persons at the table, none were unduly sober, Doc saw. He tried to calculate how many thousands of dollars their jewels, minks, and tailored tuxedos represented. The total was impressive—if one was impressed by such flauntings of wealth. He was not.

Dryden aimed a finger at Breckenridge. "Don't shush me, you!" he said mushily.

A pretty redhead in a yellow dress arose from the table, handed Doc a drink, and asked, "World's greatest what?"

Doc accepted the drink and gave a typical Banner answer. "Gibbon trainer," he said, straight-faced.

Much to his embarrassed relief, the redhead thought this was hysterical. "You can train my gibbon anytime!" she shrieked. Her table companion, a crew-cut young man with a thick neck, scowled.

Dryden was nudging Doc, but pointing at Breckenridge, saying, "You know what that little scut has been trying to pull? Steal my job, that's what!"

The redhead threw her arms around Doc's neck. Her breath smelled of crème de menthe. Under his bleached skin, the bronze man's neck turned red.

"Marylou!" said the crew-cut young man. He gathered both feet under him, as if he contemplated arising from his chair.

"Please!" Breckenridge was saying. He addressed those at the table. "If you will excuse us, we'll be going," he said. "Excuse us, please." Anger was making his cheeks flat.

Two of the aerialists, men this time, made a daring

swoop overhead. Doc was forced to duck, which gave him an excuse to detach himself from the giggling redhead.

Dryden was now shaking his fist at Breckenridge and demanding, "Who told you to follow me, you . . . you lackey?"

"Please! Ladies present," said a fat man blearily.

"I like you," the red-headed girl was telling Doc. "I want my gibbon trained. What's a gibbon anyway?"

"A gibbon is a kind of monkey," Doc said dryly.

The redhead turned to her escort. "Dan, I think he called me a monkey," she said indignantly, waving long gold-colored fingernails. "You gonna lettum get away with that?"

The crew-cut young man arose and assumed a John L. Sullivan pose. "Put 'em up!" he challenged.

"Damn it, I knew we shouldn't have come in here," Breckenridge moaned.

Dryden switched his interest to the crew-cut young man. "Who you fixing to fight?" he wanted to know.

"Him. Dogface, there." The young man indicated Doc Savage. "He come in here, insult my girlfriend," he complained. "Gonna knock him silly."

"Why," demanded Dryden, "are you trying to commit suicide? Are you crazy, boy?" He seemed genuinely, if drunkenly, alarmed. "Look at that face. Look at the size of him."

The red-headed girl picked up a partly consumed sandwich and threw it at Doc Savage. Doc twisted without seeming to move. The sandwich missed.

"Please, please!" Breckenridge was more angry than anyone. "Please!"

While everyone's attention was on Breckenridge, Dryden knocked the crew-cut young man unconscious with a blow to the chin. The young man fell loudly, making a great thump.

Dryden clucked over the young man, saying, "Saved his life. I really deserve a medal." The young man remained stretched out on the floor. His girlfriend was pouring champagne on his face when the headwaiter and three assistants arrived.

Doc Savage and Breckenridge permitted themselves to be ejected meekly. Dryden, however, took a wild swing at the headwaiter. He received a black eye in return. After that, Doc assisted him to the door.

They had walked a short way in the blowing snow when Doc Savage remarked bitterly, "If the night's events are an indication of how Special Security operates, I am not at all impressed."

Dryden lowered the handkerchief he was holding to his eye. "How does my eye look?" he asked.

Doc regarded the optic. "It has a touch of frog green already."

Dryden made a fist, pulled his sleeve up to his elbow.

"It needs a sister." His normally high-pitched voice was flutelike with fury. "And I'm gonna give it one," he added, looking in Breckenridge's direction.

"Cut it out, chief," Breckenridge said, sounding dejected. "What's the matter with you, anyway? What have I done?"

"You followed me, you spy," Dryden said angrily.

"Oh, rats!" said Breckenridge.

"Hold it, Dryden," Doc warned, the fabric of his patience in the face of this childish display wearing down to bare threads.

Dryden was paying no attention to Doc. He tugged furiously at his own sleeve. "Can't even have one last drink in peace!" He began a wind-up.

"Hold it, hold it." Doc got between the two men. "Hold it. I was the one who wanted to see you, Dryden."

"Follows me all the time!" Dryden yelled. "Damn it, I'm entitled to one last soaking. Considering what's ahead of us, I'm entitled to it." Dryden stabbed a finger in Doc's general direction. His aim was bad. "If you knew what was ahead of us, you'd be tying one on too," he insisted. "But you don't, do you?"

"I think I do," Doc said levelly.

"No, you don't," returned Dryden hotly.

"Nothing is ahead of me," said Doc. "Nothing dangerous, at any rate."

"Oh, my God!" cried Dryden, grabbing his snow-moistened hair in surprise. " 'Nothing dangerous,' he says." He peered past Doc at Breckenridge. "You hear that? Nothing dangerous, he thinks. After all the preparations we went through to create Banner."

"Savage says he's quits, chief," said Breckenridge dully.

"I've had it," said Doc.

Pale glow from a streetlight fell across Dryden's face. It showed no change in his expression, no real comprehension. He was too intoxicated to grasp developments.

"Ah, let's get a drink," Dryden muttered at last.

"Not tonight, thank you." Doc looked at Breckenridge and shrugged. "He's too tipsy to talk sense, or even understand."

"Who's tipsy?" They were now in front of the Moonwinx nightclub, having circumnavigated the block. The bulletproof green limousine was parked at the curb, collecting snow on its long hood. Dryden seized each of them by the arm. "Let's get a drink," he urged, evidently forgetting that they had just been ejected from the establishment, or perhaps not recognizing it in the first place.

Doc Savage shook free of Dryden's grasp and turned to Breckenridge.

"When he gets sober, Breckenridge," Doc said coldly, "tell him I've decided to take my chances with Anna Gryahznyi alone. No Special Security, no Moonwinx—whatever that is—and no more hiding from the world as the brutal Mr. Banner."

Dryden's voice exploded a shrill curse. "Damn you!" His fingers twitched. "You don't have to tell the world! What if that Anna Gryahznyi vixen did get to me!" His eyes were insane. "I was lucky to get away with my skin. What happened to the others is on her head, not mine!"

Doc Savage was taken aback by this unexpected outburst.

He pulled Breckenridge aside. "Did you say Dryden was in Russia when he went to pieces?"

"That's true," Breckenridge told him.

"Sounds as if Dryden had a brush with the notorious Red Widow, as they call Anna Gryahznyi."

"Damn you, make fun of me, will you!" Dryden's voice was rattling. "It's not right!"

Without saying any more, he stormed off into the whirling snow.

Doc Savage, his tone tinged with disgust, turned to Breckenridge, and said, "If this is an example of America's Special Security agency in action, count me out for the indefinite future."

Without another word, the bronze man signaled a taxi. It whisked him off into the busy night.

After he was gone, several men came out of the nightclub to see what all the shouting had been about.

"A woman," Breckenridge told them acidly. "They were arguing over a woman."

"Always trouble over a dame," one of the curious patrons sniffed. They went back inside the Moonwinx, leaving Breckenridge to stand in a vortex of gathering snow and to curse the future, which looked very bleak indeed.

For the world.

V

BRONZE MAN

Doc Savage had the cab driver let him off at a subway station along the wide boulevard that was Broadway. After paying the hack, he descended into the station.

The hour was late, the subway platforms all but deserted. There were only two individuals waiting on the near side of the tracks.

A rattling train pulled into the station, its doors sliding open like the lens apertures of some impossibly ancient camera mechanism.

At the token booth, Doc made a pretense of fumbling for change. He finally slipped a dollar through the slot on the booth, but only after the train had swallowed the waiting passengers and departed. None left the train, which was unusual even at this hour. A convenient piece of luck, he decided.

Doc dropped the token into the turnstile and walked to the far end of the platform. Across a forest of concrete support columns, he saw no passengers on the opposite platform. More luck.

Quickly, he dropped to the rail bed, and slipped into the cavernous tunnel. Several yards along, he came to a tool locker set in a wall niche. He had to carefully step over the third rail to reach it.

Ignoring the padlock, he felt around the place where the back of the locker lay flush to the crumbling concrete of the tunnel wall. He found an ancient rust-scourged push-type doorbell. He thumbed it three times, and waited.

The locker sank back into its niche, disclosing a dark opening. Doc slipped inside; the locker returned to place with only a faint grating noise, like the side of a truck scraping a brick wall.

The tunnel was narrow, and lit by exposed light bulbs of low wattage. Doc traversed the tunnel a distance approximating a short block and came to a steel door. This opened inward at the touch of another push-bell. Doc entered.

The bronze man found himself in a bare garage in which a modest collection of vehicles were stored, his personal automobiles. There was a single elevator in the rear wall. He crossed the cold concrete floor and took the lift in the only direction it could go from this, the sub-basement garage of his skyscraper headquarters. Up.

The elevator, which Doc Savage had actually devised himself, operated like a pneumatic tube on a large scale. Compressed air whisked him upward with breathtaking speed.

Stepping off at the eighty-sixth floor, Doc soon found himself in the reception room of his vast headquarters.

On the massive inlaid table that served as a desk, Doc checked with a device which consisted of a very modern tape recorder attached to a telephone. It was designed to answer the telephone in his absence and record messages any callers wished to place. From the amount of tape that had been eaten up during his absence, Doc Savage saw that the messages were many. He decided to forego playing them back. He had, after all, been gone three months.

Doc passed by a wall painting of his father and continued on to the door that entered into the vast, dusty library that housed shelf upon shelf of scientific volumes, and walked the equivalent of a city block to the great white-walled laboratory that was one of the most complete in existence.

He checked another device, this one mounted on a wall, which was actuated by short-wave radio. It was designed to indicate which of his aides—he had five associates who assisted him in his strange life's work—were in the country.

To his surprise, he saw that none were. This was unusual, but not unprecedented. The five were highly skilled in their respective lines, most of these scientific, and were much in demand. Like the bronze man, they loved action. But when he was absent from Manhattan, as he had been, they pursued their occupations with vigor. In this case, they had been led to believe Doc was at a secret retreat in the Arctic, where he often lost himself in intensive scientific research he conducted at a laboratory even greater than the one in which he now stood.

Doc weaved his way between massive hulks of machinery and apparatus to a corner where a modest living quarters was set up in a private room. It was enclosed, a virtual cubicle. Doc had not been residing in his skyscraper headquarters for many months. Even before he had assumed the identity of the fictitious roughneck known only as Banner, he had taken to residing in hotels, changing accommodations frequently. This was to foil Soviet-inspired attempts on his life. There had been many, and his eighty-sixth-floor headquarters, while well-guarded, was simply too public. Doc had no wish to imperil the ordinary citizens who worked in the building.

Going to a mirrored table illuminated by a border of frosted light bulbs, the bronze man attacked his artificial physiognomy with solvents and cold creams. He washed away the metallic dye that had given his skin a garish, coppery tint. The deep natural bronze of his skin showed around the rubber fillers that had been applied to his chin and cheeks with spirit gum.

Removing these proved to be an ordeal. They were designed for extended use. After removing the chin piece, he temporarily gave up and pried loose the mud-brown contact lenses, revealing his remarkable flake-gold eyes. They whirled under the lights, like pools in which golden flakes were circulating. It was an optical illusion, and one of the physical attributes—his bronze coloring and muscular physique being two others—which made him live up to his outlandish reputation.

And which also, he thought grimly, made him such a wonderful target.

He finally got the cheek fillers off. These resembled flat snails of copper-colored rubber. He laid them on the makeup table and, picking up a pair of tweezers, extracted moist cotton pads which had been used to distort the shape of his face from within. His nostrils, once the wire rims were pulled out, lost their markedly bovine flare.

The features that were revealed were handsome in a regular way. Not prettified. Not quite matinee-idol perfect, but strong and reassuring to behold.

Regarding his own face staring back at him for the first time in many weeks, Doc Savage was not reassured. In fact, he was disgusted. Three months setting up Banner wasted. Weeks of back-breaking work, consorting with ruffians and criminals of every stripe, for nothing. Carefully laying the groundwork for he still did not know what, getting into endless brawls to establish Banner as the bad boy of Scandinavia, and all he had done was confound the Russian assassination squads by being in almost every one of the last places they would think of looking for the great enemy of the state, Clark Savage, Jr.

Including Soviet Russia itself.

Doc gave his face a final toweling, and decided to leave be the copper tint that covered his neck, hands, and other visible parts of his epidermis. It would be much harder to remove than the facial dye, and he was exhausted. He felt as if he had chopped down half the forests of Siberia.

He had made a fair dent in them, he recalled with a grimace.

There was a fold-down cot in one corner. Doc got this ready and undressed for bed.

He switched off the light and threw himself on the cot, feeling tired, angry, and alert by turns. It was no recipe for slumber.

There was a narrow window that looked out on the night sky. It happened to frame a full moon. Doc felt too fatigued to get up and pull the blind, so he simply stared at the lunar disk for several minutes.

He could see the pattern of pockmarks and icy-colored patches mankind had called the man in the moon since the first humans set up housekeeping in caves, probably. He knew it was simply an optical illusion, composed mostly of craters and the so-called lunar "seas."

Still, it made him think of Moonwinx, and the cryptic hints that had been dropped when Dwight Wilcox of the State Department had first approached him about the matter. He had never worked with Wilcox before. But he had agreed. The matter of the death sentence the Kremlin had imposed upon him and the fearsome reputation of the Red Widow, better known as Anna Gryahznyi, had convinced him to go along, even though Wilcox had declined—really refused—to divulge what was back of the whole scheme.

In truth, Doc had not been impressed with Wilcox, he recalled now. Wilcox had asked too many ignorant questions, particularly in regard to Doc Savage's background. It was as if the man had never heard of him, Doc remembered.

It would have been hard to find a grown American who had not known of Doc Savage's life's work, which was to roam the globe, dispensing justice to those who had none. Doc had been trained for this Galahadian endeavor almost from the first breath he drew. It had been his father's idea. It had been an interesting life, too. One for which he took no pay.

During the past war, Doc had found himself at the beck and call of the U.S. government as a kind of last-ditch firebreak. A troubleshooter of final resort. He had done interesting things in that line, too. After the war, the State Department had taken to dumping all manner of impossible tasks on him. And he had always come through. He had been prepared to come through again, even for an ass like Wilcox, who seemed to think that Doc Savage was some mere footloose soldier of fortune. The man had actually been unaware of his scientific achievements. Doc was known for his genuine modesty, but Wilcox's ignorance came as a shock.

The moon continued its slow ascent. Soon, it would pass beyond the upper border of the window and cold lunar light would cease to bathe his sore features, and he would sleep at last.

Before sleep overcame him, he decided to talk to Breckenridge about this Moonwinx business. Merely out of curiosity, he told himself. He was through with the State Department, and especially with Special Security, which seemed to be headed by drunkards and fools.

In no way was he about to place his life in their hands, he thought sleepily. He would be safer on a deserted island with the heartless Anna Gryahznyi.

Just before he nodded off, in that twilight between wakefulness and slumber, the bronze man thought the man in the moon winked at him.

He could not imagine why.

VI

UNPLEASANT DISCOVERY

At a quarter past four that morning, a probationary patrolman named Rourke needed a smoke. He had finished his preliminary police training quite recently. He very well remembered there was a regulation in the manual against smoking in public while in uniform. But his craving for a cigarette was urgent. As he walked his beat on Carsey Avenue in Brooklyn, he kept an eye out for a spot where a man could have a couple of drags unobserved. He brushed fallen snow off his uniform from time to time.

"Ah," he said. He had discovered a secluded alley.

The tobacco flavored Rourke's lungs most agreeably. The cold nibbled playfully at his ruddy cheeks. He held the burning cigarette encased in his cupped hands protectively. He kept eye and ear open for the sergeant. He thought about his future, about becoming a detective maybe. A detective holding his coat-tails open to a warm radiator, on a night like this. His cigarette burned short.

Still keeping the red end covered, he leaned down to stub it out on an ash-can. Curious, he poked at something that was sticking from under the much-dented lid.

A few moments later, Patrolman Rourke bolted out of the alley in search of a call-box.

"That smell!" He gagged into the phone mouthpiece.

"Hey now!" said the station-sergeant. "Get a grip on yourself!"

"She's stinking!" choked out Rourke. "Even cold like it is, she's stinking like everything."

"Who is this?" demanded the sergeant.

"Rourke, sir." He gasped it out.

"Well, what's the matter with you, Rourke?"

"It smells like she had been there anyway a couple of

days," Rourke jerked out. "This dame I just found in an ash-can, I mean. She's cut all up in pieces."

Presently, the various experts assigned to any homicide reached the alley. The medic, the fingerprint man, the photographer, the men with the tape measures, the others. They began building evidence methodically.

The medical examiner's opinion of time of death, which coincided remarkably with Rourke's snap guess, was based on the following: twelve hours allowed for development of rigor mortis, an additional eighteen hours while the whole body was in rigor, then three or four more hours for the disappearance of rigor from the upper part of the body. The result: total probable elapsed time since death, thirty-three hours.

Fillets of flesh in the ash-can proved to be her face and her fingertips, diced into small pieces. There was hardly enough for the Police Department's moulage expert to produce results.

Meantime, Patrolman Rourke got a kidding.

"Just exactly how did she smell, Rourke?" asked the check-sergeant.

"Oh, go to hell!" snarled Rourke.

Actually there had been no strong odor from the body. Rourke had an imagination. This was his first murder body. Shock had encouraged his imagination to take over and do him a dirty trick. For weeks, he was to undergo a relentless ribbing about it.

The murdered girl had a bandaged little toe. It was found at the very bottom of the can.

Four hours after the body was found, the police located the chiropodist on Central Park West who had removed the corn. He was the one hundred and eleventh chiropodist the police had called in that four hours. None of the others, fortunately, had removed a corn from the little toe of a blonde very recently. The police considered this amazing good fortune. Blondes are just as addicted as other women to corn-making tight shoes.

The chiropodist's care record showed: Name, *Eva Baker*. Residence, *Ellenby Hotel, West Twenty-third Street*.

From there on, it was easy.

"Well, that's that." The detective hung up the telephone. "She worked for the government."

"What department?"

"Damned if I know. It's hush-hush. They're even sending a man down here to shut everything up."

"Who do they think they are? You can't shut up murder."

"I dunno. I guess they're gonna handle it themselves." The detective made a few notes on a form. "They did want some guy located and picked up." He tore off the sheet, handed it to a messenger. "Maybe they think he done it to her. Name's Banner."

VII

ARREST

"This is lovely weather," Breckenridge said, beating his numbed fingers together and stamping his feet.

The shipyard employee waded in the snow around the yawl. A flat sky the color of a mouse promised more bad weather. Far out on Long Island Sound, far away over the wind-scratched blue water, a bell buoy rocked from side to side, banging its clapper.

"It's sorta nippish," said the shipyard manager.

The yawl had been in storage four years. However, she looked fresh, due to the recently applied copper bottom paint and tophull white. Breckenridge examined the vessel, pleased. He liked her when he bought her; he liked her now. She had deep draft for her waterline length, nice run, a good deep forefoot.

The shipyard man shouted at an employee. "Getta

move on with the ladder!" he yelled. "Mister Breckenridge wants to go aboard."

"I'm in no sweat." Satisfaction felt warm on Breckenridge's bestubbled face. "I kind of like to stand back and look her over."

"I know how you feel. I know just how you feel," said the shipyard man approvingly.

"You like my boat?" asked Breckenridge, pleased.

"Yep, I sure do," replied the shipyard man.

"I paid three thousand for her," Breckenridge admitted. "And I don't know when I'll be able to take her out again."

"I'll give you five," offered the shipyard man.

"Is that right?" said Breckenridge.

"I could resell her and make myself a couple G's, I don't mind telling you," declared the shipyard man. "You couldn't duplicate her now for over twice what you say you paid. If you was to build her new—Lord breathe on us!"

"How about that?" Breckenridge looked at his boat with deep pleasure. "Well, that makes me feel better about the storage bill."

Their feet punching holes in the knee-deep snow, two men brought a ladder long enough to reach from the ground up to the yawl deck. Breckenridge and the shipyard man climbed up, found themselves on board. The deck had been scrubbed, brightwork polished.

The shipyard man produced a sealed envelope. He tore it open and handed Breckenridge the boat keys, which he took from the envelope.

Breckenridge unlocked the hatch, descended the cabin companionway. Four years of disuse fell on his nostrils. That, and it seemed a great deal colder in the cabin.

"I never happened to see her inside," the shipyard man said from the deck. "We never unlock a customer's boat, unless there's a fire or something."

"Come on below," Breckenridge invited.

They descended.

The shipyard man looked about him. "Say, she's nice," he breathed. "Say, she *is* nice."

"Want to see my ham shack?" The boat had a stateroom forward. "It's in here." Breckenridge threw open the stateroom door.

The shipyard man looked into the stateroom for a few minutes. He scratched his head.

"What'd you call it?" he asked.

Breckenridge beamed with pride. "My ham shack," he explained. "A damn snazzy one, too."

"It looks kinda like a radio broadcasting station," muttered the shipyard man, while scratching his chin.

"No, it's an amateur," explained Breckenridge, his voice losing the slight tension that had remained since the night before.

"You mean you broadcast on the radio from here?" the shipyard man said wonderingly.

"Sure, that's the basic idea," said Breckenridge, warming to the subject. "How'd you like to see how it works? Have we got city juice plugged in?" He snapped a switch and dials lighted. He launched into an enthusiastic dissertation on ham radio, flipping switches and turning dials as he talked. "We'll fire up this hundred-watter on ten meters," he said. "I hear ten's been lousy for DX lately, but we might hook a local mobile for a ragchew. If sporadic E is right, we might even work some short-skip."

Breckenridge listened to the speaker hiss and splutter, shook his head. "Hell, ten is dead. Let's see how twenty is."

The shipyard man was getting a befuddled look. But he pretended comprehension as he listened to Breckenridge saying, "There's a VK calling CQ. I'll phase him in on the crystal. I'll spot him with the VFO and give him a shout. If this quarter-wave puts out, we'll have us a QSO with Australia."

Presently, a vaguely British voice emerged crackling from the loudspeaker.

Pointing at the apparatus, the shipyard man asked, "Is that fellow talking from Australia?"

"Sure." Breckenridge winked elaborately at the other. "Watch me snag him." He picked up a microphone, threw the transmitter on, and said into the mike, "VK2LW, VK2LW, VK2LW, this is W0CBL slant two nautical mobile. Whatcha say, old man?"

He threw switches.

The loudspeaker sighed loudly for a moment.

The Australian said, "W2ENR, W2ENR, this is VK2LW. Reading you five and nine, old chappie. . . ."

The voice trailed off like a cotton ball being pulled apart.

"Nuts!" spat Breckenridge, snapping off his outfit.

"Ain't you gonna talk to him?" asked the shipyard man.

"A W2 got him," Breckenridge said indignantly. "Some bird running a kilowatt, probably." Breckenridge was angry.

The shipyard man scratched his head some more. "This is sure wonderful." He sounded confused. "It sure looks complicated, though. Say, I'd like the anchor and chain to see this."

He put his head out of the hatch.

"Anna! Anna! C'mere, hon," he shouted.

Breckenridge started violently.

"Want the little woman to see this." The shipyard man turned from the hatch through which he had called. He saw the sudden pallor on Breckenridge's face. "Say, something wrong?"

Breckenridge wiped his forehead, breathed a gusty, "Whew!

The shipyard man examined him solicitously. "Don't you feel well? You want a doctor?"

"No, just a touch of flu," Breckenridge said. He composed himself, putting the name Anna Gryahznyi out of his mind. Nerves. The way Dryden had acted when her name had come up must have gotten to him. Imagine that. Fear of Anna Gryahznyi must be catching, like measles.

He heard someone climbing the ladder. He concluded it was the shipyard man's wife. He said, "This ham radio stuff is my hobby. I used to dream of doing plenty of hamming while sailing the Caribbean in this boat. I'll be glad to show your wife—"

Breckenridge fell silent. He had lifted his face and found himself looking at a coppery bulldog of a face he had never expected to see again.

He swallowed, said, "Banner! What are you doing here?"

"Your . . . office said I could find you here," said Doc Savage without inflection.

Casting an eye to the shipyard employee, Breckenridge remarked to Doc Savage, "Change your mind?"

Doc replied, "Not really." He, too, regarded the shipyard man in a lengthening silence. The man took the hint.

"I'll leave you two to talk," he said glumly. "The wife probably wouldn't be that interested in your radio. She has enough trouble figuring how to work the television."

The man took his departure.

Looking around, Doc asked, "Planning a cruise?"

"I wish I were," Breckenridge said. "This is my retirement boat, if I make it that far."

Doc was examining the ham set. "You're young to be thinking along those lines," he commented absently.

Breckenridge shrugged. "It was a vacation boat when I bought it. Before the war. Times are different since the war. I've skipped more vacations than I can count."

Doc nodded wordlessly.

"How *did* you find me?" Breckenridge asked, to fill up the silence.

"I went to the Cory Hotel, and asked around."

Incredulity swept over Breckenridge's bestubbled face. "And they told you!"

"I showed up as Banner." Doc smiled tightly. "Banner has a reputation. No one seems to have the stomach to refuse him. Besides, it's still not safe for me to walk around in my own skin."

Breckenridge nodded. "I'm sorry it's turned out this way. I take full responsibility."

Doc looked at him. "And Dryden takes none?"

"You know how it works when things go wrong in our line of work. The chiefs keep their scalps. Us lowly Indians have to carry ours from the scalping ground in our hands."

Doc nodded again. "I took this on partly because Dryden had—" He caught himself. "—is a good man. A man of judgment."

"You weren't sold a bill of goods, Savage. I guess Dryden let Wilcox do his snaring for him. He was afraid you'd say no if you saw what he'd . . . become."

"I wondered why Dryden was unavailable during the weeks before I set out for Scandinavia."

Breckenridge said nothing. There seemed to be nothing to say.

Doc spoke up. "How important is all this? Moonwinx, I mean."

Breckenridge expelled an explosive grunt that was part laugh, part something full of inarticulate surprise.

"How important is it?" he snorted. "How important is the future of manki—"

Breckenridge's voice trailed off because he found himself looking into the end of a revolver. He swallowed once.

The policeman who pointed the revolver had a large drop of mucus clinging to the end of his nose.

"Someone here named Banner?" The officer's breath steamed. "Don't get excited," he added, and sneezed.

Doc Savage saw the pistol was cocked. He hoped the officer would be damned careful if he had the urge to sneeze again.

Breckenridge raised both hands.

"It's no heist," said the officer. "You Banner?"

The shipyard man shoved his head into the stateroom. He was pop-eyed with concern. "No," he said, thrusting his chin at Doc Savage. "That's him. He's Banner. I heard him called that by the other one."

Little heaps of snow rode the thick black toes of the officer's shoes. "They want you downtown, Banner. I'll just give you a little frisk before we start." He sounded calm, experienced. He did not take his eyes off the bronze man.

Breckenridge started to protest this, then realized whatever he said would sound foolish, if not complicate matters tremendously. He subsided into a puzzled silence when Doc Savage calmly submitted to the frisking.

"I'll inform Dryden," Breckenridge told Doc Savage as the latter was placed in the back of the waiting police squad car.

"No," Doc said. "Wilcox. Dryden's back of this, obviously."

That realization settled over Breckenridge's features like a buzzard alighting on a flat rock.

"He'll need all the lawyers you can round up for him, pal," said the officer to Breckenridge, "with what your friend here is facing." The officer blew his nose in a handkerchief, got in with Doc. The driver mopped steam off the windshield with his elbow before putting the machine in motion.

"I'd like to know what this is about," Doc asked quietly.

"Better ring him to the robe-rail, Mike," said the driver in a bored voice.

Doc Savage found himself handcuffed to the robe-rail. The officer had holstered his pistol. But now he drew it again, cocked it, and held it on his lap pointed at the man he knew simply as Banner.

"I hope you don't feel another sneeze coming on," said Doc pointedly.

The squad car traveled rapidly. At the second corner, it skidded and turned completely around on the snow-packed street.

"Doncha want to get us there alive?" the officer guarding Doc asked the driver indignantly.

Twenty minutes later, the police car halted before a hulking building long enough to take aboard a passenger. The young man carried a briefcase and an air of self-importance. "This the suspect?" he asked. Assured it was, he surveyed the silent prisoner. "I'm Grunewald, assistant D.A.," he announced. "I must say, with that face, you've got the looks for it."

"The looks for what?" asked Doc.

"Murder, as if you didn't know," said Grunewald.

Doc Savage said nothing. His arm was growing stiff from being fastened to the cold robe-rail.

The machine made its way to Manhattan, turned downtown. Big, grimy Sanitation Department trucks were swallowing the snow with the aid of mechanical loaders. The assistant D.A. frowned impressively, looked important. The bronze man—he was more copper than bronze—took an instant dislike to him, but offered no further comment.

The entire group, with the exception of the driver, entered the hotel where Doc Savage had made his contact with Breckenridge the previous night. Brown-suit and gray-suit were in the lobby, just as last night. They led the way to the anteroom. In a few moments, Dwight Wilcox of the State Department arrived, Breckenridge in tow.

"I think we can take the hardware off him," Wilcox said, after introducing himself. He indicated Doc Savage, who stood, wrists shackled together, looking not at all pleased with developments.

"Wait a minute." Grunewald gave his importance full play. "Let me see your credentials. How do I know you are who you say you are?"

"You might look at these." Breckenridge gave him some documents. They were examined with an air of skepticism.

"Very well," muttered Grunewald. "But I'll just accompany you to see that he doesn't put anything over on you."

"You will like hell!" Wilcox flared. He looked tired. His freshly shaven face was powdered to perfection. "You want a receipt for this man, officer? Hand it over and I will sign it. Then your day's work is done."

The assistant D.A. drew himself up importantly. "This fellow Banner is a murder suspect—"

"Goddamn it!" Wilcox snapped. He glowered at the man. "Take your receipt and get out of here!" His voice lifted in an intimidating shout. "And take those handcuffs off this man! He's a federal agent himself, I'll have you know!"

This last was merely a fib for effect, but it worked. Doc Savage was unfettered. The representatives of the law departed the hotel, albeit grudgingly.

Dwight Wilcox drew Doc Savage aside and they spoke for some minutes, low-voiced. Breckenridge watched this intently, overhearing nothing but straining to catch any stray word.

In the end, the two men shook hands somewhat stiffly, and Wilcox departed.

After he was gone, Breckenridge approached the bronze man, trying to read his face and feeling foolish when he recalled it was composed mostly of copper-colored rubber.

"What did Wilcox tell you?" Breckenridge asked.

"Not much. He gave a speech."

"Did you like it?"

"Did you notice me applauding?" Doc said tartly.

"You *are* in a fine humor," Breckenridge clucked. "You should be a match for Dryden, at any rate."

"I don't care to see Dryden," Doc said shortly. "He had no right to have me arrested like this, Banner or no Banner. What kind of childish trick was this, anyway? I quit, remember?"

"No," said Breckenridge. "I don't think you did. Otherwise you wouldn't have come by my boat to talk."

"Perhaps," Doc admitted. "But that doesn't explain Dryden's cheap stunt."

"It was no stunt. If you'll come with me, I'll explain everything." Breckenridge waved in the direction of the lobby elevator.

They boarded. The elevator, grinding its way upward, trembled and clanked.

"There has been much discussion this morning," said Breckenridge grimly. "Everyone agrees that they must have sent this Russian wench over to eliminate you."

The mechanical grumbling of the old elevator caused Doc to miss most of Breckenridge's subdued statement.

"Eliminate me, or Banner?" he asked sharply.

"Banner. Unless you think it's likely the Russky has figured out that one plus one equals one where you are concerned."

"Unlikely," said Doc.

"You think so?"

"I'm fairly confident on that score, which admittedly is the same as saying I've seen no evidence to the contrary."

"Well, you know that Russian wench better than we do," said Breckenridge.

Doc Savage was extremely quiet for a moment. The elevator door was rattling noisily.

"What wench is that?" he asked, his voice not quite as it should be.

Breckenridge said, "You know that woman you caught trailing you, the one you nabbed in the park?"

"Yes." Doc felt cold alarm seize him. "Special Security Agent Eva Baker, I believe you said."

"That is what I said." Breckenridge's voice was thin.

"Has she filed a complaint against me?"

Breckenridge glanced sidewise at him. "She hasn't filed any complaints, not exactly," he said dryly.

"Good for her," said Doc. There was a little relief in his voice now, but not much. "I was afraid she wouldn't be so broad-minded. I did give her a scare."

"She's dead," Breckenridge said.

Doc Savage opened the elevator door when it stopped.

"What happened?" he asked, brittle of voice.

"Murdered." Breckenridge watched the bronze man's coppery face intently.

They walked down the same corridor as the day before. The same man was working with wastepaper in the hallway. For all Doc could see, it was the same wastepaper.

"I sincerely hope no one believes I had anything to do with that," Doc said.

"Oh, we know you didn't," said Breckenridge.

Doc Savage allowed a flicker of interest to come into his mud-brown eyes. "You seem certain," he said.

"About the time she was murdered, you were climbing aboard that TWA Constellation in England to cross the Atlantic," Breckenridge informed him.

Doc Savage came to a sudden stop. His brutal, rubber-warped mouth opened slightly. His eyes were suddenly opaque with fright.

"The truth?" he asked.

Breckenridge nodded. "That's straight. A beat cop found the actual Eva Baker stuffed into a trash can, rendered like an old nag sent to the glue factory. It was a real hot potato. The police notified us this morning, according to what Dryden told me. We couldn't have Manhattan's finest poking into Special Security business, but we couldn't sweep it under the rug without throwing them a bone, either."

"And Banner was the bone," Doc said grimly.

"You had quit. Dryden figured the police would spend a few weeks looking for Banner, give up, and the matter would be closed. Except you showed up here as Banner. Dryden felt he had no choice but to tell them you'd gone to see him. He feels terrible about the arrest, he tells me."

Doc said nothing as they continued along.

"I understand Wilcox dressed him down in no uncertain terms," Breckenridge added.

"Good," said Doc. "So who was the young lady I accosted in the park?"

"Can you make a guess?" Breckenridge suggested.

Doc Savage shuddered visibly.

"I'd rather not," he said.

"Dryden thinks the Russky has sent Anna Gryahznyi over here to knock off Banner," supplied Breckenridge.

"And I've been walking around wearing this devil face as if it were safer than my own," Doc said feelingly.

"So? Just peel away the greasepaint and be done with him."

"Not that simple," Doc told him. "If the Red Widow can't find Banner, she'll probably go after Doc Savage so as not to waste the price of her plane ticket."

They approached the door at the end of the corridor, their pace quickening.

"She must be a special kind of dame, the way you and Dryden act," Breckenridge remarked, reaching for the doorknob. "Strong men shake in their boots."

"They die in their boots, too," retorted Doc Savage. "That's what bothers me."

VIII

MOONWINX, ACTUAL

Doc Savage listened to a red-headed man, who was obviously one of Special Security chief Arthur Dryden's subordinates, explain the hardships of anyone who tries to buy a single tennis ball in New York City stores. It seemed that tennis balls came packaged in airtight cylinders, three to a tube, and this was the sole way they were offered for sale. You bought tennis balls in multiples of three, or you didn't buy tennis balls.

Arthur Dryden listened glumly. He was dressed neatly enough in seal-brown slacks and tobacco-hued sport coat, but he looked as if he felt very bad indeed. In fact, he wore the demeanor of a man who badly needed a drink, but who also knew it probably would not stay in his stomach.

"So I had to buy three tennis balls," concluded the storyteller. "Here they are."

"Thank you," Dryden said crisply. "That will be all for now." He sounded polite, suave. He had steadfastly refused to meet the bronze man's gaze, which was quite striking inasmuch as he had removed his mud-brown contact lenses for comfort's sake.

Peter Breckenridge drew Doc to a chair, saying, "Sit down." Behind his hand, he added, "Don't mention the subject of Anna Gryahznyi just yet, will you?"

Doc could see Breckenridge's hands were unsteady, and he imagined they were a trifle numb.

"I wish everyone would stop bringing her name up," he said tartly.

Covertly observing Dryden, it became Doc Savage's conviction that Dryden wished to resume their acquaintance on a friendly footing.

Bearing this out, Dryden bestowed a pallid, sour grin upon Doc Savage.

"I hear the local constables gave you a hard time," he said sheepishly. "You have my apologies."

"Don't let it bother you," Doc told him. "Apologies accepted."

Nodding, Dryden returned to his desk and gathered up the tennis balls. His hands, fingering the hard white spheres, were lean, hard, bluish-white.

"We assigned an agent—a woman—to follow you," Dryden said slowly.

"Yes, I heard."

"She was killed."

"So I'm told."

"A different woman seemingly took her place."

"That is my understanding," Doc said. "*Now.*"

Doc noted Dryden's calm self-control, which deserted him a moment later when he fumbled and dropped one of the tennis balls.

"What we want you to tell us is this—who took her place?" Dryden asked, eyeing the ball on the floor as if debating the wisdom of bending over to retrieve it.

"I had hoped that you would have the answer to that question by now," Doc admitted.

Dryden started. "What do you mean?"

"Just that. Your Special Security boys would have rounded her up by now, catalogued her, and have her life story neatly tabulated on index cards."

Dryden became agitated. "You're the one who saw

her!" He shouted, "Don't sit there and tell me you have no idea who she might be!"

"I didn't say I don't have an inkling," Doc admitted. "The trouble is, I don't much care for the conclusion I'm forced to reach. I was hoping you would have one I liked better."

Dryden dropped the remaining two tennis balls. His hands clenched emptily. He scowled at Doc Savage. Apprehension chilled his eyes, made his face lie in flat, pale planes.

"Was it—Anna Gryahznyi?" he demanded thickly.

"I wish I knew for sure," Doc said honestly.

"But you saw her."

"In the park. It was dark. There was no moon."

"How close were you?"

"I had hold of her," Doc admitted, uncomfortably. He decided he might as well tell the rest of it. "I had her by the throat," he added. "I thought she was Anna Gryahznyi at first. Somehow she talked me out of that notion."

"You had the Soviet's top assassin by the throat and you didn't throttle her?" Dryden exploded, his words as fierce as daggers.

"That is not how I do business, and you know it, Dryden," Doc said indignantly.

Breckenridge watched them with growing wonder. "I have been hearing strong things about your doings inside Russia, Mr. Savage," he interjected. "And I have always felt Mr. Dryden to be courageous. Why so fearful of one Red dame?"

Dryden swung on him furiously. "I just hope you tangle with her one fine day, that's all!" he snarled.

"Let's hope otherwise," said Doc fervently. "I do not wish that fate on any man."

"Oh, I'm beginning to anticipate meeting her," said Breckenridge airily.

"You just keep her occupied getting acquainted, while I take to my heels," Doc Savage told him. "They call Anna Gryahznyi the Red Widow in much the same way a certain species of spider is known as the black widow. She's no widow in truth."

"But she is a Red, eh?" Breckenridge said, cracking a lopsided grin.

"There is some argument on that score," Doc answered. "One version of the legend has it that the Red part symbolizes the blood on her hands. She's a murderess, torturer, and worse."

Dryden grunted. He began to pace. Below the window, a radiator gave off waves of heat. Outside on the windowsill lay a cottonlike roll of snow, pure white except where freckled with soot.

Dryden did not break his pacing. "You still want out of Moonwinx?"

"I'm willing to suspend disbelief, at least through the briefing," Doc allowed.

"We'll accept that," Breckenridge said quickly.

"We have no damn choice," muttered Dryden. "Savage is our linchpin. The one man who can bring home America's bacon."

Alarm continued to make Dryden tense, alert, wide-eyed. Doc's flake-gold eyes shifted from him to Breckenridge. The dark stubble on Breckenridge's face gave him a disheveled and bedeviled look, although he was probably the calmest man in the room, Doc reflected grimly.

"Savage," Dryden asked, "Do you know why we asked you to go to Norway and establish the character of this two-fisted alias of yours, Banner?"

"No," Doc admitted.

"Yet you went. Why?"

"Two reasons," Doc told him. "First, because the State Department asked me to do so."

"You've become quite the State Department's secret weapon in this unhappy little postwar world," Breckenridge put in—simply for the sake of flattery, Doc thought.

"And the second reason?" Dryden prompted.

"I needed a vacation," Doc said dryly.

Breckenridge laughed. "A vacation, he calls it!"

"You found yourself at the top of the Kremlin's death

list," Dryden said grimly. "And a public figure like yourself makes a large target. A very large target, indeed. Becoming Banner was a way to kill two birds with one stone. You do your country some good, and maybe you discourage the Soviet killer apparatus."

"Something like that," Doc admitted.

"All the time, all those months up north, you had no idea why you were playing at being this rough fellow we have named Banner."

"It's common practice to keep as much from an agent as possible, in case of capture and interrogation," Doc said impatiently. "So let's get on with it."

"Yes, let's." Dryden picked up the dropped tennis balls. "Take these and stand at the other end of the room, please," he instructed. Noting Doc's puzzled expression, he added, "This is just a little demonstration that will give you the whole idea in a nutshell."

Carrying the three tennis balls, Doc went to the east end of the room.

"Savage," Dryden explained, "the part of the room where you are standing represents, for the purpose of the demonstration, Russian territory. Let's say you are standing on one of the Ural Mountains. Got it?"

Doc nodded.

Dryden added, "Now, pretend you're a radio transmitter. A secret American radio transmitter. The tennis balls you are holding represent urgent messages you must send home by radio."

"Got it," said Doc.

"One thing more—you've just seen the Russky start taking atomic bombs out of his Ural Mountain storage caves," added Dryden. "You know that means war. An attack on us. That's what your radio messages are. A warning we're to be attacked. Very urgent."

Doc Savage nodded. "An exceedingly important message, in other words."

"Breckenridge"—Dryden jerked his head toward the opposite end of the narrow room, where Breckenridge stood—"represents a radio receiving station in U.S. territory. You've got to get your messages to him."

Dryden took up a position in the middle of the room, midway between Doc Savage and Peter Breckenridge.

"Okay," he directed. "Throw one of the tennis balls to Breck, there."

Doc Savage threw one ball toward Breckenridge.

Dryden snagged it, intercepting it before the white sphere reached its destination.

"Is there a point to this game-playing?" Doc asked tightly. "I can't send him a message if you snare it in flight."

"The idea exactly." Dryden thumbed his own chest. "I represent, in our demonstration here, the Commie radio jamming stations. You can't get your message through. They can jam any damn frequency you use. Am I right? Try again."

Doc threw swiftly, trying to slip one past Dryden. But Dryden, prepared, knocked it down. "See!" he said.

"Isn't this a little oversimplified?" Doc asked, unhappy with the play-acting he had been drawn into. "I've been dabbling with radio, man and boy, since I was in knee pants. I know what a radio can and can't do. Lord knows, I've set up several clandestine radio stations behind the Iron Curtain. Every one of them turned out as useful as a hat on a squirrel."

Dryden replied by pointing at the ceiling.

"See the moon up there?" he asked smugly.

Surprise coming over his rough, coppery features, Doc Savage noted for the first time the flat white ceiling. Someone had used yellow chalk to draw on the smooth plaster a ring some four feet in diameter. The ring was located approximately over Dryden's head. There was a cartoon face drawn inside the ring. It very much resembled the neon man in the moon in the window of the Moonwinx nightclub, except that neither eye was winking, of course.

Comprehension came to Doc Savage. He felt the beginning stir of excitement in his chest. "Pretty large for the moon, isn't it?" he remarked.

"Never mind. You can hit it, can't you?" Excitement seemed to take possession of Dryden also. His voice fluttered like insects inhabited it. "Bounce a message off it to Breckenridge. Try to make the man in the moon wink, while you're at it."

Doc let fly with a tennis ball at the chalked representation of the moon. It hit well out of Dryden's reach, struck one chalky yellow dot that was meant to be an eye, and glanced downward. Breckenridge caught it easily.

"See!" Dryden was elated. Above his head, the man in the moon's left eye was now a blurry smear. It looked remarkably like a knowing wink.

Impressed, Doc said, "If you mean what I think . . . !"

Dryden cut him off by making patting motions with his out-facing palms. "Hold it. Wait until you hear part two of our modest demonstration." Dryden waved at a chair. "Sit down and relax. What you're about to hear is a tape recording."

Bringing out a portable tape recorder, Dryden pushed the plug into a light socket. While he waited for the tubes to warm up, he explained, "I don't need to tell you, you being an acknowledged expert in radio, that the Federal Communications Commission has monitoring stations which listen in on the amateur bands all the time, checking up on the hams to make sure they're not lousing up the air with bum transmitters, or using vulgar language. Traffic cops of the air, as it were."

"Speaking as a radio ham myself," Breckenridge muttered, "I've seldom heard the F.C.C. called anything so polite. Them and their damn blue-tickets!"

"Let's hear the tape," Doc suggested.

Dryden prepared to start the machine, paused.

"This is a recording the F.C.C. monitor made of two hams talking in the midwest," he explained. "Later the hams caught hell." Dryden flipped a steel lever.

A ham's voice came out of the recorder loudspeaker.

"This is W0LAL back to W0BXB. I just looked in the callbook, old man, and I see your home OTH is Cedar

Rapids. Which reminds me of something. I was flying across Iowa the other day and set down at the Cedar Rapids airport to take on gas. I saw something on the edge of the field that puzzled me. Maybe you can straighten me out about what the gadget was. It was a trumpet affair, seventy or eighty feet high, with clockwork at the base. Had a radio nameplate on it, the company I understand you work for. Can you brighten me up about what the thing is? Here it comes back to you. W0LAL over to W0BXB.

Dryden lifted a hand dramatically.

"Talk about letting cats out of the bag!" he said. "This guy threw 'em out nine at a time. Just listen."

The other ham said:

"W0BXB back to W0LAL. Five and nine and solid, old man, but your transmitter still has that goldurn hum. Now, about the gizmo at the airport. It just happens I helped build it. That one is an early model of our moon trumpet. Yeah, moon trumpet. An experimental uni-directional ultra-high-frequency beam antenna for beaming to the moon. The signals are bounced off the moon. Currently they are being picked up on an experimental basis by the Bureau of Standards in Washington. We're finding out some funny stuff, Jake. The signals take about three and a half minutes to go up there and back. That mechanism you called clockwork at the base of the trumpet keeps the antenna tracking the moon. You know, like an astronomer's telescope."

The voice was abruptly buried under a loud buzzing.

Presently the other ham came on, and said in an annoyed tone, *"You're a fine one to accuse me of having hum on my signal. I can't even read you now."*

"That was when the F.C.C. put a jamming signal on top of that guy," Breckenridge explained.

Dryden switched off the recorder. "I hope they drowned him out in time," he said fervently.

In spite of himself, Doc Savage was deeply impressed. He knew that employing the moon as a giant radio-wave reflector was theoretically possible—he had worked out the calculations for himself, as a matter of fact—but he had no clue that it had been accomplished in practice. This was clearly top-secret stuff.

"What was done about those two hams?" he asked, curious.

"Aw, one of them was a lawyer," Dryden said sourly. "When the government threatened him, he threatened right back. No action was taken against him, which is more than I can say for the Cedar Rapids ham. It was kind of a good thing it all happened, because it showed how sloppy security precautions were at that radio company." He grinned. "They tightened down after that."

Doc Savage cleared his throat. He realized he had not been breathing during some of the time he had been listening. His flake-gold eyes were briskly animated.

"How bulky is that moon-bouncing device?" he asked at last. "How awkward to move around?"

"Move where?" asked Dryden coolly.

"Don't be coy, Dryden," Doc said, brittle-voiced. "If I'm to pack that gadget into Soviet Russia on my back, I want to know how heavy it is."

"It's lighter than you think," Dryden said, his eyes glowing with amusement. Breckenridge suppressed a smile of relief.

"How much lighter?" Doc asked.

"The latest refined model weighs complete, a few ounces over five hundred pounds," said Dryden.

"Five hundred!" Doc was shocked. "Only five hundred?" He computed mentally. "From the Pechora estuary southeast to the Soviet's Ural atom cache is a thousand miles airline, give or take fifty. Ducking and dodging the Red Army can double the distance. How many ton-miles is that?" No one said anything, so Doc added, "It's almost a thousand ton-miles, isn't it?"

"It's nearer five hundred ton-miles," supplied Breckenridge.

"Just a feather's weight," Doc said aridly. "Either of you ever try to pack a thousand tons a mile through tundra snow?"

"You won't be alone, Savage," said Dryden. "Breck

and I will carry our share of the Moonwinx transmitter, if it comes to backpacking."

Doc Savage became still. The fine golden flakes in his aureate eyes seemed to pick up circular velocity. He regarded both men, his face an inscrutable copper mask. He folded his cabled arms, the action pulling his sleeves back from his wrists and exposing large sinews and rather fine bronze hair.

"You two plan on going into Russia?" Doc demanded, amazed.

"Yes," said Dryden.

"The secrecy of the mission requires top people, and top people only," explained Breckenridge. "My ham experience qualifies me. You're the man who knows the terrain."

"Rubbish!" Doc snapped. "You'll be about as much help as boils." His attitude was skeptical. "You've never experienced the tundra in winter, have you? That country separates the men from the boys, usually in a few minutes."

Dryden flushed scarlet. "You haven't got a corner on courage, Savage," he said sharply.

"Who said anything about courage?" Doc's voice grew testy. "I'm just telling you that a couple of hothouse boys, who have been training by brightening the seats of their britches in swivel chairs, will have a tough time of it. I'll probably have to pack you both on my back, and the gadget, too."

"Nerts," Dryden snorted.

"You innocents just don't know what you're in for," Doc went on. "The snow country has driven more men to drink than all the blondes of history."

"Why do you think we were whooping it up last night?" Dryden asked firmly. "For all we knew, it might just have been our last night on the town until—well, ever."

Doc received that revelation with something akin to relief. "I see," he said slowly. "I was concerned you didn't understand what you would be getting into."

"We know it will be tough," Breckenridge said.

"Tough!" Doc shuddered. "It will not surprise me if

we are frozen solid, shot by the Red Army, devoured by wolves, and kicked to death by reindeer. Even if we make it in, set up your Moonwinx safely, there remains the small problem of getting out of Russia again."

"We have arrangements for two men to be slipped out by submarine," said Dryden.

"Two?"

"I'm staying," Breckenridge said quietly.

Doc looked his disbelief.

"Moonwinx is automated," Dryden explained. "But someone has to maintain it, do repairs, and, of course, act as a lookout and observer of the atom cache."

Doc turned to Peter Breckenridge and said simply, "I'm impressed by your courage. I hope it carries you through to the end of the trail before us."

"Then you'll go?" Dryden asked quickly. "You agree to the mission?"

"I do," said Doc, still looking at Breckenridge.

Breckenridge returned his gaze without flinching.

"It strikes me, Savage, that you're awfully quick to change your mind and take on all these hardships."

Doc Savage nodded vehemently, said, "You are very right. I am."

"Why?"

"It's important," the bronze man explained. "It's probably as important a matter as my country could ask me to undertake." Doc paused. "And because I happen to believe that Anna Gryahznyi is here in New York, which means that she can't be in Soviet Russia." His voice was quite somber. "That makes Russia the safest spot for me to be right now."

"And me," echoed Dryden.

To which Breckenridge added a puzzled, "Amen."

IX

THE USEFUL WIDOW·

His ears, like cats after mice, searched the Norwegian voices for danger.

The third-class bar jammed, bulged, and howled. A whaler had come in. A whaling ship from the Antarctic. They were having a *dansen,* a wingding.

Outdoors where Doc Savage had paused to reconnoiter, thin snow fell in the night. Noise sprang out of the place in bunches at the bronze man—he was as copper as the Indian on an old penny now, thanks to a fresh application of a chemical skin dye—disorganized goblins composed of uproar. The darkness swallowed this noise, replied with snow. The darkness was black and moist, cold and static, like a lost fragment of outer space.

The name of the place was *Nyttig Enke.* This was a Norwegian name, which Doc mentally translated to mean "Useful Widow." It was a startling coinage, under the circumstances.

He reflected: *I hope I locate that Russian, Poltov, before any strange females—widowed or otherwise—become involved.*

Doc Savage opened the door of the *Nyttig Enke.* So much noise met him that there did not seem room for anything else in the place. The whalers had not been home to change clothes, so they smelled of fletched whale meat and rendered oils and favillous whalebone. Doc pushed into the surging mass of humanity, and found its components to be large, active men. The bronze man felt like a log in a whirlpool, butted by their hard, seafaring hips, as he moved among them. He was astonished by their howling, and appalled by the way their women screamed and laughed hysterically. Beer foam splashed his rough clothing.

Customers howled at him. *"Opvarter! Opvarter!"*

"Nei, herr! Nei opvarter!" he retorted indignantly, letting them know he was not their waiter.

His ears and eyes kept a wary watch for danger, although joy jigged all over the place. He wore heavy, brand-new Norwegian buskers, which were wool trousers built for utility and warmth. His Norwegian sea jacket was also brand-new, as was his dark blue stocking cap, more commonly known as a *hode-sokker*. His knee-high boots were hand-sewn reindeer. Somebody thrust a beer stein in his hand.

"Mange takk," he said, before discovering the stein empty. Obviously, someone was playing a prank. It made no difference. The bronze man eschewed alcohol.

Four whalers were singing. They leaned together, their sea-cured bodies forming a cone of brawn. They accompanied themselves by shaking half-krone coins in their cupped palms, making a sound like green crystal waves scooting across steel decks. Doc paused, intrigued. They startled him by singing the words in English:

> "They gave him cake and whiskey,
> *Ranzo,* boys, *Ranzo!*
> Which made him rather frisky,
> *Ranzo,* boys, *Ranzo!*"

The chanters had their eyes closed. They swayed, afloat on their private sea. The bartender listened to them, too, absently swabbing the bar. There was enough loose beer on the bar that his towel threw a wake like a motorboat.

As Doc listened, waving his empty stein in time to the chantey when he remembered who he was supposed to be, a small blond girl attempted to duck under his arm in passing. She failed to make it, his elbow colliding with her head.

"Unnskyld!" said Doc. "So very sorry."

She was a wide-faced girl. Her skin was the color of rich cream with a touch of coffee in it.

"I am so very sorry," Doc repeated, searching her face.

She wore a blue sequin dress, as shiny as a fish skin and fitting her like one.

"Hei!" She rubbed her forehead. "You pack a mule's kick in your elbow, *fremmend.*"

Doc bowed gallantly. "Won't you aid your recovery by having a drink with me?" he said.

"Will that aid me?" she asked, forgetting her hurt.

Doc observed her face. "I am sure it will," he said.

She wore her hair long and like a soft frame around her features. She did not look like a Russian, but there were so many types of Russian face that this was inconclusive. Her bumping of his elbow could have been accidental, but he had to be certain. Hence the offer of a drink.

"Do you suppose my friend will mind?" she asked.

She spoke Norwegian with a slight touch of Danish, Doc noted.

"Is your friend male or female?" he asked.

"He is very much male," she replied.

"That so?" said Doc. Her legs were long and curved. "Is that so, now?" he added. "Do you suppose he would mind?"

"I don't know," she said, smiling slightly.

The smile reassured Doc. There was no hardness in it.

"Shall we try some of this aid, and find out?" he suggested.

Without consulting the lady, the bartender placed a champagne cocktail before her. "What'll you have?" he asked Doc. The bartender wore a high, tight, celluloid collar striped vertically in black and white, the effect being that of large teeth trying to swallow his head. "I would suggest something strengthening," he added meaningly.

"What do you have that is muscle-building?" Doc asked. He presumed the bartender meant he would need to become very strong to cope with the cute little blonde's boyfriend. He was not frightened, though.

"Might I suggest reindeer milk?" said the bartender.

The little blonde laughed.

Doc frowned. Giving a snarling inflection to the gruff,

cured-in-brine voice that he had cultivated as Banner's, he barked, "What the hell! You think I'm a Lapp?"

"Sure," returned the bartender. "From the north, anyway. Maybe around Tromso. I been noticing that monotonous way you got with your words, half singing. That's Bodo Tromso. And those boots you are wearing. Made by a reindeer-chewer, weren't they?"

Doc decided to accept this as a compliment, although at first wondering if an insult had been meant. They were speaking Norwegian, and Doc had been trying to put in the Lapp accent. The bartender was probably an old hand at spotting home areas; bartenders usually were good at that. If he was deceived, then Doc felt himself doing very well.

"Hard one to fool, aren't you, Ole?" he said to the bartender.

"If you was to ask, I would place you as from around Flammerfest."

Doc slapped the worn bar top. "Why, this fellow is good! He is very good." He turned his attention to the blonde. If she was a party agent, her voice might give her away. It was hard to school the harsh Russian enunciations from a Soviet-trained agent.

She didn't seem to mind his rough ways. She said her name was Nina. Nina Kirkegaard. "Hello, Lapp," she said, putting out a small, warm hand.

Doc accepted her hand. "Meeting you is a great delight, a truly wonderful event," he said, putting effusion in his tone.

"You really want a shot of reindeer milk?" asked the bartender.

"I think not," Doc said hastily. "Just a bit of kummel in a large glass with enough vodka added to kill the taste of caraway seed."

The bartender departed, but came back to lean on the bar. "The taste of caraway don't kill so easy."

"That's what I mean," said Doc, winking.

The bronze man turned to Nina. Her mink-brown eyes watched the dancers struggle on the floor.

"Should we . . . ?" he suggested.
"If you like."

He found he had overestimated her smallness, for she was well up to his shoulder. She gave an impression of tawniness in his arms, and she danced superlatively. Her hair was spun fine, and its blonde was almost a white. It smelled faintly of good clean oat straw. He did not think its hue came out of a peroxide bottle. She proved adept at not getting trampled. He was no dancer.

When a waiter carried a tray of drinks to the orchestra, the music came to an abrupt end. Feigning disappointment, Doc guided his dancing companion back to the bar. He had not made up his mind if she were the genuine article, or not.

Their place at the bar was now occupied by an enormous man who was built in the shape of numerous squares. He stood, his back to them, questioning the bartender. The points of the man's shoulders, the edges of his fists, the sides of his head, all were squares.

The bartender seemed to be quite afraid of the fellow. Doc read disquiet on his features as if it were written there in Braille.

The blonde, however, crowded in at the square man's left to reach around him and pick up her champagne. "Oh, stop frightening the bartender, Paul," she said in an exasperated tone.

The square man turned to her. A hardening glint came in his eyes, and he said, "Nina, it isn't like you to pick up the first bum you bump into." He sounded furiously angry. "And a walrus-eating Lapp at that," he added. His fists were big brass-colored cubes streaked gray with sinew. He had not noticed Doc Savage standing directly behind him.

Doc tapped the fellow on the shoulder, saying, "If you are hungry enough, a walrus isn't so bad."

The big man turned around and saw the battered face of Banner, which resembled an old copper pot that had been struck many times over a period of many years.

The brass leaked out of his own face until it became the color of a recently boiled bone.

Nina watched them brightly over her half-filled glass of champagne.

"You boys have met?" she asked.

The big man's mouth was hanging open, but the lips were drawn in over the teeth. This made him look toothless from fear. He was a huge anvil of a man, a blacksmith anvil with legs. His face, with its brass coating, held remarkable evil. The overwhelming physical foulness of the man was shocking, although he was built with the shapes ordinarily called handsome. His eyes glittered at Doc in bloodshot fright.

"You!" he muttered.

Doc was smiling tightly, but his tinted eyes were watchful. "Yeah!" he said. "Banner."

"Ah?" The big man's tongue moved visibly back of his numb lips.

The blonde viewed Doc Savage thoughtfully. "I thought you said your name was Adam Eggmelk," she said, frowning.

Ignoring this, Doc said, "Paul Poltov." He put out a hand to the big man. "How are you, Paul?"

Paul Poltov seized the offered hand. He pumped it heartily, holding it in both of his. Having pumped the hand, he continued to hold it while rubbing it briskly. "God, you gave me a start!" He panted with relief. "To tell you the truth, it was like being tapped on the back by the devil. I thought my time had come." His lips were quickly moist.

"Your time is long overdue." Doc recovered his hand. He resisted an impulse to borrow the bartender's towel and wipe his palm off thoroughly. "I was sort of hoping to run into you, Paul."

"You are seeking me?" The returning color stopped at the level of his chin. "I am always delighted to see you," he said. He made an effort to control returning fright.

"I'm not going to hurt you, Paul," Doc assured him.

Poltov's eyes were on the bronze man. "I hope that is true," he said sincerely.

Nina, between sips of her drink, watched them. "How about me?" she asked. The minks in her eyes were bright with curiosity. "Do you plan to harm me?" she asked Doc.

The bartender placed a very large glass of liquor on the bar in front of Doc Savage.

Doc straightened his jacket self-consciously. "No, I have other plans for you," he told Nina.

The whalers singing chanteys finished a number. The jingling coins in their palms brought to mind a silvery wave rushing up on a clean beach and bursting into sound. Ear-splitting whistles, applause, and foot-stamping complimented them.

"Nina, you must meet this man." Poltov started to place his arm over Doc's broad shoulder, nervously changed his mind. "See his ugly face. Keep it in your mind, Nina. He has one of the worst reputations in Europe and Asia. You will almost never hear of him by his real name, which is Banner. You will hear of him as The Face. When you hear of a terribly evil devil called The Face, it is this one. The Soviet is terrified of him. He is not an enemy of mine, which I consider most fortunate." Poltov eyed Doc anxiously. "That is right, is it not?"

Doc nodded his acceptance. "You are very flattering. In a way." He discovered his drink, and looked at it with some alarm.

"You are a Lapp, though?" asked Nina.

"He is everything," said Poltov quickly.

"I am a Lapp too," said Nina. "A Danish Lapp."

"I didn't know there were any Laplanders in Denmark," said Doc.

Nina signaled for more champagne. "I'm not in Denmark," she said.

"It is good to see you, Banner," said Paul Poltov nervously.

"My father was in Denmark." Nina's teeth were very white and very even. "My mother was in Lapland."

"I understand perfectly." Doc did not think she was any more Lapp than he was. "The stork brought you," he added.

The blonde blinked at him over her drink. Then, to his surprise, she blushed. "You are vulgar," she said. Doc thought it a schoolgirl blush.

Poltov fell to mopping his face with a large green handkerchief. "Did you say you were seeking me?" he asked.

"Yeah, sort of." Doc pretended to taste his drink. It burned his mouth, even so. He handed the tall, well-filled glass back to the bartender. "Heat this up," he commanded.

"I hope you had little trouble finding me," muttered the Russian.

Nina looked at Poltov. "I thought you were in hiding, Paul," she said. "How did he find you?"

Poltov moved a shoulder vaguely, explained. "Banner finds anybody anywhere."

"Heat it!" The bartender held the tall glass. "Heat it?"

"That's right," Doc told him, straight-faced.

"Why?"

"I like to have it burn going down." Doc made his voice casual. "Sterilizes the throat, you know."

Nina said to both men, "You two are old friends, I take it?"

"Yes, indeed." Doc looked on critically as the bartender lit a gas flame under the huge drink. Several other customers had started watching also. "We have had our times together, haven't we, Paul?" he added.

Poltov paled visibly. "Oh, yes," he said.

"Where did you meet?" Nina asked.

"Meet Paul?" Doc wondered what had possessed him to order such a drink. "I forget. Was it in Warsaw, Paul? Or Czechoslovakia, or Moscow? Or Archangel?" Doc's fist shot out suddenly, giving Poltov a hard poke in the ribs. "I seem to recall Archangel, Paul."

Poltov gasped, holding his side. "Mother of little reindeer!" Pain was not what made him pale again. "It was not my doing, that business at Archangel. I swear not!"

Doc eyed him thoughtfully. "I still wonder."

"No, Banner! I swear!"

Nina giggled with curiosity. "What was this in Archangel?" she wanted to know.

With a feeling of terror, Doc Savage watched the stuff in the glass abruptly start boiling. "Let's see if I recall what did happen," he said. "Oh yes, some son-of-a-seacook told the Reds I was smuggling a shipload of American cigarettes and nylon stockings, and they chased me three hundred miles up the Dvina River. I followed them, though. I joined up with a crew of Russian lumberjacks. Saints, I chopped down half the trees in the Karelian country that time." Doc had fixed Poltov with his eye. "Nobody knew I was a Lapp."

"My, you're adventurous," Nina said. "What happened to your shipload of smuggled goods?"

"Oh, my partner unloaded that at a sweet profit." Leaning toward Poltov, Doc added in a fierce whisper, "Where's my share of the money, you thief?"

"I—I'll pay you, Banner!" Poltov gasped.

Poltov's tongue was hardly visible in his mouth for the saliva.

"I'm glad to hear that," Doc said, calm-voiced.

"My goodness, you'll be rich," Nina said. She beckoned for more champagne. The bartender brought Doc's huge glass when he came to serve her. The stuff in the glass bubbled, steamed, stank.

Doc Savage indicated the glass. "You call that hot?"

"I can't get it any hotter," the bartender apologized. "It will boil away. It seems to have a low boiling point."

Poltov's mouth was working agonizedly, leaking some saliva.

"I got no money," he croaked. "Banner, I'm sorry, I got no money."

Doc asked, "You mean that you have squandered my share?"

"I—well, yes."

"You can't pay off?"

"No. I am sorry."

"You may not suffer from sorrow for very long." Doc's nostrils were assailed by the steam arising from the potion in the glass. The odor was awful, but it suggested an idea. Doc Savage did not wish anyone to think Banner would order something he didn't dare drink, but he did not care to drink it either. He seized the boiling drink and shoved it into Poltov's hands. "Drink that, you welching skunk," he said. "We're taking a walk. You'll need liquid support. Drink it." He dropped his hand into his coat pocket and made a convincing pretense of a gun with a stiffly extended finger.

Poltov did not argue. Using the bar towel for a pad, he picked up the drink and dumped it down his throat. He emitted scalded moans. Doc assisted him in placing the empty glass back on the bar.

"Now we'll take that walk." The bronze man had to support Poltov toward the door.

"May I come?" asked Nina, a little too quickly, Doc thought.

"Yes," Doc told her gruffly. "You can even serve as next of kin for the deceased, if you like."

"I doubt if I qualify, but I'll try." Nina did not seem unduly alarmed about what might happen to Poltov. The bronze man greatly admired her composure, until it occurred to him she might have a gun in her purse and be intending to use it to defend her boyfriend when they were outside.

"His coat?" prompted Nina.

"He won't need it," Doc returned. They approached the door. "He won't feel the cold very long, if he doesn't pay up," he added warningly.

"Well, if you think I am going out on a night like this without my coat, you can guess again." Nina stood on tiptoes, waved a hand overhead. "Olga, Olga, honey!" An older girl wearing a waitress's apron gave them her attention. "Olga, will you bring my coat?" Nina called.

"You must come here often," Doc said. It suggested that she was a regular, and less likely to be a Red agent.

Nina accepted the short fur jacket which the waitress brought. She cast it over her shoulders. "Why shouldn't I know the help here?" Siberian wolves had furnished the furs for the jacket, Russian sables the lining. "Seeing I own the establishment," she added airily.

"You own this joint!" Doc blurted. He had the presence of mind to retain his Banner-like tone despite his surprise. He opened the door and boosted Poltov out into the night. The snow nipped at their faces with tiny teeth. Along the top of the sign that bore the name of the place, *"Nyttig Enke,"* snow lay like a line of roosting white sparrows. The bronze man pointed at the sign and asked, "Are you the Useful Widow mentioned there?"

Her eyes touched him briefly, glinted.

"You think it unlikely?" she asked.

"No, I don't." Doc revised his earlier opinion of her schoolgirl innocence. "I bet you can be very useful." He kept a tight grip on Poltov. "But I wouldn't be too useful to Poltov here, if I were you," he added.

"Does he really owe you money?" she asked.

"You didn't hear him deny it, did you?" said Doc.

Poltov coughed hackingly as they walked into the darkness and falling snow. The snow sang like tiny violins underfoot, indicating intense cold. The streetlamps were as yellow as handmade diamonds.

Nina held her coat together at her throat with one hand.

"What do you plan to do to Poltov?" she asked.

"Collect," Doc said grimly.

"He has no money."

"Then I'll have to knock him off," Doc said, matter-of-factly.

Both Poltov's hands were clutching his throat. He coughed in deep, lung-rending barks. Sweat came out on his face and steamed. It was working, Doc reflected. The fearsome visage of Banner, The Face, did most of his intimidating for him.

"Are you serious?" Nina asked, more out of curiosity than concern, Doc thought.

"I can't have business associates putting the double cross on me," he bit out. The aura of steam about Poltov's face made him wraithlike. He added gurgling to his barking. "A thing like that can be catching," Doc went on. Poltov made the gurglings before each paroxysm of coughing.

Nina looked blank.

"Catching to other business associates, I mean," Doc explained.

"I think Paul is trying to tell you something," Nina said.

"Yeah?" Doc slammed Poltov against the side of a darkened building. "Speak up, you wretched thief!" He shook his head at the sounds Poltov made. "Can you understand him?" he asked Nina.

"No."

"I can't, either."

They resumed walking. Poltov endeavored to turn toward the more populated part of the city. Seizing the Russian's collar, Doc Savage steered the man toward the waterfront. "I might as well drop you off a dock," he said fiercely.

Nina made almost no noise walking in the snow. "I think that drink you forced on him burned his throat terribly," she said.

"He must have a chintzy throat," Doc said with false bravado. "A man's drink like that never bothered me." He neglected to add that he had never tried swallowing one.

Nina's eyes glinted up at him. "You seem an unusual man."

"Why? Because I can drink a warm vodka toddy?"

Nina indicated Poltov. "I have never before seen Paul afraid to fight, or resist a man," she said.

"I don't believe he is afraid of me," Doc said. Poltov's hands no longer clutched his throat. As if afflicted with St. Vitus, he jerked as he walked. Doc added, "But I do think he knows it might make me angry if he put up a battle."

"I have an idea that might help," Nina said.

"You have?"

"Poltov owns a half interest in a small steamship," she told him. "Perhaps if he signed over his half to you . . ."

Doc shook his head. "No," he said. "I don't want to get in the steamship business."

"You wouldn't be interested?"

"Nope."

Nina shrugged. "Well, I was just trying to help."

After walking a few more steps, Doc Savage abruptly hurled Poltov against another building. "Stand there, you!" The building—sprawling, grimy, windowless—seemed a warehouse. They were alone. "What you just said about a ship gives me an idea," Doc told Nina.

"Yes?" she said, expectantly.

"If you don't mind, I'll discuss it privately with Poltov," Doc told her.

"Oh?"

A strong smell of fish indicated the harbor was nearby.

"How about walking on ahead a ways?" Doc suggested.

"I'd like to listen," said Nina frankly.

Doc Savage shook his head. "This is private business. You trot on ahead, or I'll plant my foot where it would encourage you most."

"You just try it!" Nina fluffed her fur coat angrily. "There's a bar around the corner. You can join me there."

Doc Savage watched her walk away, disappear to the left. He felt a creeping admiration for the little blonde, but he was shocked by her resolute calmness.

"She isn't worrying much about you, is she?" Doc asked Paul Poltov.

The Russian kneaded his throat with both hands, then spat a yellow stain on the snow. His bloodshot eyes glittered moistly, fearfully.

"I don't want to harm you," Doc told him truthfully. "But you understand how it is. You got something coming."

Poltov endeavored to speak. At the first sound, he clutched his neck convulsively.

Doc Savage said, "Nod your head, yes or no. That will do. . . . The first thing, is it straight that you own half a seagoing vessel?"

Poltov nodded.

"Okay," said Doc, "maybe you can pay off what you owe me by doing a job for me. Or do I fill your pockets with rocks and drop you off a dock."

Poltov nodded again, unable to muster words.

Doc made a clucking sound of approval. "That's fine. Give us a chance to be square. . . . Have you been doing any smuggling business around the mouth of the Pechora River lately?"

Poltov nodded once more.

The bronze man glanced about. They were very alone.

"Think you could take me, a couple of friends, and a few boxes weighing about five hundred pounds, and put us ashore in the Pechora, or near it, without the Soviets knowing it?" Doc asked quietly.

Poltov hesitated. He was genuinely frightened.

Doc said, "Of course if you can't . . ."

Poltov nodded hastily. Doc wondered if he had bitten his tongue. The lack of blood at the corners of his mouth suggested not.

"Good. That's all the settling it needs. I'm glad we hit on something sensible." Doc was talking in a friendly tone now. "Say, you haven't got on enough clothes, and I'll bet you're cold. You go on back to the Useful Widow. I'll meet you there at two o'clock this morning, and you can load us on your vessel." He put out a hand. "Is it a deal?" He withdrew his hand hastily when he saw Poltov's hand was wet with sweat and drool.

Poltov endeavored to speak, but Doc Savage could not understand him. "Yes, you take us to the Pechora, and I'll see she gets home safe," he said. "I'll look after Nina."

Poltov scowled, but turned and left. After a few steps, he fell into a trot, beating himself with his arms for warmth.

Without trouble, Doc Savage found the small bar the blonde had mentioned. Sitting on a stool, Nina Kirkegaard poured brandy in a cup of steaming coffee, added a lump of sugar. Two men were taking turns telling her a humorous story. They frowned at the bronze man.

"Business transacted," Doc told Nina amiably. "The evening is free."

The little blonde said coolly, "I'm going home."

"I merely said the evening is free."

"And I've decided I don't like your manner," Nina said, frost riming her tone now. "You are a brute."

Her two men companions stood shoulder-to-shoulder. They measured Doc Savage with hostile eyes. Each was slightly larger than the bronze man—which meant they were large indeed.

Doc spoke to them mildly. "Poltov wants her taken home. I promised him to do so," he explained, addressing his words to the pair.

The two men exchanged startled glances. After a brief hesitancy, they departed.

Doc said, "They must know our friend Poltov."

"You're impudent," said Nina. She slung her fur coat over her shoulders. Doc inquired if she wished to finish her coffee, but she shook her head angrily. "I knew you would find a way to make up to Poltov. You're a great big phony," she said, flouncing off.

"You mean a mega-phony—all noise?" Doc hastily followed her to the door and back out into the night.

Outdoors, she walked rapidly, keeping ahead of him. She made small, firm footprints in the snow.

"Maybe you would like me to get a taxi?" he called ahead to her.

"Drop dead," she said.

Doc knew the quick pace would soon tire her and he would overhaul her. Padding along a few paces behind her embarrassed him. It made him feel like a puppy dog trailing after his mistress following a scolding. He pretended to turn off a side street, and as if by magic, his big body shed the awkwardness that characterized Banner's movements. He melted into a long patch of shadow and reemerged on the street, well back of the blonde. His footsteps were eerily silent as he followed at a decorous distance.

To the bronze man's surprise, Nina turned on to a

wharf. His quickened steps enabled him to observe her stepping into a motor-equipped dory.

Doc drew near, astonishment at this unexpected turn of events making him shed all caution. "Where do you think you're going in that motorboat?" he called out.

The boat was more launch than dory. A fancy one. Its mahogany and bright brasswork peeked through its coat of new-fallen snow.

"I'm going home." Nina flipped the launch mooring line clear of a cleat, freeing the craft from land.

"You live out in the Shetland Islands?" he asked, slightly incredulous. They lay due west of Bergen. A mere two hundred and fifty miles due west.

"Hardly! And I do not appreciate being followed." Nina seized a boat hook, a formidable thing which Doc felt she would not hesitate to use upon him. He kept his distance, but asked, "Say, where *do* you live?" Blue exhaust smoke spurted from the pipes under the launch stern. The engine had a powerful, throaty voice.

"I live on a ship," Nina flung back. "I own half the ship, if you must know. Poltov owns the other half." Nina spun the wheel and the launch settled by the stern, then swung away from the dock strongly, its propeller already throwing up a plume of water. "I'm captain and co-owner of the ship," Nina called back to him.

The harbor waters rushed darkly together behind the launch, and its wake pursued it away from shore.

Doc stared thoughtfully. He wondered if he should shout after her the news that they were associated in a business deal.

"She doesn't know she's being snippy to a good customer," he remarked to himself. And he wasn't entirely satisfied that she was what she seemed to be, and only that.

He turned away from the wharf and disappeared into the frigid Bergen darkness.

X

RENDEZVOUS IN EVANGER

Doc Savage decided to rent a small truck which he could drive himself, and use this to pick up Moonwinx, the UHF radio apparatus designed for reflecting signals from the moon surface. It was not windy enough to drift the snow and block the road to Evanger, the small town near Bergen where Arthur Dryden and Peter Breckenridge were supposed to await Doc's arrival. They would have the UHF radio equipment, packed for transporting, with them.

They would, that is, if there had been no hitches.

They will be there, Doc thought, *if Anna Gryahznyi hasn't hit their trail.*

Thinking of Anna Gryahznyi caused Doc to break out in a thin film of sweat under his disguise. He was forced to stop and make his mind a blank. Should the Banner face slip at an inopportune moment, all these months of careful hard work and trouble would have been for nothing. And the bronze man suspected that a great many inopportune moments lay before him.

It was hard to put the Red Widow out of his mind. He had first heard of her during the war. Anna Gryahznyi had been a Russian resistance fighter. It was said that the Nazi invaders feared her more than the Russian winter. The savagery with which she had dealt with captured German soldiers—breaking their will to keep their secrets by practically dismembering the ectoplasm that held their souls together and then dismembering their bodies with the casualness of a child plucking apart a spider's web—had seemed to be one of those many examples of patriotic brutality that war brings about.

After the war, Anna Gryahznyi had not returned to her civilian life, in which she was rumored to have been everything from a schoolmistress to a hospital nurse. She dedicated her awful skills to advancing the Kremlin's country-crushing agenda. In peace, she became even more of a monster. Or perhaps, Doc reflected, it was just that without the barbarism of a world war to blend in with, Anna Gryahznyi only seemed more fearsome.

Doc composed himself sufficiently to visit an *Automobilstald*, select a pickup truck, and argue bitterly with the proprietor over the deposit, which he was ultimately forced to pay. Muttering direly, Doc climbed into the vehicle—an ancient model—and started the engine indoors. The sound brought forth was deafening. He thought for a moment a battle had been started with shotguns, rocks, and empty tin cans. However, the vehicle plunged fiercely along the snow-quilted streets, and its racket outdoors did not seem as objectionable.

It was not snowing in the country, but there was a thick fog, like cotton packed around him. Doc managed not to become confused in the fog, and drove straight to a residence on King Harald Street in Evanger. All the other houses on Harald Street were prim, neat, unlighted, the good burghers who lived in them obviously asleep. How they could sleep with all that noise coming from the house before which Doc had halted was a mystery. But they had always managed this, the bronze man recalled.

Doc Savage eyed the house, which emitted great gout-like bursts of revelry. He grinned inwardly. For he had recommended the place to Breckenridge and Dryden as a hide-out, and he wondered what they thought of it. Particularly Dryden, whom Doc felt deserved a comeuppance for his past behavior.

Two men came out of the house and walked away, hastily turning up their coat collars and averting their faces when they noticed Doc's approaching figure.

A window flew open. A gentleman's brown hat sailed from it. The window banged closed.

Doc's firm knock was answered by a strange butler. Fearing the place had changed ownership, the bronze man demanded, "What has become of Rafael?" His alarm subsided when the butler said, "Rafael is taking a night out."

Yellow light from an ornate chandelier made a halo about the butler's white hair. Waves of brassy music, cries of hilarity, came from many parts of the house. A dignified man in a brown suit made his way past Doc and the butler. The man retrieved his hat from its resting place on the snow in the yard. When he attempted to reenter, the butler shut the door firmly in his face.

"The gentleman has been ejected from the establishment, sir," the butler told Doc apologetically.

Doc grinned. "I bet he wishes he had let his hat stay out there."

"May we give you service, sir?" asked the butler.

"I am supposed to have a couple of friends staying here," Doc told him. "There names are Dryden and Breckenridge."

"And your name, sir?"

"Banner."

The serving man's eyes flickered. "I believe I have heard you mentioned, sir. Will you step this way?"

Breckenridge sat in the parlor playing cards with a dark-haired girl in a cheap yellow dress. There were two stacks of five, ten, and fifty kroner banknotes on the table, the far larger stack in front of the girl. The girl's name was Agnette. Her eyes lighted up at sight of Doc Savage. "Welcome back, Meester Bean-neer," she said. Breckenridge gave a guilty start, arose.

"I see you fellows got here," Doc said, shaking Breckenridge's hand.

"Yeah." Breckenridge had shaved and powdered recently. "We've been here three days." His eyes were bloodshot. "What kept you?" he asked.

"I'll tell you about that later," said Doc quickly. "Is Dryden around?"

"Upstairs."

"I think we'd best have a talk with him." Doc was looking at Agnette. She avoided his eyes. "Agnette, honey," said Doc, affecting the easy manner of Banner. "Breck, here. He's a pal of mine."

Agnette leaned back. A faint color came into the blue shadows over her cheeks. Her little mouth became sullen. She counted out most of the money before her, handed it to Breckenridge. He flushed.

"Take it." As they moved to the stairway, Doc Savage advised Breckenridge, "Agnette dealt blackjack at Monte Carlo once, but they fired her in time to save the place from bankruptcy."

Breckenridge became indignant. "Hell, she was letting me teach *her* the game!" he complained.

In the upstairs hall, a wonderfully incandescent red-headed girl walked past. Her carriage was statuesque, dignified, provocative. She was lovely. Once past them, she called back gaily, " 'Allo, Meester Bean-neer." The maroon mules on her feet were flamboyantly trimmed with red ostrich plumes. They were the most conservative scrap of attire adorning her form.

"Flashy slippers, didn't you think?" Doc Savage asked, pretending not to have noticed the girl. He wondered if he was blushing under his disguise. He added, "I wonder if Dryden could be too busy to see us?"

"I doubt it," said Breckenridge. "I don't think Mr. Dryden quite approves of this place."

"He doesn't!" said Doc, feigning surprise.

"No," affirmed Breckenridge.

"I rather thought this place would suit him," Doc said, innocent-voiced.

Dryden jumped up from his bed at first sight of them, casting aside a copy of *Pravda* which he had been reading. "What held you up?" he demanded. "Did you run into trouble?"

Doc shook his head. "I imagine I was on a slower plane." He thought Dryden looked much more fit than in New York. "This climate seems to agree with you," he added. "Or maybe it's the Norwegian hospitality."

Dryden crossed to kick the door closed. "The damn incessant noise!" Doc Savage did not think closing the door had made the room noticeably quieter. Dryden added, "You picked a hell of a place for our rendezvous!" He was genuinely indignant. "Some joke! A gambling casino masquerading as a hotel!"

"I agree with the boss," said Breckenridge. "The place is a novelty, I'll admit. But the novelty soon wore out."

Doc Savage was secretly delighted over his little joke. But he kept his brutish face impassive.

Dryden came around a chair to them. He held himself erect and aloof, like a parson decrying sin.

"What kept you so long? That's what I want to know." Dryden was really furious.

"Keep your shirt on," Doc retorted, keeping up the pretense of being the notorious Banner. "I had work to do." Amusement created wrinkles at the corners of the bronze man's brown-tinted eyes.

Dryden scowled. "I hope you accomplished something," he said bitterly. "Did you?"

"Oh, sure," Doc said airily.

"What?" asked Dryden. "Let's have it."

Doc shook his head warningly. He moved casually about the room. He peered behind a painting of a milkmaid gazing up at another milkmaid in a gnarled tree. "I think we'd best do our talking in the truck I've hired," the bronze man said, low-voiced.

Alarmed, Dryden wrote a question on a sheet of paper. The question: *Is the place wired?* He looked at Doc Savage anxiously.

"I don't see any sign of it." Doc pulled an airman's canvas bag from under the bed. "This all your luggage? Let's be on our way."

With Breckenridge carrying a similar airman's bag, they went downstairs. The butler appeared silently and listened to Doc ask about the other baggage the gentlemen had brought. "We've been called away suddenly," he explained somberly.

* * *

By the time he had backed the truck around to a shed in the rear, Dryden, Breckenridge, and the butler were dragging the UHF radio equipment out of hiding.

The Moonwinx apparatus was in five aluminum cases. All seams had been welded and carrying handles had been riveted at convenient places. Any single case could be lifted by one strong man. Carrying it all day would be another matter.

The pickup engine popped and clattered as they drove off, sent echoes banging around in the dark street.

"I'm glad no dampness can get to the gadget," Doc offered. "Somebody really packed that stuff. Only I hope it's all there." He became thoughtful. "With a book of instructions," he added dryly.

"You better be able to make the damn thing work, is all I can say," said Dryden, turning to Breckenridge. "That's why you were chosen, because you're a radio ham."

"I'll make out," Breckenridge said sourly. "And if not, Sav—" He caught himself, swallowed audibly. "Uh, Banner is our man."

Dryden scowled. "Let us hope your confidence isn't premature," he said. "It is a long way to our destination."

Doc Savage dismissed all concern. "I'll have you lads in the middle of Russia, watching that Moonwinx gadget percolating, before you know it."

They lit all three cigarettes off one match. Doc pretended to smoke. He detested tobacco, but it made a good prop.

"See? We're not only bold, we defy superstition," said Doc carelessly.

"I noticed you're more optimistic than you were in New York." Dryden, now that he was no longer residing in the hotel, seemed less irritable. "In New York, you sang the glooms," he added.

"The New York climate didn't agree with me," Doc said soberly.

Breckenridge pointed about them at the snow and fog. He shivered.

"This is an improvement?" The outdoor cold was bringing his carefully guarded ill humor to prominence.

"You bet." Doc was convincing. "Dig this pure air. Not a whiff of Anna Gryahznyi in it." He glanced sidewise at Dryden. "Makes a man feel more healthful—doesn't it, Dryden?"

Dryden said thinly, "I do not care to discuss it." His lips had almost disappeared into his mouth. The sinews were standing out noticeably in his neck.

Although he would have liked to know exactly what had befallen Dryden at the hands of Anna Gryahznyi when Dryden had last visited Russia, Doc Savage kept the question to himself. He understood how Dryden must feel. A man was entitled to privacy in the part of his mind where his profoundest secrets of terror were kept. Dryden was not a man to be permanently affected by the dangers of being garroted, shot, poisoned, run over, or toppled from high windows. After all, the act of dying takes but a moment. The really enormous villainies are the ones which move slowly and defy eradication, much like an attack of the warts.

I know how he feels, Doc thought. He wouldn't have cared to discuss his fear of Anna Gryahznyi himself. There was something unnerving about being singled out for death by an enemy nation. Knowing the name of one's intended assassin made it worse. That the assassin was a woman—a faceless woman who could be anyone—made every turn in the road ahead a place where terror lay coiled to strike.

Evanger lay behind them, its streetlamps losing themselves in the fog like dim eyes closing. Snow-draped countryside surrounded them—peaceful, darkened, cold-looking. Doc drove with more care, not wishing to slide into a ditch. A farm dog ran out from a gate in a fieldstone fence, barked at them furiously, the dog's breath spurting from its mouth with each bark like smoke from a Gatling gun loaded with black powder.

"Did anyone remember to pay our bill back at the hotel?" Breckenridge asked suddenly.

"Money is a viper, wealth is a sturdy character," said

Doc cryptically. When they both looked at him in silence, he added in his natural voice, "Mr. Banner's credit is always good in that particular establishment."

Presently, they and the headlights of a train approached a crossing simultaneously. Concerned over being blocked long enough to attract the attention of the local authorities, Doc Savage bore down on the accelerator, but the train won the race, and then perversely stopped with its cars blocking the crossing.

Fuming, Doc switched off the engine, and watched a trainman carrying a lantern tap on bearing boxes. "Why on earth do trains always stop so they block a crossing?" he wanted to know. The roof of the little stone station, the flower boxes around it, were heavy with snow that could have passed for powdered sugar.

"I still can't figure out why you were two days late joining us," Dryden told Doc.

The bronze man, still watching the train, let his breath run out between his teeth. "We're stuck here. I might as well tell you all about it," he said. He rolled up the window to keep out the cold air. "While you two were enjoying Norwegian hospitality, I have been combing Denmark, Sweden, and Norway, hunting up what our mythical friend, Banner, would call a patsy, who could be persuaded to smuggle us and our gadget into Russia."

"I'm glad you've found time to tell us where you have been," said Dryden grumpily.

"I had to find transportation, didn't I?" asked Doc. "How did you plan to get to the Arctic coast of Russia? Swim?"

Dryden said, "The United States Army has airplanes and parachutes."

"The Soviets have radar and firing squads," Doc said bleakly.

Dryden said, "The United States Navy has submarines, too."

"The Russians have a gadget for detecting them, as well," Doc said crisply. "If you can get a sub within a hundred miles of any Soviet coast without their knowing, you will be accomplishing something."

The trainman with the lantern had stopped to light his pipe.

"And since we intend to make our escape by submarine, I don't believe taking that risk on both legs of this trek would be advisable," Doc added.

Breckenridge cleared his throat. "We've been over this before."

"Yes, we have," sniffed Dryden. "And were overruled by our Russian expert here."

Doc Savage said, "Tonight I snared a dupe who agreed to put us ashore in the Pechora River, snug as a flea in Malenkov's pants."

"Can he deliver on his promise?" Dryden sounded skeptical.

"I hope so," Doc said sincerely. "He had better."

The bronze man related in detail his experiences in the waterfront cabaret known as *Nyttig Enke*. He went into particular detail about Miss Nina Kirkegaard.

"You hooked up with a strange woman!" Dryden said, going apoplectic.

"She hooked up with me," Doc Savage explained. "I'm not altogether certain if our meeting was an accidental accident or a deliberate one."

In bringing Paul Poltov into his story, Doc Savage held back the fellow's name as a surprise for Dryden. He related events much as they had happened, not omitting to play up Poltov's huge size and terrible reputation.

Dryden interrupted once to ask, "When this guy double-crossed you and tipped off the Russky, and they chased you into the woods—was that the time you were missing for over a month?"

Doc nodded. "That was the time." The bronze man narrated how in the end Miss Nina Kirkegaard had turned out to be half owner and captain of the ship that was to carry them. This surprised his companions as much as it had Doc Savage.

Dryden saw reason to be apprehensive.

"One of them cutthroat Commie dames, that's what she sounds like to me," he said harshly.

"Yes, what are you getting us into, Sav—uh, Banner?" asked Breckenridge, worriedly.

Without any warning other than two whistle toots, the train crashed into motion. The trainman with the lantern was taken completely by surprise.

"I'm not worried," said Doc firmly.

Dryden blinked. "It's safe?"

"Nothing in the days ahead will be safe," said Doc grimly. "Of course, we will have to watch this Paul Poltov like a hawk."

Dryden started. "Poltov! Is that who . . . ?"

"Yes."

The trainman held his lantern high over his head and stared angrily at the boxcars increasing speed. Doc knew he was thinking that it was a long, cold walk back to the caboose on top of the cars but that if he waited, the caboose would be going too fast to catch when it arrived. However, the trainman's dilemma was nothing compared to Dryden's agitation.

Dryden groaned. "Poltov!" he said. "A murderer! A scoundrel! A smuggler!" His roaring filled the car, was louder than the train. "That's the kind of man you have hired to help us!"

"He will get the job done," said Doc Savage.

"He'll cut our throats!" cried Dryden.

"I imagine he will try," said Doc, dryly.

"He can't be trusted!" Dryden exploded.

"Of course not."

"He's a double-crosser!"

"If he sees the opportunity for double-crossing," Doc admitted.

"Poltov will sell us out to the Russky!"

"I will think up something to cope with that," Doc assured him.

"I don't like it!" Dryden fumed.

"I don't either, if you want the truth." Doc Savage watched the trainman, who had started to run alongside the cars. "But beggars cannot be choosers," he added. The train was moving faster than the trainman thought, and he put on full speed. He lost ground. He threw away his lantern. Thus lightened, he overtook a car, seized a handhold, was jerked off his feet, and smashed against the car side. Finally, he clung safely with one hand and shook his other fist in the direction of the engineer. He vanished in the fog. The caboose finally snapped past, pulling a fat tail of snow behind it.

"He'll have to pay for the lantern, I'll wager," Doc said thoughtfully.

He got the truck moving again, sending it jouncing over the hard, snow-dusted rails.

XI

TWO BLACK SHEEP

Paul Poltov had been a Communist during all but three years of his life. Only from birth to the age of three years had he not been a Communist. Paul had been born on Big Diomede Island, his ancestry mostly Chukchi. The Chukchi are supposed to bear the closest likeness to the American Indian of any people in Asia.

Big Diomede was a godforsaken wart of rock and ice. But even on Diomede, they took the babies away from the parents who had any capitalistic taint and put them in the party *shkola* for Bolshevik training. Paul Poltov had reached his thirty-second birthday two weeks ago. That meant twenty-nine years in the party. This long experience had made him well-acquainted with the shifty, buck-passing, fear-bedeviled state of mind which was standard equipment when transacting business with an upper-echelon Communist. Paul would not have felt natural without it.

On a Communist-to-Communist basis, Paul trusted Jon Gahs about as much as any comrade. This did not imply he trusted Jon Gahs very much.

Jon Gahs was the name of the local ranking Communist agent, the one to whom Paul was making his report about the smuggling proposition of the man he knew only as Banner.

Very few Communist agents look the part, but Jon Gahs was an exception. He was a double for the cartoonist version of a bomb-tosser. His beard and hair were a frenzied black, very disheveled. His body was not worth much and he kept it sloppily clad. Generally, Jon Gahs resembled the northern exposure of a frightened southbound skunk.

Jon Gahs worked as janitor in a Bergen apartment house. He was a trusted employee. He had held his position eighteen years. He was also corresponding secretary of the Apartment House Workers Union committee for the expulsion of Communists from Norwegian labor unions.

Paul Poltov looked intently at the turning spool of a tape recorder. "I guess that is all." They were in Jon Gahs's room in the apartment house basement. The walls were shaggy mortared stone. Overhead were soot stains and steam pipes. Paul drew a finger across his throat suggestively, eyeing Gahs. Paul wanted the telltale tape recorder shut off. Gahs switched it off.

"That Banner!" he shouted. "That snake in the grass! That capitalist!"' The lower lids of Jon Gahs's eyes drooped outward from his bloodshot eyeballs like gaping pockets. "What do you think is in his boxes? Money? American currency for paying imperialistic bribes to weakened workers of the people's republic? How big are the boxes? How much money is in them?"

"I do not know what is in the boxes," said Poltov, truthfully.

"Money? Do you suppose it is American currency? This is important to know, comrade." Around the edges of Gahs's eyeballs, the blood vessels looked as if they had ruptured.

"If it is money, Banner will steal it before we can get our hands on it," Poltov suggested. "He is a devil."

"Do you think there is a chance we two could steal it first?" asked Gahs.

"From Banner? From under his nose? I doubt it." Paul Poltov's voice was in bad shape. It sounded like a chair being dragged across a concrete floor a little at a time. "I do not know if money is in the boxes," he repeated.

"Since we cannot steal it for ourselves," Gahs muttered darkly, "I suppose we must pass it along to the greater thieves." He paused. In the back of the room, a boiler digested coal with contented rustling sounds. "I will telephone Moscow," Gahs said at last. He did not sound happy about it.

Gahs pulled a telephone to him.

Poltov waited. His hands, resting on his knees, were hard as bricks and hairy as pigs. His breathing sounded like sand sloshing in a tin can.

Gahs got through to Moscow on the telephone with little trouble. The long-distance operators were party girls, so he was sure his call would be bypassed around any wiretapping the Norwegian authorities happened to be doing. Gahs identified himself to Moscow. Then he put the tape recorder on playback and held the telephone where it would pick up Poltov's oral report.

Presently, the telephone receiver emitted sounds similar to the part taken by the hounds in a fox chase. Gahs reduced the tape machine volume while he asked into the phone, "Isn't it coming through? Comrade Poltov's voice . . ."

The phone receiver bayed back at him. Gahs listened attentively. One hand pawed foolishly at the tape machine, turned it entirely off. Either the lids were sinking farther from his eyes, or his eyeballs were getting bigger.

Poltov was silent. He knew someone in Moscow was cracking the corners off of hell and heaving them along the wire at Jon Gahs.

"Dah! Dah! Dah!" Perspiration was appearing on Gahs's head like droplets of nasal secretion. *"Dah, soodar!"* he said. He looked at Poltov. Gahs's lower lip began to thrust out in rage; it protruded until it looked as if he were trying to swallow his nose. *"Dah! Dah!"* he said to

Moscow. *"Dah! Dah! Dah!"* His beard bristled like black-painted steel wool.

Gahs dropped the telephone on the hook with a shaking hand. He said to Poltov, "You snake! You bishop! You priest!" His words were mumbled as if he were chewing them as he talked. "I'll teach you to make me trouble!"

Poltov began to say, "I assure you—"

Gahs advanced angrily. "All was so peaceful until you came!" He looked like a buzzard making a charge. "I'll teach you to come to me like a sick dog and empty yourself on me!"

"I have to report to you," Poltov protested. "Those are my instructions. You are my superior officer."

Jon Gahs directed an open-handed slap at Poltov, which the latter avoided.

"No, comrade, no!" screamed Poltov. He placed a hand on Gahs's face, pushing him away. "Swine!" he cried. Gahs had bitten through one of Poltov's fingers to the bone. Poltov seized Gahs by the nose and twisted until the finger was free.

Then Poltov stepped back, as if realizing the full import of what he had done.

"We must not fight, comrade," Poltov said, no thread of hope in his scared voice.

Hands poised like talons, Gahs charged. "I'll kill you!" Blood fell out of his tweaked nose. Poltov stepped aside. Gahs's momentum carried him past and as he tried to turn, he stumbled and lurched against the hot furnace.

There came a sizzling sound of meat searing. Gahs cried out and toppled back from the furnace to flop on the floor. His mouth worked. "You are right," he moaned. "We must not fight." There was an odor of singed cat in the room.

Poltov was pale, shaking. "I am sorry," he blubbered, near collapse.

"Moscow is so angry," Gahs mewed. His eyes filled with tears. "Sometimes it is more than a man can bear." He staggered to his feet. Already one side of his face was filling out in a horrible pale blister. "Salve. For burns. In that cabinet there," he moaned weakly.

"I will get the salve," said Poltov, anxiously.

"No, never mind," Gahs said. "It can wait. Thank you, comrade, it can wait. I am so sorry I lost my temper, comrade. I am sure you did not know this is a terribly big matter when you came to report to me."

"All I know," said Poltov, "is that Banner wants to hire me to smuggle him and two others and some boxes into Russia."

"No, it is bigger than that." The blister grew like a child's pink toy balloon slowly filling with water. "In the Kremlin, it produced an earthquake. You heard?"

"All I heard was a lot of barking on the telephone," allowed Poltov.

"Ah," spat Gahs.

"Well, I suppose I can avoid taking Banner," said Poltov. "That is if I can get out of town before he catches me. Comrade, can you get me a travel card to, say, the Crimea? Quick?"

Gahs shook his head. "You are to do as Banner wishes."

"I am!" Poltov said, dumbfounded. "I thought Moscow . . ."

"You are to find an excuse to put your ship in at Tromso en route," said Gahs.

"Tromso? That's not hard. Banner will expect that. He knows I always put in at Tromso to make arrangements with the Russians for an illegal ship clearance."

"Yes, Moscow mentioned that you usually did it that way," said Gahs.

"Really?" Poltov was dubious. "They know more about me in Moscow than I supposed," he said thoughtfully.

"In Tromso," continued Gahs, "you will take on a passenger who will be one of our high-ranking agents."

"Good," said Poltov. "That will take the responsibility out of my hands."

"Yes, I imagine."

"I won't have to worry about Banner," Poltov

promised. "That will be a relief. Who is our agent who will come aboard in Tromso? Anyone I know?"

"No, comrade, you have not met her."

"Her? A woman?"

"Anna Gryahznyi." Gahs fingered his bulging blister. His eyes were shiny with revengeful satisfaction.

Poltov ducked his head slightly.

"Anna Gryahznyi . . . will join my ship in Tromso?" He could feel the hairs on his nape crawling. "Is that what you said?"

"You are lucky, Comrade Poltov." Gahs touched his blister as gently as if it was an exposed wound. "Anna Gryahznyi is a notorious person. She will save you from Banner."

"Yes, I am a lucky fellow," said Poltov gloomily. "I will get your salve, comrade."

The salve for burns was in a screw-top jar. There was also a bottle of raw turpentine beside it in the cabinet. Without hesitation, Paul Poltov mixed some of the turpentine into the ointment.

"Here you are, comrade," he said, handing the re-closed jar to Jon Gahs. He suppressed a grin of anticipation, remembering how dogs howled when turpentine was applied to their wet noses.

This memory cheered him slightly as he took his hasty departure.

XII

A WALL CLOSING IN

At half past ten the following morning, Doc Savage came on deck. Their ship, which was named the *Norge Pike*, seemed to be engaged endlessly in sitting in a world of pale fog, jabbing wave-edges, chill dampness. Alarmed lest they be hove to for some reason, the bronze man peered over the side. The smart cut-wave being thrown by the bow reassured him.

Doc started off on a brisk constitutional around the deck. The damp feel of danger was strong. But he did not mind. Anna Gryahznyi was back in New York City, he was certain, seeking him under two separate identities, so he did not mind at all. He felt good.

Dryden was sagging on the rail. He had no hat. Doc said, "Good morning." Dryden did not respond happily. He had been vomiting over the rail. He was seasick.

"How soon does a man die of this?" he wanted to know.

Doc drew in deep health-giving breaths of morning air. "I don't think it ever kills you," he said jauntily. Doc indicated a nearby open hatch. "Is our coworker down below watching that no one steals our Moonwinx?" he undertoned.

Dryden nodded. "We've got to get the boxes out of that hold. It's awful down there, Banner. Awful!" Dryden clutched the rail with one hand and his stomach with the other. "A man can't stand it."

"Oh, it can't be so bad," said Doc in Banner's breezy manner. "It's probably warm and cozy down there."

"I would rather be swallowed by a hog," Dryden said bitterly, "as go down there again."

A cargo boom squeaked and tugged gently at its lashings on the foredeck. Fog moved in nebulous patches. The sky was the color of rabbit fur.

Doc descended the hatch into the hold, lowering himself on a steel ladder. "A happy good morning to you, too," he said to Breckenridge. The hold did smell a little gamy, he noticed.

"Hello." Breckenridge was not going to admit he was seasick. "How goes it?"

"Fine. Fine. Was it rough down here?"

"No more than could be expected."

"No thieves in the night?" asked Doc.

"No."

"Any visitors?"

"Not a single one."

"I wonder why not." Doc pondered. "Norwegians are a friendly, curious folk. I don't see how they could resist sticking their noses into the mystery of why three men are guarding five boxes night and day." He decided the bilge smell in the hold was rapidly getting worse.

"Maybe they aren't curious-type Norwegians," ventured Breckenridge.

"Maybe they're not Norwegians," Doc suggested pointedly.

Breckenridge stiffened. "Are you kidding?"

"Yes, I am." Doc paused, listened to a rat fight which had started in the piled cargo nearby. "At least I hope I am."

It seemed to Doc Savage that the stink of the hold was increasing intolerably. He assured himself this sensation was the result of a strong imagination rather than a queasy stomach. He could see that Breckenridge was not bothered by it, outside of being slightly pale, with just a little green thrown in. If Breckenridge could stand a little stink and some rolling by the ship, then he could, too.

"It's sure nice and warm down here," Doc said robustly. He inhaled a deep, healthy breath, and almost wished he hadn't. "It's safe, too," he added.

"Safe from what?" asked Breckenridge. "Air you can breathe?"

"Oh, air like this is very healthy," the bronze man told him. "When you take in a lungful of this, you've got something substantial."

"Nourishing, you mean?" asked Breckenridge bitterly.

"Something like that," said Doc. "Well, I'll see you later. I am now going to have a hearty breakfast of Swedish ham and fried eggs and . . ." Breckenridge suddenly went a shade greener. Doc decided not to mention food further. "I will also look around to see how imminently our lives are menaced," he added. He started for the ladder.

"By the way," called Breckenridge. "Don't forget you

go on watch down here in half an hour. Each of us stands an eight-hour watch. That was the deal."

Doc paused with his foot on the first rung of the ladder. "I'll be on the job," he said, with less confidence than he had begun the conversation. His sense of smell was quite acute, the legacy of years of intensive training designed to heighten his senses. He did not look forward to his time on watch.

He climbed out on deck, wondering if he was actually up to a spell in the noisome hold.

The fresh air was reviving, and seemed to settle his sudden unease. He wondered what had caused it, the hold-stink or the fear that had never really left him. Fear of the dangers that lay before them and the deadly Red Widow that had been left behind in New York.

Dryden had removed his fur cap and was fanning himself with it. Doc noticed one of his ears had a chewed look to it, as if a dog had gotten to it somewhere in his past.

"Your Breckenridge," said Doc, "is not a very tough lad. He doesn't like it down there in the hold."

Dryden nodded listlessly. "Well, you'll soon be on duty down there. We'll see how you like it."

"Probably not very much." Doc was very serious now. "First, I'd better see if the coast is clear."

Dryden started. "You think it isn't?" he demanded.

"I think," Doc said in an emphatic tone, "it is better to be sure than to assume."

He walked briskly around to the other side of the deck house. He was not sure he was sick, but the morning did not seem as charming as before. The ship was doing a slow, distressing series of corkscrew rolls as if hell-bent on wetting every outside rivet in each wave, a performance he had not noticed when he first arose.

He thought of what Breckenridge had said about no visitors. That wasn't like the friendly Norwegians, not to come around to gossip or crack a joke. Doc decided to investigate, learn why the three of them were being treated as pariahs. Instead of acting like Norwegians, the crew was acting like gloomy-Gus Russians, Doc thought worriedly.

If it should turn out that the crew is all Russian, he reflected with a tightening expression, *that would cure my confident mood rather fast.*

Doc Savage walked to the bow. A lookout stood there peering intensely into the fog ahead. Damp black oilskins made him seallike, and he kept both hands cupped back of his ears, listening for the small sounds waves would make breaking on any obstruction in their path.

"Dobraye ootra, gaspadeen," said Doc in Russian.

"Kakahya rabdast? Pashahlooista ne bespakoites," returned the lookout. In Russian. The man turned his face, which was round, stupid, slightly greasy. He was a Russian. He scowled at the bronze man, surprised.

Doc's first thought was that someone was playing a joke on him. They'd be in a tight spot if the crew turned out to be preponderantly Russian. Any Russians on a ship making calls on Soviet seaports would be okayed by Moscow. No anti-Communist, he knew, if one managed to get as far away from home as Norway, would ever set foot voluntarily on a vessel returning to a Soviet port.

Doc scrutinized the Russian closely, memorizing the fellow's glum face. *I had better keep an eye on this fellow in the future*, he reflected.

"You're a tough-looking cookie, Ivan," Doc said in Banneresque English.

The Russian said, *"Dah."* A few hairs grew out of his chin like wheat.

"Well, I'll see you later, but not up a dark alley, I hope," Doc said lightly.

"Dah," said the Russian. He plainly did not understand English.

Doc walked toward the stern of the vessel. He wondered if there were more Russians aboard.

There was only one way of finding out, he realized. Take a look. Most of the crew would be found in the forecastle, of course. He walked briskly in that direction.

Doc shoved open the forecastle door. Through tobacco

smoke the color of saliva he saw men, mostly heavy-faced. He saw sock-covered feet sticking out of bunks. A man sat in a chair with a towel around his neck; a second crewman whom the bronze man briefly mistook for a barber was sprinkling the first one's head with insect powder. Four men sat at a table and played cards. There was almost no conversation. The cards made soft, greasy, slipping sounds. The man getting his head powdered sounded as if he were getting his head sandpapered. The ceiling of the forecastle was papered solid with pinups.

Doc Savage eyed the pinup photographs, first with disinterest, then with opaque surprise, and finally with up-springing alarm. One by one, the eyes of the men in the forecastle found Doc Savage. Once finding him, no gaze moved on. Silence came.

"Nice productive kind of babes there on the ceiling," Doc said jauntily.

Unwavering stares transfixed the bronze man.

Silence continued.

"What's the matter, boys? My taste bad?" asked Doc.

A man spat noisily.

"It's been nice seeing you," said Doc.

He got the dickens out of there. In his haste, he slipped and skinned a shin on a ladder rung. Big drops of sweat crawled down his backbone. He was scared, Doc thought. He was damned scared.

A breeze was kicking up. It had swept away some of the fog. Waves traveled across the sea toward the vessel like puffs of air moving under a soiled bedsheet. A wave hit the bow quartering, drenched the lookout, who did not move, did not seem to notice. A hissing plume of spray from the same wave raced along the rail, trying to climb aboard. When it got aboard, it fell on the deck with a sound like running feet. The sound frightened Doc Savage further.

Dryden eyed Doc with surprise moments later.

"Trouble," Doc said tightly. "Be calm, and just answer this question: Did you bring a machine gun?"

"What would I be doing with a machine gun?" asked Dryden. Seasickness had made his lips lead-colored.

"I don't know yet," Doc told him seriously.

"When you make up your mind, let me know and I'll get it out of my trunk," Dryden said blandly.

Breckenridge put his head out of the hatch. "My time on watch is up." He looked at the bronze man.

"Have you got a Gatling gun up your sleeve, or haven't you, damn it!" Doc asked Dryden.

"What's going on?" asked Breckenridge. "What has happened to our Mister Banner, the legendary Face? Not up to a stint with the rats?"

"Cut it," snapped Doc.

"Okay, but it's your turn at watch," said Breckenridge.

"Yes," said Dryden. "I have two, as a matter of fact."

"How many boxes of cartridges did you fetch?" Doc demanded.

Breckenridge climbed out on deck. "I don't know what is going on, but I'll be damned if I stay down there one more minute!" He separated his feet somewhat so he would not upset.

"Ten boxes," said Dryden.

"What size boxes?" asked Doc. "How many shells in a box?"

"Fifty," Dryden said.

Breckenridge had wiped his mouth and tongue on a handkerchief. He stared at the handkerchief. "What is the fuss here?" The handkerchief had a brownish stain. "I refuse to stand another watch in that hold," he said.

Doc mentally tallied the number of shells. "Ten boxes of fifty shells each is five hundred shells," he said. "That will keep one machine gun doing business for about seven tenths of one minute, isn't that right?" Doc eyed Dryden. "You did say you had two machine guns in your trunk, didn't you?"

"Correct," said Dryden.

"It's your turn to go on watch below," Breckenridge said to Doc Savage in a tight voice.

"No," Doc said firmly. "We will move the boxes to our cabin."

"What's that?" asked Breckenridge.

"We're going to move the boxes to our cabin now," Dryden said, his mood brightening at the prospect of no more tricks in the smelly hold.

Breckenridge thought about this for a moment.

"The hell we are!" he exploded. "The chief stood watch in that stinking hold for eight hours. I stood watch in that hold for eight hours." Breckenridge's voice swelled with indignation. "Now, by God, you'll take your turn in that stink-hole for eight hours! *Then* we will talk about moving the boxes."

"I favor doing it that way, too," Dryden said blandly. "But maybe we had better find out what got him so excited all of a sudden."

"He probably has feet of clay," Breckenridge said acidly. "A lot of the glory-hounds are like that." Breckenridge was quite determined that the bronze man should sample the disagreeable conditions in the hold, even if it meant baiting him into it.

"That was uncalled for," Doc said pointedly.

"Banner would pull his weight," Breckenridge retorted.

Shrugging, Doc prepared to descend into the hold. "No one can say I'm not willing to do my share." A fountain of warm foul air poured up from the hatch, almost gagging him. "But if I were you, gentlemen, I would be particularly careful about taking strolls around this ship."

Dryden frowned. "What do you mean?"

"Go take a look in the fo'castle," said Doc. He descended the ladder. "Don't miss the fo'castle ceiling. The decor is very interesting." He found that he did not feel seasick at all when he stood in the hold, probably, he imagined, because he was frightened.

Doc Savage heard Dryden and Breckenridge depart together. They went in the direction of the forecastle. Doc imagined they would be back shortly. He found the coil of line which had been used last night to lower the aluminum boxes into the hold. He secured one end of the line to a handle on one of the boxes, using a bowline knot.

Dryden and Breckenridge returned even sooner than Doc had expected.

Without comment, they seized the line when the bronze man tossed it to them and hauled the boxes out of the hold. To their starboard, beyond four or five miles of slowly squirming sea, the rugged Norwegian coast could be seen. The ship steamed parallel to the coast. There were scabs of snow on the hills, which dived at the sea in sheer cliffs.

Not until all five boxes were stowed in their cabin, with little room left over, did they pause to wipe their steaming faces with handkerchiefs.

"How did you like the pinups on the fo'castle ceiling?" Doc asked dryly.

Dryden returned bitterly, "I liked them as much as you did." He opened a fiber traveling bag, one of several which had accompanied the aluminum cases from New York. The two submachine guns were disassembled, wrapped in oiled paper. They were Thompsons. Dryden handed Doc Savage one to put together.

"Where are the cartridges?" Doc asked.

Breckenridge broke a long, puzzled silence. "Would you two mind telling me what you saw in those pinup pictures?" he asked.

Doc Savage and Arthur Dryden exchanged looks.

"You mean you thought they were all right?" Dryden asked Breckenridge.

The cartridges were sealed in airtight tins, Doc discovered.

"I didn't think the pictures were sexy enough to offend you two," offered Breckenridge. "In fact, I never saw a bunch of more fully dressed, plainer-looking, frumpy dames."

"Nor I," added Doc.

After a minute Breckenridge asked, "Well, what is so scary about those pinups?"

Dryden loaded a clip, snapping the cartridges in place smartly.

Doc Savage also loaded a clip. "The women in those pictures are People's Worker Heroines," he announced. Doc examined each cartridge with care before clipping it. "Didn't you notice the Russian writing on them?" He found grease on one shell. "They're a Russian substitute for our movie stars." He carefully wiped the shell on a piece of waste rag, wishing he had one of his supermachine pistols, which were not only small enough to conceal in his clothing, but fired nonlethal bullets faster than a Thompson. But such equipment would give him away as Doc Savage, and risk jeopardizing the mission. He wondered which alternative was worse.

Breckenridge looked at Doc. "Even if I was a true-blue Commie, I don't think I would stick such cows on my ceiling."

"You would," said Doc grimly, "if you were sailing on this ship under party discipline."

Alarm opened Breckenridge's eyes wide. "Cripes! You think we got an all-Commie crew?"

"How else do you explain a ship fo'castle without any pictures of movie actresses?" demanded Doc Savage, testing the safety of his rapid-firer.

Breckenridge thought about it only long enough for it to dawn on him that he should have a weapon, too. He complained bitterly when informed there was no third Thompson.

XIII

VIOLENCE FOR BREAKFAST

Doc Savage offered to do his sleeping on a pallet made on top of the five metal cases containing the Moonwinx UHF radio apparatus, there obviously not being room in the cabin for all three of them at once, unless someone slept on the boxes.

"You fellows had it tough in the hold, so I'll make out here," Doc offered. "This way they can't get the gadget without stealing me too."

"Fair enough," said Breckenridge, mollified. He seemed vaguely annoyed that the bronze man had escaped standing an eight-hour watch in the miserable hold.

"I want you two to see something," Doc said, unbuttoning his shirt. He opened it. His companions expressed amazement at the dull, silvery shade of the undershirt he was wearing.

"Bulletproof," Doc said, slightly embarrassed. He had for years worn a chain-mesh protective undergarment. It was his one concession to the life of danger he lived.

Strips of adhesive tape held a plastic envelope to the skin under the bronze man's armpit. He jerked the tape off the metallic fabric.

"If anything happens to me, don't either of you forget this," Doc told them. He unfolded a large sheet of paper that had been in the plastic envelope. A map. "I drew up the original of this map when I was lumberjacking for the Soviets," he explained. The chart possessed considerable detail about airfields, roads, town, factories, negotiability of terrain, military occupancy, and the inhabitants' degree of enthusiasm for Communism. "This is a pretty good map, the U.S. military intelligence thought," he added. "They found some items on it that surprised them," Doc explained modestly. "I showed it to them before I left New York." He allowed himself a grim smile. "They thought I did pretty well for a wood-chopping Lapp."

Doc showed them a line he had drawn on the chart, beginning at the mouth of the Pechora, following the river south, then ending at Ust Taylma, a town near the great bend the Pechora took eastward.

"This is our route," Doc told them. "The first part, at least. I didn't mark it all out, for obvious reasons." He tore a paper match out of a packet. "You two know where the

Soviets are storing their atom bombs in a cave, don't you?" Doc used the match as a pointer. "Right here. Edge of the Ural Mountains." He used care not to touch the map with the matchstick, and explained why. "Let's not make any marks on the map around there," he said. "I don't think Ivan suspects we know where he is hiding his big eggs." Doc eyed the map with contained self-satisfaction. "This map could save the day for you fellows, in the event I don't survive. Don't forget it."

"What are these numbers written down by some of the towns?" asked Dryden.

"Probably phone numbers of babes, from the way the girls at that Bergen clip joint acted toward our friend, Banner," joked Breckenridge.

Dryden straightened up from the map. "That's a hell of a way to talk about a map as important as this!" Dryden flushed angrily. He turned to Doc. "What are they, anyway?"

"The numbers are a code key to anti-Communists in the towns who can be depended upon for reliable information and assistance," Doc explained, eyeing Breckenridge coldly. He was beginning to find the man's ways grating.

While Doc was refolding his map, a knocking sounded on their cabin door. Dryden and Breckenridge dived for the guns.

"Who is it?" Doc pasted the map back on his ribs with alacrity.

"Me." Paul Poltov's voice was still hoarse. "Poltov."

"Just a second, Paul." Doc gestured to conceal the submachine guns under a blanket on the bed. Then he extracted two false beards from his suitcase. "Here, put these on," Doc whispered. The beards were bushy and black. "Disguises I brought along for you fellows," he explained.

Dryden retreated from his beard. "This is absurd! Me wear that thing!"

"Paul hasn't seen your faces," Doc reminded them as he adjusted one false beard on Breckenridge's face. "These will make you look like a couple of czars. I'll introduce you as returning royalty."

"Confound you, Banner!" Embarrassment mixed with Dryden's anger. "I expected stuff like this. I warned Wilcox you might turn this into a farce for screwballs. One reason why I insisted that your aides not be involved in this mission!"

Doc buttoned his shirt as he strode to the door, saying, "Coming, Paul."

Hastily, Dryden grabbed up the remaining set of whiskers.

Doc paused, waited until Dryden was done affixing them to his reddening face, and opened the door.

"What's on your mind?" he asked.

Paul Poltov bulked in black oilskins dripping with deck spray. The smuggler looked enormous. His face was a square brass block the size of a building stone. He would not have been able to enter the door without stooping and turning sidewise.

"I hope you are comfortable." Poltov ducked his head to peer into the cabin. "I came to see if you wanted anything." His eyes widened when he saw Dryden and Breckenridge and their beards. "And, I see you have your friends with you."

"That's right. You haven't met them, have you, Paul?" The bronze man turned to Dryden and Breckenridge. "This is Baron Adeen and Baron Dvah." Doc did not explain which baron was which.

Both the "barons" said, *"Kahk vy pazhyvahyete."* They spoke the Russian language excellently. Their how-do-you-dos were very convincing.

"It is a pleasure, gentlemen." When Poltov opened his mouth to speak, it looked as if he had been eating chocolate recently. "Is there anything I can do for your comfort?"

The barons shook their heads.

"What'd you really want, Paul?" Doc asked, slipping into the careless English that characterized the fictitious Banner.

Words were giving pain to Poltov's throat. "Well, I did think I should tell you I will have to put the ship in at the Norwegian port of Tromso." Poltov winked evilly with one eye. "I have to make certain arrangements, and certain payments, to certain representatives of Russian officials. I do this, and we will get a Russian naval coastwise clearance. You understand?"

"Yeah, I know that's the way you work it," said Doc. "But thanks for telling me."

"Good," said Poltov. "Will you gentlemen join me for breakfast?"

Doc Savage glanced at the barons. They shook their heads. They weren't that hungry, they muttered.

"I guess not, Paul. Maybe later." Doc adjusted his collar. "The truth is, I was figuring on looking up Miss Kirkegaard and having breakfast with her."

Poltov closed one eye. "Ah?" His other eye looked evilly at Doc. "You will watch your step there, no?" His fists tightened with some repressed emotion.

Doc Savage, in his nastiest tone, said, "Don't you tell me what to do with a babe, you welcher!"

He slammed the door shut in Poltov's face. Immediately, the bushy black beards came off the faces of the Special Security men.

"What was the idea of all that?" Dryden roared, shaking his false whiskers at the cabin rafters. "You don't think these skunk pelts fooled him for a minute, do you?"

"No," said Doc calmly. "I do not."

"Then why? For God's sake, you made us look like blithering idiots!"

"Exactly. And no one would confuse an idiot for a secret agent."

Breckenridge snapped his fingers. "I get it! They were a psychological disguise."

"Something like that," Doc admitted.

Dryden was so taken aback by this answer that he sputtered for a full half minute. When he ran out of sputters, he fell into a moody silence.

Breckenridge broke the silence after several minutes.

"Now I ask you: Isn't there some slight risk in telling a guy as big as Poltov that you are going to have breakfast with his dame?" he asked. "That bird may be the original Russian Giant. I don't think I ever saw a bigger Russky."

"He will not be a problem." Doc began hunting a mirror. "Banner can bounce him around like a basketball, and Poltov knows it." Not finding a mirror, he polished one of the aluminum cases with his sleeve and examined his disguise on its surface. "I don't think Miss Kirkegaard is his dame, as you so inelegantly put it," he added.

"Well, Poltov's eye glittered when you mentioned her," warned Breckenridge.

"He has a glittering eye," said Doc. He decided he looked like an Eskimo in the stuff he was wearing. But he also remembered it was cold outside. "Shall I change to a business suit for my breakfast date? Is it better to be presentable, or comfortable?" he asked.

"You haven't even got a breakfast date," Dryden said acidly.

"I'll get one, don't you worry." Doc decided to be comfortable. He washed his hands and combed his dyed-black hair. "Poltov told us he was putting in at Tromso to bribe the Russians. That means he is following routine. That is what I expected. If he had tried to go straight to a Russian port, I might have become worried," Doc remarked.

"Oh, now you're not worried?" said Dryden.

"Not about that," Doc said. He prepared to depart, adding, "I'll see you later."

"Not if our all-Russian crew sees you first, I bet you don't," said Dryden darkly.

Doc looked serious. "I'll have to ask Miss Kirkegaard why all the Russians." He drew a revolver from his clothing and ascertained it was loaded. He hoped he wouldn't have to use it. It was another Banner prop.

The entrance to the ship's bridge bore a sign in Norwegian, *"Ingen Adgang,"* meaning no admittance, but Doc Savage ignored it. There were but two people on the bridge. One was the helmsman; the other was Nina Kirkegaard. She wore an old overcoat, felt pants, and rubber boots.

"Pass Skanland whistling buoy to starboard," she was saying. "That will put us through the narrow part of Vags Fjord and past Senja Island in daylight." The helmsman nodded.

"You!" Miss Kirkegaard had discovered Doc.

"Hello there!" Doc pretended to be surprised. "I just dropped by to see where we are, on my way to breakfast."

"Indeed?"

Her blond loveliness was enhanced by the rough clothing and rubber boots. "I sure didn't expect to find you here on the bridge." Doc added.

"I told you I was the captain."

"I thought you might be fooling."

"I navigate."

"Thank God," said Doc. "I was afraid Poltov was navigator, and we might wind up in Greenland. Where are we, by the way?"

"Why"—Nina Kirkegaard's mink-brown eyes were defiant for a moment—"why, I guess you've a right to know. You're our employer." She pointed to the chart. "Here." The spot was inside the Vestfjord, exactly where the bronze man thought they were.

"Fine. Will you join me in breakfast?" Doc saw she was going to refuse. "I have something very important to talk to you about," he added.

"Important?" she asked suspiciously.

"Yes."

"What?"

"The crew." Doc indicated the helmsman with a glance. "It's private."

"I'm on watch," Nina Kirkegaard said. "But I suppose I can take off a few minutes."

The ship indulged in a series of very slow rolls. It seemed to lie on its side and rush forward. Doc found it expedient to grasp Miss Kirkegaard's elbow to help support her as they walked.

"Isn't it sort of difficult for a woman to work up to the job of captain?" Doc asked casually.

"No, not when you own half the ship," she said matter-of-factly.

Hissing, crackling, frantic whistles of Morse code came from a doorway. The room was the radio shack. The operator came and looked out at them. He stuffed a newspaper in his hip pocket. It was a copy of the Russian party organ *Trud*.

Doc Savage ignored the radio operator. "I'd say that was the hard way," he said to Nina. "I'd venture it would be even tougher to save enough money to buy half a ship like this. I'd say you got to be captain the hard way."

"It wasn't so hard."

The radioman spit on deck and wiped his mouth on the back of his hairy hand. He watched Doc Savage as a bulldog would watch an unfamiliar canine. There were no front teeth in his mouth.

"We might as well go in here," Nina Kirkegaard said, a few paces farther on.

The door she opened had a six-inch-high threshold to discourage entrance of seawater. As they stepped through, the vessel gave another of its great tired rolls, tossing them together.

Reacting quickly, Doc caught Nina Kirkegaard in his arms.

He was never clear on what happened after that.

Someone simply put a thumb in his right eye. The warm body in his hands was suddenly no longer there. Whether Nina had wriggled free or had been snatched away, he had no idea.

With a gasp, the bronze man backpedaled—he hoped—out of danger. The raised threshold of the door tripped him and he landed asprawl on the deck. He arose with as much speed as he could muster—just in time to have the radioman's fist catch his mouth. Doc was sent sprawling. He attempted to stabilize himself with an outthrust hand, but collided painfully with the deck house.

Men were coming out of the radio shack, Doc realized. One, two, three, four of them. They advanced in attack. The radioman rushed again, but the bronze man sidestepped, then hit the man's jaw with his fist. Doc did not recall drawing his gun, but it was in his other hand. The radioman plunged face-down at the feet of his companions. They hesitated, eyeing the gun in Doc's big hand and their fallen comrade by turns.

"Want something?" Doc flourished his gun. He could taste salt in his mouth—blood.

The radioman rolled over on his back, peered at Doc Savage's imposing form. He began to crawl away, fingernails scratching on the deck. He crawled into the radio shack. The four men followed him into the radio room. One closed the door. Not one of them had spoken a word, except Doc.

Miss Kirkegaard had disappeared, he noticed.

Holding his head forward so the blood dripping off it would miss his clothing and fall on deck, Doc glowered at the radio room door. Anger pulled at his wire-distended nostrils, made them flare like a bull's. He cocked his revolver, seriously considered firing a few shots through the radio room door for effect.

His blood spatted measured drops along the deck. Finally, he decided against it. He might inadvertently kill someone, not to mention possibly damage the ship's radio.

Doc Savage ignored the questioning looks from Dryden and Breckenridge when he reentered their cabin. When he examined his reflection in the side of the aluminum UHF radio packing-case, he was surprised to find no visible blood, no swelling. He did not even look very disheveled.

"Well, did you enjoy your breakfast with the blonde?" asked Dryden curiously.

"Not exactly," Doc said. "It was served cold on the plate."

After he had explained the attempt to bushwhack him, both Dryden and Breckenridge lost what little healthy coloring they had retained.

"What do we do?" Dryden asked thickly.

"Play it by ear," Doc recommended.

"You mean, just do nothing?" Breckenridge's eyes were emerging from his head like white grapes being squeezed from two bloodless fists.

"No, I mean let's continue acting as if nothing is wrong."

Dryden sputtered, "But what possible good can that do us?"

"Perhaps none," Doc admitted. "Perhaps a great deal. If they want to take us, they can do so at any time—or so they must think. There may be no more sinister a reason for all this cat-and-mousing than that Poltov's harassing me for his mistreatment at Banner's hands, but we gain nothing by forcing the issue and bringing matters to a head."

"So we act nonchalant?" Breckenridge said blankly.

Doc nodded. "And remain prepared to act when events force us to, and not before. Agreed?"

From the expressions on the faces of the two Special Security men, they clearly did not care for such a plan of action, but could think of no sounder strategy.

They fell to rechecking their weapons.

XIV

PASSENGER UNKNOWN

The harbor of Tromso was smooth as leaded glass, so when the launch belonging to the *Norge Pike* left a wharf, it dragged an ostrich plume of wake that spread and reached for the foot of the sullen-looking hills. And inshore the wake ran knocking along the dock piling, ranging the bases of the boxlike wooden fishery buildings.

"Six." Breckenridge counted the figures in the launch. "There should be five." He and Doc Savage stood at the *Norge Pike*'s rail. "Either that, or I miscounted when I got eight in the other launch load," Breckenridge added.

Doc brought binoculars to his eyes. "I see Dryden. That must be the last launch."

"We gained one," Breckenridge grunted.

"I see Dryden has removed his whiskers," noted Doc. He chuckled. "Is he trying to unmask us?"

"I don't think he wore them ashore," Breckenridge said.

"For a while I believed Dryden thought I really intended for him to wear that alfalfa for a disguise." Mirth made Doc's eyes glint. "I wasted two hours in London hunting up those beards." The binoculars became fogged and Doc lowered them. "Truthfully, I never imagined I would get those whiskers on Dryden. But when Paul Poltov knocked on our door, I knew Dryden would be just scared enough to put them on. He was." He turned to Breckenridge. "Weren't those beards awful? Dryden looked like Ivan the Terrible. And how did you like the names I introduced you by? Baron One and Baron Two?"

Breckenridge did not fully share Doc's amusement. He wore the sour expression of a farmboy who had swallowed a tadpole while swimming in a pond.

"Six and eight," Breckenridge muttered, as if to himself. "Five and eight." He nibbled a thumbnail. "It doesn't come out."

"Eh?" asked Doc, his humor fading.

"Six and seven make thirteen," said Breckenridge. "Six and eight make fourteen. Thirteen people went ashore from this ship. Fourteen came back."

"This may be one instance where thirteen might not be the unlucky number." Doc Savage handed the binoculars to Breckenridge. "You want to count again? I'm going to hunt up Poltov."

Breckenridge accepted the glasses absently. "I could have miscounted, of course."

"It's possible." Doc made a fist preparatory to setting out on his promenade of the deck. "I just hope I run into that radio operator and his friends," he said ominously. "Or Miss Kirkegaard, who seems to be avoiding me."

* * *

On the pretext of inquiring about a case of Irish whiskey which he had asked be brought from shore, Doc Savage sought out Paul Poltov. He found Poltov, stripped to the waist, changing from town clothes to working gear. "It is all arranged." Poltov's eyes glittered, darkly unfriendly. "I saw the right Communists ashore. It cost me plenty. But this ship is cleared to make calls at north Russian ports, including the mouth of the Pechora."

"I was more interested in the case of Irish," Doc said. "I wasn't much worried that you couldn't get us up there to the Pechora. You know how I trust you, Paul."

"I noticed you had your friend sniffing my heels the whole time I was ashore." From the amount of fur on Poltov's chest, he could have been wearing a bearskin vest. "That is trust, eh?"

"It's my kind of trust." Doc discovered the case of whiskey beneath Poltov's bunk. He seized it. "Were you trying to steal this, you sneak?"

Poltov's denials were nearly inarticulate.

Doc carried the case in his arms. "I wouldn't put petty thievery past you," he said. He paused at the door.

"By the way, who's the new passenger—the local commissar?"

"I do not know of what you speak," Poltov said, sullen-voiced. "There is no new passenger."

"I'd better not find out differently," warned Doc. He kicked the door shut with a heel in leaving.

Dryden had joined Breckenridge in their cabin. He saw the whiskey. His eyes took on an avid shine. "The U.S. government wouldn't approve of that," he said happily, "but I sure do."

"I wasn't about to offer either you or the U.S. government any," Doc said dryly. He looked for a safe storage place for his burden. "How long did Poltov spend with that tall, skinny sardine dealer on Karl Knutson Street?"

Unhappily, Doc placed the whiskey on the radio cases. "We have to guard this stuff carefully. No proper storage here."

Dryden's jaw had sagged. "How'd you know Poltov would confer with a sardine dealer?" he demanded.

"Because his name would be mud if he didn't," said Doc. "That sardine huckster is the Commie bigwig in these parts. He is the guy to see if you want to smuggle a shipload of contraband into the people's republic." He frowned, adding, "This stuff is good for reindeer bites. Remember that."

"How'd you know that?" Dryden was really surprised.

"I've tried it. Externally, of course."

"I mean about the sardine dealer."

"It's my business to know these things," said Doc, lapsing into his breezy Banner persona. "I'm careful. I'm foresighted. I'm trustworthy and brave. So knowledge just comes to me." His tone grew serious again. "Dryden, how many came back in the launch with Poltov?"

"Eight."

"That's what I counted, eight," said Breckenridge.

Dryden paled.

"Did you notice a new face?" Doc asked.

"No, but I wasn't looking for any," Dryden admitted. He swallowed. He eyed the case of Irish whiskey. "Isn't it common to take on new crew at ports?"

"Not on a smuggling run, which this is," Doc said flatly, dashing cold water on Dryden's hopes.

"But it is possible, isn't it?" Breckenridge pressed.

"We would all be better off not looking for silver linings in any prowling shapes that happen to scud by," Doc warned them.

"I feel we should settle this eight question right now," said Dryden suddenly. "I feel we should settle it by having eight for the sea." He attempted to tear open the whiskey case with his hands.

Doc intervened. "No," he said sharply.

"What did you have it brought aboard for, then?" he snapped.

"Two reasons," Doc explained. "To live up to Banner's fire-eating reputation and because where we are going, we will have no medicines available. What I said about reindeer bites is true. Not to mention gunshots, knife wounds, and other injuries we may sustain along the way to our destination."

Grudgingly, Dryden subsided. He and Breckenridge repaired to their bunks.

The er.gines began to vibrate underfoot. The anchor winch swallowed anchor chain with a loud iron gobbling. The customary warm, greasy odor left the engine room and wandered through the ship.

Dryden abruptly announced that he needed a drink to defend himself against the smell. Breckenridge agreed.

Reluctantly, Doc allowed this. He realized it would be just a matter of time before one of them—Dryden probably—sneaked a drink. Better to get it over with now than have problems after they left the comparative sanctuary of the ship.

Grinning, Breckenridge advanced on the case. He grabbed up Doc's revolver from where it lay on one aluminum case, reversed it, and prepared to smash open the case with its hard butt.

"Stand back," he warned.

Dryden shoved him aside. "Are you crazy? You might break a bottle." He demonstrated how to pry open the case with his sheath knife.

"Look!" Breckenridge stared at the revolver. It had no front sight. "When did that happen, do you suppose?" He put the weapon away hastily to have his hands free to accept a bottle of Irish whiskey.

Dryden said, "I bet that radio operator stole the sight off the thing during that scuffle."

Doc Savage said nothing. He imagined it had broken off during the scuffle. He was coming to believe that was the least of his worries at this moment.

Dryden and Breckenridge fell to imbibing. From the bottle.

The harbor was slick and shiny. The ship moved on it like a turtle.

Dryden announced the need of another drink to defend themselves against seasickness.

Breckenridge said, "I'll second that."

In an effort to make them think twice about overindulging, and not because he absolutely believed it, Doc Savage said, "There is every reason to believe that someone new has boarded this vessel. A clear head is advisable."

Dryden hoisted his bottle, saying, "A toast to the new crewman. Let's hope his last name isn't Molotov!"

XV

DARK ENCOUNTER

On the cabin floor, three empty bottles rolled with the ship's motion.

"We mustn't be untidy," said Dryden, blearily. "Besides, a man could turn his ankle or break his leg."

Dryden carried the three expired soldiers out on deck. He found it to be surprisingly dark. It was also bitterly cold.

About to toss the bottles over the rail, he discovered a Russian sailor following a flashlight along the deck. On the unlikely theory it might be a Russian commissar, he hurled a bottle at the fellow. It was a miss. The sailor fled and presented such an elusive target that Dryden missed with the remaining bottles, as well.

"It's darker than the inside of an owl out here!" he muttered. Dryden dashed back into their cabin. He neglected to close the cabin door behind him.

"A man could get lost out there," he puffed. A frown caused his features to prune. "Where is that breeze coming from?" he demanded suddenly.

"You forgot to close the door," said Doc Savage, disapprovingly. He had not participated in the drinking-fest, but had had no other choice but to witness it.

"Why, yes," said Dryden, surprised. "So I did."

Breckenridge was grinning at Dryden. "Can I throw away the empty bottles next?" he asked gaily. "It sounded like fun."

"You certainly can," said Dryden, magnanimously.

"There are no empties left," said Doc Savage, an edge creeping into his voice.

"No problem at all," said Dryden. "We will make some."

"Do you think we should?" asked Breckenridge. "After all . . ."

"No problem, no problem at all." Dryden grasped a full bottle by the neck. "Gentlemen, I propose a dedication."

"To the king. . . ." said Breckenridge.

"No, to action," said Dryden.

"What kind of action?" asked Doc Savage, alarm coming into his voice now.

"Action without reaction, of course," said Dryden. He uncorked the bottle, held it over his head. "Immediate action. Fast action. Quick action." He drank deeply and passed the bottle from hand to hand. "What other kind of action do you want?"

Breckenridge was amused. "What other actions do you have?"

"Gentlemen!" Dryden lifted his Thompson. "Gentlemen, it is no empty toast—dedication I mean—I give you. I give you . . ."

They watched him. Doc Savage was alarmed by the careless manner in which Dryden waved the dangerous weapon around.

"Action," said Dryden. "I give you the best action of all . . . immediate action." He lunged for the door. "Come on! Forward, men!"

Doc Savage blocked his way. "Where do you think you're going?" he demanded.

"Into action," said Dryden. His eyes swam in his face.

"Be more specific. After all, we are on a ship crewed by Soviet citizens."

"I'm going to capture the ship," boasted Dryden.

Doc started. "You can't be serious!"

"You may watch and see," said Dryden, weaving on his feet.

"You are completely drunk," said Doc. Disgust tinged his voice.

"I beg your pardon," said Dryden. "On Irish whiskey, one does not become intoxicated. One becomes an Irishman."

"I guess we'll have to put you to sleep," said Doc Savage, unhappily.

Breckenridge seized Doc Savage's arm warningly as he moved toward the bronze man. Breckenridge had seen that Dryden was very angry. Dryden bristled at them, shouted, "If I go to sleep, it won't be on the same boat with those chicken-livered you-know-whats!" He was so furious his hands shook. "Another thing!" he yelled. "Another thing . . ."

"One moment . . ." said Doc Savage, trying to reason with the man. Dryden's finger was close to the Thompson trigger. Doc eased away from the muzzle, an action which regrettably cleared a path to the door. But it was the better part of valor, the bronze man decided.

"And another thing!" Dryden pocketed the half-emptied bottle. "I'm damn sick of sitting around waiting for these damn Russians to cook up God knows what kind of a scheme. I'm through waiting, brother." He struggled with the doorknob. "I'm gonna kick their playhouse to pieces. That's the way to handle a Commie."

Dryden got the door open and plunged outside.

Breckenridge turned to Doc Savage. "You don't suppose he's serious?" His voice was cold sober now. Fear sometimes does that to a man who's had too much to drink.

"I have no idea," said Doc wearily.

"The fool!" said Breckenridge hotly. "The utter fool!"

"He is beginning to act like I feared he would," said Doc, neglecting to point out that Breckenridge was only slightly less soused than Dryden. "I think the party is about to start."

"Should we help him?" wondered Breckenridge.

"Have we any choice?" Doc retorted bitterly.

They stuffed extra cartridges into their pockets. Breckenridge locked the cabin door behind them. "Hope we don't get side-tracked so long that somebody makes off with those packing cases," he said. "Which way'd he go?"

It was easy to hear Dryden's feet hammering the deck as he made his way through the darkness. He sounded like a clubfooted tap dancer.

"Headed for the radio shack," Doc decided.

Hands feeling the way, they followed Dryden. Breckenridge smashed the bridge of his nose into a wire brace. "Egad! How does Dryden get around that fast without falling over something?" He felt blood crawl over his chin, down into the collar of his shirt. The darkness was blacker than tar.

They saw a blade of light come out of an opening door and stab the deck. Cat-quick, Dryden stepped through the door, which then closed.

"Hurry!'" Breckenridge cried. "Drunk as he is, they'll tear him to pieces!"

Headlong, they rushed toward the noises that now came from the radio room. Not loud noises, but remindful of the stirring within a schoolroom as the recess bell sounds. They did not last long. Nor did there seem to be a particular climax.

Doc Savage reached the door first, threw it open. He saw the sprawled shapes of two of the crew on the floor. The radio operator sat on the floor, on the wreckage of his chair. One of the radioman's ears was split just like on an earmarked calf; half his shirt was off. The man held both hands cupped over his face as if playing a game. Dryden stood over him.

Dryden saw Doc Savage and Breckenridge. He swung on them. He looked pugnacious. "What's this—reinforcements?" Dryden bent over the radioman again. "I'll be with you as soon as this guy moves. I don't like to swing at a sitting target."

The radioman slumped over backward. He was unconscious.

Dryden expressed surprise. "I don't recall even touching him," he remarked.

Breckenridge laughed with relief. "Was he born with that split ear?"

"I don't know," confessed Dryden. "I didn't see him born. I wouldn't want to, either."

Grimly, Doc Savage sprang to the door, peered outside nervously. Lights were springing out toward the bow, in the vicinity of the forecastle. "Quiet!" he warned. Doc was able to distinguish gathering figures. "They heard the rumpus." He closed the door hurriedly. "I think we're going to have trouble," he added.

"How many of them?" asked Breckenridge.

"They're just getting a gang together," said Doc.

"Didn't you count . . . ?"

"Nine or ten, I think," the bronze man reported. "But they're just beginning to . . ."

Dryden was tush-tushing their fears by patting the air before him with his hands. "Relax, will you?" His eyes were shiny with excitement. He had forgotten to remove a set of knuckle-dusters from his right hand. "What's the matter? Don't you think I know what I'm doing?" Dryden asked cheerfully, the Thompson cradled in the crook of one lifted arm.

Breckenridge's face was wild. "Let's get out of here!"

"No. Not until I finish what I came here to do." Dryden discovered the bottle of whiskey in his coat pocket. He eyed it with alarm. "Good grief, I've spilled half of it jouncing these guys around!" Apparently, he had forgotten he had been drinking from the bottle. He had another drink. "You didn't think I came here just to bounce these jokers, did you?" he demanded. "Well, I didn't. I have a plan I'm following."

In a leisurely way, nerve-wrecking to Doc Savage and Peter Breckenridge, Dryden removed the brass knucks and dropped them in his pocket. He went to the rack of radio apparatus. The radio panel was the one neat thing in the cabin. Dryden opened one of the racks, thrust his head inside. "They got a real transmitter here," he remarked. "Take a gander, Breck."

Breckenridge jumped to his side. His whistle of appreciation sounded muffled. "Copy of a Collins job, looks like." His arm disappeared into the radio rack alongside his head. "I hope to God the filter condensers are all bled. Could knock a man cold sober if they aren't," Breckenridge added.

"Come on, Dryden," Doc warned. "If they corner us in here—"

"Say, this is a nice transmitter!" said Breckenridge, his interest overcoming his natural fear.

"If you two do not get a move on," Doc warned, "I might just leave you here!"

"He's right, chief," Breckenridge said.

"Go ahead," said Dryden indifferently. "No, wait. Take this with you." His hand came out of the radio transmitter. The power tube his hand held was a shining fist-sized affair of glass and intricate internal elements. "Don't drop the damn thing," he added as Breckenridge took the component. "We may want to put it back so we can talk to the Russky or somebody."

Breckenridge had to hold the tube with both hands, he began shaking so hard.

Dryden withdrew his head from the apparatus. "I got their oscillator crystal. Crossed a couple of wires too." He frowned at Breckenridge's symptoms of nervousness. "Say, by Gadfrey, you keep on shaking like that and you'll drop the tube. We bust that tube, we're up stink creek without a radio transmitter, because I don't see any spare. Why don't you give that tube to our pal, Banner, to carry?"

A hard object whacked the door outside.

"What is going on in here?" It was Poltov. His voice was belligerent.

"I wish we had a radio receiver in our cabin," mused Dryden. "It would be nice to listen to the Philharmonic on short-wave." He examined the rack of panels containing the ship's receiving equipment. "We could keep tab on the

Russky radio activities too," he added. "And enjoy good music."

Poltov kicked the door.

"Who is it?" Doc Savage challenged.

"Open up!" bellowed Poltov.

"It shouldn't be much trouble to extract one of these receivers and take it with us," said Doc to the others.

Breckenridge offered a nervous suggestion. "Why not just move our residence to the radio shack? Wouldn't that simplify things?"

No one took that fear-induced suggestion seriously enough to reply to it.

"How're we going to get out of here?" asked Dryden, suddenly. He watched the door with pop-eyed tension.

Poltov's voice roared through the door. He was cursing them. He cussed them in Norwegian, Swedish, Italian, and Russian, most fluently in the latter.

"Holy Hell, look at this honey of a receiver!" Breckenridge pointed at the radio rack excitedly. "An old Super Pro, one just like I got in my shack on the yawl," he added. "You gotta say one thing about these Commies—they know the best stuff to steal!"

Paul Poltov struck the pane violently several times.

Doc Savage crossed to the door.

"Stop making so much noise, you sticky-fingered lout!" called Doc in his most intimidating Banner tone.

The door-banging came to an end.

"There's too many noisy people around here," Dryden said angrily. He returned and unsnapped the radio receiver from the rack. "Who wants to carry this? The loudspeaker too. . . ." He heard a moan. He glanced down. He saw he was inadvertently standing on the hand of one of the unconscious crewmen. "Anything else we need?" he asked. He continued to stand on the hand.

In his arms, Breckenridge juggled radio, loudspeaker, and Dryden's Thompson gun.

"I got the radio tube," Breckenridge said.

"Let's get back to our cabin before somebody steals Moonwinx," Doc Savage said.

"I can't see them letting us go back to our cabin," moaned Breckenridge. "It would be a miracle."

Doc Savage yanked one leg of the shattered chair from under the unconscious radio operator. It made a well-balanced club.

"You better let me hold their attention," he said. "You two run for our cabin. I'll join you there later." He made several swings to test the club for balance.

"How do we do this? Just take off?" Breckenridge was at the door.

Doc Savage restrained him. "Suppose they have guns trained on that door?" he asked. "We better be cute about this," Doc added. "Dangling this outside the door should show whether they plan to shoot on sight."

He yanked open the door, thrust the makeshift club outside, ready to flick back at the first sign of impending violence. No shots came.

Doc faded back from the door.

"All right," he said. "It appears safe to run for it. But you'd better get going," Doc added. "They may have anxious trigger fingers."

The pair slithered through the half-open radio shack door.

Stationing himself at a tiny porthole, Doc Savage peered toward the bow.

The men he had seen earlier could be distinguished in the forecastle vicinity. Poltov, himself not in view, was shouting orders at the men. Doc could not catch the gist of the commands.

Moving to another position, the bronze man saw that Dryden and Breckenridge had passed from view on their way back to the cabin. Doc was tempted to follow them, but he was also curious about what could be going on near the forecastle.

Suddenly a rod of light, stiff as a white-hot poker, sprang skyward from the group of men on the forecastle. They had hooked up a searchlight.

Alarmed, Doc Savage thought they might be preparing

to signal someone. That, or they were going to blind him with the light, the way a frog-hunter fascinates a frog with a flashlight beam.

Doc drew his revolver and sank to a knee to aim. He would, he decided, fire into the air twenty feet or so over their heads. This would serve as a warning. If it went unheeded, he could follow up by shooting some splinters out of the deck near their feet. He did not feel there was a need to shoot anyone. The lack of a sight on his revolver was a handicap in selecting a spot twenty feet over their heads. However, he squeezed off a shot.

To his profound astonishment, the lens sprang from the searchlight, sounded like gnashing of glassy teeth as it hit the deck. The ship forepart lit up a glaring blue, as if a welder had struck an arc. After this, darkness. All over the vessel, darkness.

In the following silence the rattle of Dryden's and Breckenridge's feet came to a halt, like marbles that had reached the bottom of steps.

"Banner, you okay?" Muffling distance did not make Breckenridge sound less alarmed.

"Don't worry about me," Doc shouted back.

"But that shot. . . ."

"That was me. I let one fly in the air." Doc knew full well he had not hit the searchlight while aiming twenty feet above it. He felt sure some startled sailor had dropped a wrench in the light, or something of the sort. He added, "The clumsy fools short-circuited the power somehow. That's why we have no lights!"

From the depths of the ship came Breckenridge's angry voice. "For God's sake, are you coming with us, or aren't you?"

Doc thought he heard concerted movement from the bow. He wondered if he was being charged. He wished it wasn't so dark. It was so pitchy that the blackness seemed to have a shine to it. It could not have looked any blacker had his head been plunged into a bucket of drawing-ink.

"Hold your horses!" he shouted.

He ran along the deck in the direction of the stern.

About where the door should have been, he fumbled for the opening. Nothing but the deck-house siding met his touch. Hard-frozen frost on the wood made it feel like sandpaper. Concluding he had underguessed the distance, he ran on while dragging fingertips against the side of the superstructure. He had no further doubt that men were coming at him from the direction of the bow. How many men had been clustered around the searchlight? Ten? Fifteen?

"Thank God!" Doc suddenly breathed. He had located a door, and he lost no time getting through it, then closing it behind him.

The bronze man leaned against the door gratefully. He was no longer quite so afraid. The warmth, the greasy closeness, were welcome. He drew in a long breath and released it, then secured the heavy bolts designed to hold the door stoutly against pounding seas.

Doc hissed, "Breckenridge? Dryden? Are you here?" into the blackness, and listened. He heard no response. Dryden and Breckenridge had continued on to the cabin, evidently.

Carefully, Doc Savage proceeded toward where he felt their cabin should be. He experienced some disorientation, which, he figured, must be due to the unaccustomed darkness. He did not feel it could be due to the vague fear that seemed to rise up inside him. He bumped his forehead into a bulkhead which shouldn't have been there.

Staggering back, he experienced the wildly ridiculous thought that they had turned the ship cross-ways. He wished he could be certain Dryden and Breckenridge had made it back to the cabin. The thought of leaving the Moonwinx gadget—the thing for which they had risked their lives—unprotected for any length of time gripped him like a vise of chilled steel.

Presently, Doc felt he had walked far enough to more than have reached their cabin.

Could he be lost?

He wondered if he dared shout for Dryden and Breckenridge. If the lights would only come on. Didn't Poltov or anyone in his crew know how to replace a simple blown fuse?

As he walked on in catlike silence, he encountered sudden soft movement in the darkness, an eddy of intriguing perfume. Was it—marrubium?

Instantly defending himself against attack, Doc lunged and seized in the black void. "Excuse me!" he said. He had captured a woman.

She was much shorter than he. She had soft shoulders. And softer hair. His hands told him that.

"Miss Kirkegaard, I believe," said Doc. It was hardly a stab in the dark. Still, his heart seemed to suspend its beating as he listened for a reply.

When Doc received no answer, and his sense of smell was too confused by the heavy ship smells to inform him whether or not the perfume he detected was in fact marrubium, he went for her throat.

He had a wild moment, a sense of stepping back into time, back to the encounter in Central Park with the mysterious woman who was supposed to be Eva Baker, but actually was not. One hand had this woman's throat. With the thumb of the other, he attempted to locate her earlobe, which would enable his fingers to find the nerve center by which he could render her unconscious.

She was a clawing wildcat in his arms, and so he thought the trouble he was having was due to her frantic flouncing. Then he realized the surprising truth. And he understood, before the blackness in front of his eyes overtook his brain, why he had been unable to overcome the woman in Central Park, the woman he was utterly certain now floundered in his grip.

The woman had no left earlobe!

Then her teeth were at his own ear, and there was a hissing that made him think of an angry cat, and the gas entered his nose, his lungs, everything.

His last hollow thought was: *If this is the Red Widow, God have mercy on my soul.*

XVI

THE SHORTENING ROPE

The ship rolled far over to the portside in the seaway, then rolled equally far to the starboard, like a pig in a puddle trying to coat itself fully with mud.

This motion caused Doc Savage's arm, the one dangling over the side of the bunk, to sweep back smartly against the bunk, rapping his knuckles. "What?" he said drowsily.

He realized with a start that he had been asleep. He could not immediately recall where he was or how he had got here. He felt exhausted. His head pounded.

It came back to him. The eerie encounter in the dark. His desperate fumblings for an earlobe that did not exist. And like ghostly cobwebs trying to suffocate him, the frightening odor of marrubium insinuating itself into his lungs.

Except that it was still in his nostrils and he recognized it now. Not minty marrubium. But ether.

He had been drugged!

Doc Savage opened one eye carefully.

His lady assailant was no longer in the room. The cabin was empty, in fact.

The bronze man sat up in bed. He noticed that he had been stripped down to shorts. His bulletproof chain-mesh undergarment was under his ordinary undershirt, apparently undiscovered by his ambusher.

Most importantly, a quick examination by touching his face indicated that his Banner physiognomy was intact. Air left his stomach in a relieved sigh.

Had his attacker gone to bring back help? Doc wondered.

He frowned at the cabin ceiling, feeling something

133

was different. It was. The light was on. The crew had finally fixed the blown fuse, Doc realized.

He went in search of his clothes. They were nowhere to be found. His eyes narrowed on the door.

The door! It stood partially open. Obviously anyone who passed would have seen him lying helpless. Doc shuddered at the thought of what might have happened had the passersby been Paul Poltov or some of his crew—the radio operator and his friends in particular.

Doc got control over his alarm.

He felt the girl—whoever she had been—had been inexcusably careless. But he wasn't about to complain about a slight smile bestowed upon him by Lady Luck. He would, he decided, simply get the devil out of here.

The bronze man sprang out of bed, immediately collapsing to the floor with a groan. The ether. His skull felt like a balloon expanded to the breaking point by the stupefying gas. One earlobe throbbed insistantly.

Resisting the nausea which assailed him, he climbed to his stocking feet. He lifted his eyes as the ship siren moaned, an evil, crocodilelike bellow that poured out and seemed to come back in echoes. A loathsome outburst of noise.

Growing increasingly light-headed, Doc Savage felt it best to find safety with Dryden and Breckenridge without delay—assuming of course that they were safe. He grabbed a rough blanket off the bunk to shield him from the elements.

There were several inches of snow on deck, far more in spots where spray had joined it to freeze into large ice cakes. Hard-hitting little flakes of snow hurtled about, tried to embed themselves in Doc's exposed flesh.

Without warning, the wind seized his blanket and disrobed him. The blanket stretched out in front of him, jerking at his hands and making popping noises. He retained his grip with difficulty. The wind made an icy-cold whistling with his shanks.

Dryden gaped at Doc Savage when the latter burst into their cabin. "What on earth!" Dryden blurted.

"Hello," said Doc morosely. He would have grinned sheepishly if his face had not been half frozen. He was immensely relieved to find them safe, along with Moonwinx.

"Where have you been?" Dryden demanded. "Where in the name of all holies have you been?"

"I have been asleep," said Doc without pleasure. He didn't want to alarm them with the horrible truth. Just yet.

"You what?"

"A man must sleep, mustn't he?" Doc asked.

"We've been worried as hell about you," sputtered Dryden. "We thought that radio operator and his friends had you."

Doc Savage stood in the middle of the cabin. "I told you not to fret about me." He felt colder than he had ever felt in his life, too cold even to shiver. "I always make out. As Banner might put it: 'Almost any creek I fall into, I come out smelling purty.'" He began to dress himself stiffly.

Dryden eyed Doc's scratches, scrapes, contusions, and abrasions.

"What's been biting you?" he demanded suspiciously.

"This?" Doc said, fingering his sore ear. He shrugged deprecatingly. "Frostbite."

"Is that so?" Dryden was skeptical. "I'd swear, if I didn't know . . ."

Doc looked at him sharply. "If you didn't know what?"

Dryden sucked his lower lip thoughtfully.

"Monkey business," he said. "If I didn't know the only lady on board, Miss Kirkegaard, had been in the engine room the whole time you were missing. . . ."

Doc narrowed his eyes. "I hope she enjoyed herself in the engine room," he said flatly.

Preparing to thrust his arms in a fresh undershirt and hoist it up around his shoulders, Doc Savage was astonished when Dryden emitted a yell. "Wait! Hold it!" Dryden shouted.

Dryden rushed around to Doc's back and stared.

"Godamighty! Where is it?" Dryden cried.

"Where is what?" Doc asked, frowning.

"That damn map you were showing us!" Dryden seized a fistful of Doc's fresh undershirt and yanked it up. He attempted to drag the side of the chain-mesh vest into the bronze man's view. "It's gone," he bleated. "Here is where the adhesive tape was. But it's gone."

In a moment, Doc resumed dressing. "I guess I haven't got it," he said thoughtfully.

"Haven't got—?" Dryden gulped. "Where did you put it?"

"I didn't put it anywhere," Doc admitted, angry with himself. Now he understood why he had not been killed outright. The map plainly indicated that he and his party were en route to Russia, although his precaution of not marking the final leg of their journey would leave their ultimate destination a mystery to whoever now had possession of the map. No doubt his attacker had intended to interrogate him upon his revival.

Dryden gulped again. "You mean . . ."

"I guess it fell off during one of our many scrapes." Doc's ugly false-face was solemn. "I wouldn't be surprised if it fell off when the radioman jumped me," he added. "In the confusion, I might not have noticed." He frowned. The answer did not seem right somehow, but his brain was too punchy from the ether to function clearly.

"You know what this means to the mission if the Commies put their hands on that map," Dryden warned. "Even without knowing where exactly we are going, they can pick up our trail during the first land leg."

"I know," Doc said absently. As he put on his pants, shirt, coat, he wondered if that wasn't the idea of leaving him to escape. He felt of the lobe of his ear where the unseen female had bitten him last night. It felt smooth and round, like a large pearl earring. Swollen. "Think I'll go see if I can hunt up that map," he said at last.

"Well, I should think you would!" said Dryden.

At that moment, Breckenridge arrived. He looked at Doc without much surprise. "You woke up, eh?" Breckenridge had shaved the dark beard off his cheeks quite recently and they were ruddy as Jonathan apples. "You look like something the cat swallowed but couldn't keep down," he added.

"How did you know I had been asleep?" Doc demanded.

"Oh, Miss Kirkegaard told me." Breckenridge was pleased with himself. "I just had breakfast with her. You know, I think we can figure that gal on our side."

Doc Savage endeavored to adjust the ear flaps of his fur cap so his sore ear would be covered.

"I hope it was a safe and sane breakfast." The cap flap caused Doc's ear to give such a throb that he winced noticeably. "Did Miss Kirkegaard happen to mention how she knew I was asleep in the cabin?"

"She got that from Poltov."

"I see." The bronze man was thoughtful.

"We owe a lot to that gal," continued Breckenridge.

"To Miss Kirkegaard, you mean?"

"Yes. You owe her a lot too."

Doc Savage examined Breckenridge's face suspiciously. He saw only innocence. "Is that so?" said Doc.

Dryden sprawled on the bed. "That's right," he said. Dryden's shoes were off. He wore at least four pairs of wool socks. "Last night that babe laid down the law to Poltov. That was when Poltov was hot and looking for you, with his crew to help him," Dryden added.

Interest flickered in Doc's muddy eyes. "Miss Kirkegaard did that?"

"Yes."

"Well, that was good of her." Doc removed the cap and carried it in his hand. It was much more comfortable that way. "When did this happen?" he asked with pretended unconcern.

"Miss Kirkegaard was here outside our cabin when we got here from the radio shack," said Dryden. "She'd heard the ruckus. She came to see if we were in trouble."

Doc silently pulled on sealskin-lined mittens, considering all that he was hearing. He cocked his head, listened to the ship siren give another of its tremendous howls. In a moment, an echo came back out of the storm. Doc opened the door. Wind instantly wrestled him for control of the door, hit him with bird-shot snow. He heard a wave break against the ship side and saw a bluish fury of spray race along the deck toward him. Instead of going out, he closed the door quickly to let the spray go past.

"You're sure," said Doc, "that you came straight here from the radio shack, and found Miss Kirkegaard waiting?"

"Yes," said Dryden.

"That's right," added Breckenridge.

"She was here?"

"Yes," agreed Dryden.

"Then she left?"

"No," Breckenridge admitted, "not for a couple of hours. She went with us to tell Poltov off, then hung around a while."

"Hmmm. I'll be hanged if I understand it." Doc listened to the wind howl in the rigging. "How long has this storm been around?" he asked at length.

"Oh, twelve hours or so," ventured Dryden.

"About that," said Breckenridge.

"I see," mused Doc.

"You see what?" asked Dryden.

"I see nothing very clearly," said Doc thoughtfully.

Spray-polished green and white ice, as slippery as oiled ball bearings, made the deck treacherous going. Hard-flaked snow came driven out of a bullet-gray sky in bucketfuls. Doc Savage found it impossible to see even as far as the bridge. The sea looked black and furious, what little of it could be seen. The waves lunged up well above the height of the rail like angry black Angus bulls. Doc was glad to find a door that let him into the deck house. He did not mind at all that the place smelled like the stomach of a large animal that had been eating lubricating grease.

He felt fortunate to remember his way to the cabin where he had woke up after his hair-raising encounter with the mysterious female. By walking tightly and defensively, arms held out to fend off the furniture, he was able to circle the gloomy room repeatedly. He left the room dark. His eyes kept busy searching. He dragged the covers off the bed. He looked under the bunk. He looked in a bucket in a holder fastened to a bulkhead. He looked in the smoke-blackened chimney of a kerosene lamp that swung on gimbals. He looked in the mattress. He failed to find the missing map. He did find a button off his missing shirt.

As Doc stood by the side of the bunk and tried to think, the ship siren moaned, sending out a raucous creature of sound that seemed to rush out into the gale and fetch back not one echo this time, but two. Doc's head came up. His pupils dilated in alarm. He listened. But the siren fooled him, keeping silent.

Haste, and air so cold it seemed to cut his throat, made him temporarily unable to speak when he stumbled back into his cabin.

Presently, he was able to ask, "Did you two know we are steaming through a field of icebergs?"

"Sure," said Dryden. "Didn't you know it?"

"I just figured it out," said Doc, dryly. "But not until I decided that was what is making the echoes when they blow the whistle. The echo is bouncing off bergs."

"Yes," said Breckenridge. "Scary, isn't it?"

"Perhaps," said Doc. "They have a radar on the bridge. I've seen the antennae, anyway. They should be able to keep from stumbling over an iceberg." The bronze man was not as unconcerned as he pretended.

"It's safe, you think?" asked Breckenridge.

Doc nodded. "Poltov will get us through."

"That cutthroat!" Dryden spat.

"He's a seaman, that cutthroat is."

"I don't trust him," Dryden snorted.

"Poltov was born in a puddle of ice water," Doc pointed out. "He knows these Arctic seas. Trusting him has nothing to do with it."

Dryden looked at Doc Savage questioningly. "Did you have a successful trip?"

Doc shrugged. "Not very," he said. The bronze man

was quietly embarrassed. He wished Dryden did not know the map had come up missing. He wished he had never brought along the map in the first place, or had given it to Breckenridge to carry. The futile part of it, Doc reflected, was that they did not need the map as long as he, Doc, remained alive and kicking. Having drawn the map, he held its every detail in his retentive mind. But the mission had been so critical that he had taken his usual plethora of precautions.

The greater the number of precautions, he thought wryly, the more potential problems could crop up to hinder them.

Dryden lay back on the bunk, listened to the radio receiver. The crackle of snow-static was intense, like a theaterful of people eating popcorn. "Could a man rig a loop aerial on this radio? Keep track of where we are?" Dryden asked.

Doc nodded and said, "Yes. A man could." He was thoughtful, and added, "If we have time."

Like a toy operated by strings, Dryden sat up on the bunk. "Time?" He was alarmed. "What's eating you?"

"Do you mind if I ask you a question?" Doc inquired.

"What question?" asked Dryden.

Doc Savage held the Special Security chief with his intent gaze. It didn't quite go with his brutal face.

"It is in the manner of a personal question," he said.

"Is it?"

"You won't mind answering it?"

"How the hell do I know if I'll mind!" Dryden said sharply. "Ask your question and we'll see."

Doc Savage watched Dryden. He decided to put the question to Dryden without any beating around the bush. "How well did you get to know Anna Gryahznyi?" the bronze man asked.

Dryden fell back on the bed. He was like a doll that had broken in the middle. He looked fixedly at the ceiling, licked his lips. "You can go to hell," he said.

"No, I have to ask this," he said. "Did Anna Gryahznyi have a missing earlobe?"

Dryden lay very still. The ship siren cut loose a shrill

volley: *Whirk-whirk-whirk!* This time there were many echoes. They were like puppies barking at their mother.

Breckenridge had observed this exchange with interest. "A what?" he asked. "I didn't catch that last part," he complained.

"Let him answer," Doc said sharply. His lips felt dry as toast crusts.

Dryden's throat moved. He spoke with amazement. He said, "If you had time to notice that ear, you're lucky to be standing there alive."

"I see," said Doc slowly. His mud-brown eyes narrowed. He felt suddenly drained.

Without another word, the bronze man sank to his knees and dragged his suitcase from under the bunk. It contained a shoulder packsack similar to those Alpine guides wear. He began placing essential possessions in the packsack.

Curiosity made Breckenridge bright-eyed. "What kind of wild plan have you got now?" he asked.

"The wisest one so far," Doc said, metallic-voiced. "We're getting off this ship."

"Off!" sputtered Breckenridge. "We're in the middle of the Arctic Ocean!"

"That's not all we're in the middle of," said Doc Savage, grim-voiced. "Anna Gryahznyi is on board this vessel."

XVII

THE BOTTOM FELL OUT

The project to make a direction finder out of their radio receiver was a great success. The loop antenna which Doc Savage built was simple in design. The loop frame, an X of sticks, was constructed from strips split off the case which had contained the Irish whiskey. For wire, lamp cord served. They each carried pocket compasses anyway; there was no problem there.

They tuned in various stations on the Soviet mainland, located the nulls, and drew bearing-lines on a chart. Just in case the Soviets had turned tricky and juggled their radio station call letters, the bronze man took additional bearings on Norwegian and Swedish broadcast stations. Eventually, they had a pencil-dot on the chart. Doc felt it showed their location reliably.

"Say!" Breckenridge expressed surprise. "We're closer to the shore than I thought. Farther along, too."

"Lady Luck must have kept a spare smile in reserve for us," suggested Doc. He wore his cap yanked down over his sore ear. He was in no mood to baby a sore ear now. "Even if it does mean she's double-crossing us," he added.

Breckenridge looked up. "How come?"

"I won't have so far to walk ashore," said Doc.

"Walk?" said Breckenridge.

"Yes," said Doc.

"Walk! Are you nuts?"

"No, he isn't," said Dryden. His white hair stood out from his head in disarray, enhancing Dryden's air of excitement. "He means walk ashore on the ice. Coastal inlets will be frozen over this time of the year."

"Oh."

Doc said quickly, "I could walk ashore on top of the water, though. Easily."

This moved Dryden to shudder, and say: "I could, too, just by thinking about Anna Gryahznyi being aboard this ship." He laughed self-consciously. "My feet get so cold, thinking of Anna, they'll freeze the water and I can walk on the ice cakes."

Doc nodded with sympathy; his fears were similarly strong. The stories of her ways with instruments of torture were horrific. He had seen a photo of one of her victims after an "interrogation." The man's closed eyelids were shadowy hollows. His eyeballs had been extracted by cold tongs. The frozen expression etched into his lineaments testified that this operation had been accomplished in life.

Breckenridge was unconvinced. He didn't share their fright. Breckenridge looked fresh-laundered, crisp and eager. He plainly showed the rejuvenating effects of having had breakfast with Miss Kirkegaard, Doc felt.

Breckenridge said, "What I was trying to ask: What makes you think Lady Luck's going to double-cross us?"

Doc pointed. "Look at the map."

Breckenridge eyed the chart. "Say! We're way the hell past the mouth of that river, the Pechora! How come?"

"That river is called the pie-chore, not the pea-cherry," said Doc, brittle-voiced. "As for why—because they've been running the ship full speed. Our speed is making this storm seem more than it is, probably." Doc tapped the map with a finger. "You see this inlet in Verandei Bay? That's where the Soviet has a weather station and an army post. Want to bet we're not headed there?"

"That so?" Breckenridge was impressed. "You think we're in a trap?" His lips visibly lost color.

"I know we're in a trap." Doc folded the chart and gave it to Dryden to carry, explaining, "Maps don't seem to stick with me."

The whiskey case still contained three unopened bottles. Dryden suddenly wondered aloud if a stiff drink would steady their nerves. He wondered if Doc Savage and Breckenridge would mind. "A shot might help us solve our problems," he suggested lamely.

Doc Savage and Breckenridge did mind. Both became visibly and audibly upset over the idea.

"My God!" Breckenridge cried. "We're at death's door, and you want to get drunk again!"

Dryden looked injured. "They haven't closed the door. . . ."

"Remember the fix you got us in last time," Doc warned.

"He's right!" Breckenridge's cheeks had turned from Jonathan apple to the hue of a yellow transparent apple. "There'll be no drinking. No, sir!"

"The hell you say!" said Dryden. He became angry himself. "The hell you say!" He moved toward the whiskey. Breckenridge sprang ahead of him, seized all three bottles, wrenched open the cabin door.

"Wait!" Doc yelled in alarm. His voice was a crash of sound.

Breckenridge threw two bottles overboard.

"You wasteful son of a gun!" Dryden cried as they struggled for possession of the third bottle. Breckenridge snatched the third bottle and hurled it overside—one step ahead of the bronze man.

"There," Breckenridge said, satisfied.

Doc gained the porthole a second too late. He peered into the raging wind and flogging seas where the bottle had disappeared. "That was a mistake!" he complained.

"We can get along without that liquor," said Breckenridge staunchly.

"Yes, and you'll get along without that map, too," Doc said furiously. "It was in one of the bottles."

Both Dryden and Breckenridge were dumbfounded, and looked it after their expressions finished settling into sagging lines.

Dryden said, "But I thought . . ."

"Yes, it was in the bottle," said Doc angrily. "I thought you two would guard it with your lives, thinking it was whiskey."

Breckenridge sputtered, "You should have told us. . . ."

"How was I to know you'd suddenly turn into a prohibitionist?" complained Doc.

"When'd you hide it in the jug?" Dryden stood glumly, hands pocketed.

"Last night," Doc told him. "It was a notion I had when your spirits were high. I was a little hazy about remembering it, thanks to what Anna Gryahznyi did to me last night. I'm still hazy. Ether will do that to a man."

"Anyway, the Russky didn't get the map," said Dryden, as if that solved the problem.

"He will when it is tossed up on the beach in that bottle," Doc pointed out. "Personally, I am not going to wait for that to happen." He dragged the two submachine guns from under the bunk where they had been hidden. "We may need these right away." He examined the gun mechanisms. "They have too much oil on them," he noted. "While I'm gone, you had better fieldstrip them and wipe most of the oil off. In this cold, oil on a gun can get you in a fix." He examined his revolver critically. "If you hear me in trouble, hurry to my rescue," he said. "Let's not have any foolishness about the radio gadget in those boxes taking precedence over my life."

"What . . . ?"

"Let's not have any choosing between me and the radio," Doc said. "In any such eventuality, forget the radio. Our chances of completing this mission successfully are very slim now. No sense in throwing our lives away in the bargain."

He placed his revolver inside his clothes, next to his skin. This was so his body warmth would keep it in operating condition. The icy touch of the steel gun gave him a chill worse than that of his two dark encounters with Anna Gryahznyi.

"What do you think you are going to do?" Dryden demanded.

"See Miss Kirkegaard," said Doc Savage.

"Nina Kirkegaard? Why see her?"

Doc was at the door. "She *is* captain of the ship, isn't she?"

"Yes. That is . . ."

"Then she should be able to explain why we've been carried past our destination, shouldn't she?" Doc demanded.

The boat was growing fat with ice. The hawsers near the bow were as thick as telephone poles with the stuff. The siren sounded an ear-hurting rooster crow of a noise and the echoes came back like the cries of excited hens in the storm. They were in a regular floe of small bergs, Doc Savage decided.

Making his way toward Nina Kirkegaard's quarters, Doc had difficulty keeping his feet. Two sailors lounged outside her door. They had heavy Slavic faces. One of the men spoke to the bronze man in Russian, after snuffling his nose moistly.

"What do you want?" he demanded rudely.

"Miss Kirkegaard," replied Doc in the man's own tongue.

Both men were Russians. "It is not permitted," one said. He had been wiping his nose on his left sleeve for some time. For days, from the looks.

"Who says so?" asked Doc belligerently. "Poltov?"

"Do not answer him, Ivar." The other guard was more cautious. He scowled at Doc. "You are one of the men with the boxes? You are not allowed here." His hands were very dirty.

"Be careful," warned Doc. "How would you like to have Anna Gryahznyi angry with you?"

"Shto!" said the Russian. His eyebrows bunched like mice which had felt a chill.

"A very suitable comment, comrade," said Doc, brushing past them.

Neither man made a move to prevent him from flinging open the door of Nina Kirkegaard's cabin and entering. He closed the door hastily behind him, lest they follow.

"Hello there!" Doc stepped across the cabin. "Hadn't you better give me that? You might nick yourself."

Paul Poltov moved to the left like a sidewinder. "You!" His right hand held a heavy clasp knife with a pearl handle and open blade. "How did you get in here?" Poltov was no longer hoarse of voice.

"The guards? Oh, I have a couple of words I use to paralyze strong men," Doc said breezily.

"Get out!" spat Poltov thickly.

"You oughtn't to use strips out of a blanket just to tie up a lady," allowed Doc. "It's wasteful."

Poltov watched Doc Savage. His nostrils, dilated, were thumb-sized holes.

Doc turned and made sure Nina Kirkegaard had not

yet been harmed. Manhandled, yes. But there was no indication the knife had touched her. The cabin's one chair was held securely to the floor with the short chain usually supplied for that purpose. Ribbons torn from a blanket in turn lashed Nina to the chair. Her face was composed, but her mink-brown eyes were luminous with terror.

Doc glanced from her to Poltov with surprise. "I thought you two were partners."

"Partners. . . ." she hissed. "Poltov was going to kill me." Her hands strained at the bonds, fingers splayed rigidly.

Doc Savage said, "Is that so?"

Nina Kirkegaard's words were ringing and brittle, like a wine glass being struck by a fork. "He wants my share of the ship!" she spat. "If I am dead, he gets it."

Poltov started. "A lie!" He held the clasp knife with both hands. "It's not that at all!" The blade pointed at Doc. "Anytime I want this ship, I just take it. I do not have to kill anyone."

"I'm inclined to agree with you," said Doc. He watched the knife with wary concern. He knew of only one sure defense against a knife attack, and that was a chair held out with its legs poised to deflect the blade. The only chair happened to be occupied. He told Nina, "You must have made him mad. Something you said, perhaps?"

"Maybe," she admitted.

"What was it?"

"It wasn't anything!" Poltov snarled.

"It must have given him a jolt," Doc prompted casually.

Nina Kirkegaard nodded. "I merely demanded—"

"Silence!" Poltov ordered.

"You better stop interrupting," Doc Savage warned.

"I demanded why the ship had not put into the Pechora as agreed," said Nina defiantly.

"I'm curious about that myself," the bronze man admitted. He eyed Poltov. "It seems a reasonable question for the captain of the ship to ask."

"Also, I demanded—"

"No, not that!" Two purple veins stood out in Poltov's forehead like engorged leeches. "It is nothing. She only imagines." His eyes were wild. "I will tell you the truth. I asked her to marry me. Over this, we quarreled. That is all."

Doc Savage looked at Poltov amazedly. "Do you always propose to the lady by tying her up and threatening her with a knife?"

"I perhaps became excited," Poltov said grudgingly.

"How does that sort of technique work out?" Doc asked. "I should think it would get results, one way or the other." Doc glanced at Nina Kirkegaard. "How did it appeal to you?" he asked, wry-voiced.

"I would as soon marry the devil," she spat.

"That would be a better deal, probably." Doc casually put his weight on his left leg. He planned to use his right foot to kick Poltov's kneecap, hoping that would disable the fellow's leg.

"Yes," Nina exclaimed. "I'd prefer Satan." Her shoulders twisted with fury. "My brother formerly owned half of this ship. He was murdered. . . . I think I know now who killed him." The look she gave Poltov was like a stiletto.

"Did you inherit your interest in the ship from your brother?" Doc inquired.

"Yes. After he was murdered."

"After Poltov killed him, you mean?"

Nina's voice was tight. "Yes."

"She is mistaken." Poltov's teeth were the color of old bone. "She is immensely mistaken."

"I am sure," Nina said coldly. "I no longer have any doubt."

"Hmmm." Doc Savage regarded Poltov. "How about that? Did you kill her brother?" He was disturbed to notice Poltov was also balancing his weight on one foot, probably preparatory to kicking him.

"Me?" Poltov shrugged. "Do you imagine I would murder the brother of the woman I love?"

"I'm asking you."

"I did not."

"She seems to think you did."

"So?"

"Doesn't that make you feel bad?" Doc asked.

"Very."

"I doubt if it made you feel bad enough to start brandishing a knife under her nose," suggested Doc. "I think it was that other question she asked you. Wasn't that what drove you crazy?"

Poltov stiffened. "There was no other . . ."

"Yes, there was," said Nina Kirkegaard. "I demanded to know who the woman is who came aboard in Tromso. At that, he became like an insane man."

"Take it easy," Doc said, looking at Poltov with apprehension.

Poltov held the knife with both hands. "Witch!" he hissed. Only the blade protruded from his fists. "I told you not to talk!" It was as if a blade of grass grew from his fist—steel grass.

Before anything more could be said, Doc sidestepped quickly. It was a wise move, because Poltov kicked and his foot whistled past the spot where Doc's stomach had been. Momentum carried Poltov's foot to the height of Doc's shoulder. Like a subject about to kneel before his king, Doc bent his knees. He reached under and over Poltov's lower leg to seize the man's toe.

When Doc straightened and put on pressure, Poltov left the floor completely.

He revolved three times in the air and made a hissing noise of alarm, hitting the floor with his unprotected face. He skidded, slammed his head up against the wall; his feet flopped up and fell back to the floor.

"Kick a man, would you?" taunted Doc.

Poltov's eyes focused on the tip of his nose. They were still there intently when Doc placed a foot on his heaving chest. Doc stepped down, twisting his foot. There was a mushy crackling of rib cartilage. Doc's weight was on the foot as he twisted. He jiggled a little. A thin stream of blood suddenly appeared at Poltov's nostrils. It shot out in a long spray. The Russian bleated like a lost lamb.

Doc glanced at Nina Kirkegaard. "The blade snapped," she said. "I am not afraid of him now."

"Care to ask him anything before I throw him out?" the bronze man inquired.

"I'd like to know who that woman is," she said.

"I can tell you that." Doc looked down in irritation. Poltov was trying to seize his ankles and lift Doc's weight off his chest. But it was no use. The Russian was outclassed.

Poltov kept a tight clutch on one of Doc's ankles. He used both hands. Poltov's teeth had been forced through his lips in three places. A small crimson fountain marked the location of his nostrils. The fountain was about an inch and a half tall. Doc observed that Poltov's knife had been dropped nearby, and he found that by squatting he could reach it. He laid the blade's broken edge against the tendons in the joints of Poltov's fingers, as if preparatory to severing them.

Poltov screamed and released Doc. Nina snatched away the knife and waved it over Poltov.

Going to the door, Doc opened it.

The two guards peered past him into the cabin. They looked at Poltov and failed to recognize him. "Where is Paul?" one asked in harsh Russian. His hair hung down over his eyes like a sheepdog's.

"Take him away," Doc ordered, indicating Poltov. "Take him to Anna Gryahznyi." His Russian was Soviet military academy crisp.

"Paul!" exclaimed one of the guards amazedly. "Paul, your face. . . ."

"Anna Gryahznyi wants him," insisted Doc, using a commanding manner. But in case the guards should decide to give trouble, he drew his revolver.

"Poor Paul!" The sailors fell to their knees beside Poltov. "Your poor face! Oh, Paul!" moaned one.

"Listen, you two!" said Doc.

They scowled at him.

Doc said, "If I were you, I'd be careful how I went around poor-Pauling an enemy of the people's republic." He watched them stiffen with fright.

"Just a word of friendly warning," he added.

"You say that Anna Gryahznyi—?" muttered one guard. The other could not seem to get his mouth to close.

"She wants him brought to her right now," Doc lied.

"But we thought . . ."

"Anna Gryahznyi is not a patient wench," Doc said. He smiled faintly at the Banneresque turn of phrase. "You had better shake the lead out of your pants, worker-comrades." He raised his voice. "And stop arguing!"

Their eyes as big as deviled eggs, the two sailors laid hold of Poltov, one taking legs, the other wrists. Poltov's wrists were slippery with his own blood and the sailor transferred his grip to Poltov's mop of wild, canniballike black hair. There was considerable stretch to Poltov's scalp, so that his head seemed to become cone-shaped as they carried him out.

"Well!" said Nina Kirkegaard. "I think you deserve your liar's diploma for what you just did." Her paleness became her, Doc thought. She added, "I thought they would tear you to pieces when they saw what you had done to Paul."

"I wasn't so worried," said Doc breezily.

"You are very brave." Nina Kirkegaard's voice was throaty and delightful. "You are brave, hard, and cruel." Her brown eyes were on Doc. "Why did you yourself become pale when you mentioned Anna Gryahznyi, who I presume is the woman who came aboard at Tromso?"

"Eh? I . . ." Doc struggled with embarrassment. "You're a quick one with a question," he said at last. He wondered if he looked the way Dryden always looked when refusing to discuss the subject of Anna Gryahznyi. "I happened to show up here because I was paying you a call to ask you if you cared to join our side. What about it?"

"Will I be safe with you?" she asked.

"I doubt it," Doc said. He wished she would put away the knife. It affected the edges of his teeth. He forced a grin. "You'll be safe from Breckenridge and Dryden, though," he added. "When they hear how you were waving that shiv at your boyfriend . . ."

Her eyes rested on him obliquely. "Poltov was not my boyfriend," she protested. Her teeth showed for a moment, and they were small and remarkably white. "I mean never."

"That so?" Doc said. He was not sure he believed her. "Glad to hear it." He opened the cabin door and glanced both directions in the corridor. He said, "When those sailors learn they were flimflammed, they may decide to come back for us. I would not want to be here if that happens. I suggest you tag along with me." He paused, fixed her with his steady gaze. "That is, if you care to throw your lot in with us."

"If you think I want to take my chances with that Poltov . . ." Nina Kirkegaard shuddered. "What have you in mind?"

"Let's join my friends," said Doc hastily.

They got going.

Snow sifted over the edge of the cabin roof like smoke. The Arctic wind, very cold, bruised Doc's face like fist blows. Shivering violently, the bronze man aided Nina Kirkegaard along the deck.

A gun spoke out with an enormous, cold voice. Doc heard the sound of the bullet quite near his head; it was as if someone had driven a cork into a bottle neck with a hard palm blow.

Doc threw an arm about Nina and hauled her down to the deck. He pulled his revolver out of the tangle of his fur garments and returned the fire with blinding flashes. He thought they had been fired at from the bridge, so he shot back in that general direction.

When his eyes recovered from the glare, he could see no one.

As he watched, a great wave rushed up to the side of the vessel and began climbing aboard. There was the noise of tons of falling water. Doc endeavored to get to his feet and help Nina Kirkegaard to hers, but the mass of water fell upon them, spinning them about, tumbling them along the deck.

"Banner!" Dryden splashed toward them, slithering on the icy deck. "Are you hit?"

"Watch out!" said Doc warningly.

"My God, what's *she* doing here?" blurted Dryden. He was gaping at Nina Kirkegaard.

"She's with us now," Doc told him.

They were speaking English, not Norwegian, which brought a startled look to Nina's mink-brown eyes. "You are all Americans?" she gasped.

"Do you mind telling me just what is going on?" Dryden demanded.

The remainder of the wave careened aft and pitched back into the sea from the taffrail.

"Somebody took a shot at us," Doc explained. "Let's get out of here before they try it again."

Dryden stared at him. "Who was it?"

"One of Poltov's friends, I imagine," ventured Doc.

"What did you do to stir them up?" asked Dryden.

"Not so much." Doc Savage, alarmed, saw another wave bearing down on them out of the night. "Merely rescue Miss Kirkegaard from his toils." He glanced sharply toward the rail. "Run for the cabin. Here comes another of those deck-washers."

All three got going.

They managed to reach their cabin and yank the door shut behind them in time to let the wave break harmlessly. It sounded like a small Niagara, or a herd of agitated goats on the deck.

Breckenridge greeted them, one of the machine guns in his hands. "Hello," he said. "Was that a shot? I suppose things have opened up, then?" He smiled in the direction of Nina Kirkegaard. It was a sappy smile. "Why, hello, Nina," he said in his fair Norwegian.

"Skip it," Dryden snapped. "She knows we're Americans."

"Oh."

Doc Savage saw that preparations had been made to abandon the ship. The aluminum cases were equipped with straps to facilitate carrying. Dryden and Breckenridge had assembled their other gear into packs. All was in readiness for flight.

When the noise of the breaking sea subsided outdoors, Doc said, "Is everyone ready to leave the ship?"

Dryden looked at him in alarm, demanded, "Can we make it in this rough water? Can we even get a lifeboat over the side?"

The bronze man, one of the cases of radio apparatus under his arm, looked at him intently.

"Personally, I think I can manage my share," he said. "But of course," he added ruefully, "I've been inspired by Anna Gryahznyi."

Nina Kirkegaard hugged herself and shivered from head to toe. She said, "The way you speak that woman's name makes my blood run cold."

No one offered any comment on that pronouncement. Nina had given words to their innermost feelings.

XVIII

FLIGHT

The *Norge Pike*'s Diesels, laboring at high speed, vibrated the whole ship. *Chug, chug, chug,* they said, and blue vapor came out of the stack. Pools of water on deck became goose-fleshed due to the vibration of the planking beneath.

Doc Savage made out a lifeboat lashed in a cradle under its davits. "How about this one?" he asked Nina Kirkegaard.

"It's a sound lifeboat," she said, nodding. "It's almost new, too. It has an engine."

"Load aboard," said Doc. "Don't forget to check for gas, water, and food."

Starting to free the lashings of the lifeboat cover, Doc sighted movement. A man had stepped out of the deck house to stare at them. Doc produced his gun, and the man vanished quickly.

"They're wise to us," cautioned Dryden.

"So it would appear," said Doc.

A moment later, the ship heeled far over in a ninety-degree turn. When it straightened, it was running broadside to the wind and crashing seas. Tons of water sprang aboard, battering the ship and the lifeboat, making it impossible to think of launching the latter.

Dryden clung to a davit. "We're trapped here," he gasped. "We couldn't lower an anvil over the side without getting it smashed."

"Oh, yes we can," rapped Doc.

He tore at the lifeboat cover. The heavy canvas was an inch thick with ice, and the wind caused it to snap at him with the sound of an alligator using its jaws. However, he managed to swing the cases of radio apparatus into the small craft.

"Get set to lower away," Doc called.

"But the seas will crush—" Dryden began to say.

"No," Doc told him. "There is an auxiliary steering gear over the rudderpost. I'm going back there to do a little steering myself." He debated as to whether to take one of the machine guns with him, and finally decided it would have a persuasive effect. "When the ship turns and makes a lee, get the lifeboat overboard," he directed.

"All right," Dryden bit out. "Don't be too free and use up all our ammunition."

The *Norge Pike* shuddered with the impacts of the sea. Green splits of seawater frequently jumped completely over the superstructure. Doc kept his feet with difficulty.

Foul air, a stout blend of grease and bilge, poured out of the little auxiliary hatch when Doc Savage pried it open.

He descended the steel ladder into a small cubicle, dank and dreary.

A moment later, by delivering a kick against a lever, he was able to take charge of steering the ship.

Confidently, he laid on to the hand wheel, spinning it to starboard.

Presently a wave struck the rudder while the ship stern was high in the water; the wheel spun, hurling the bronze man against a bulkhead. He set his teeth, waited until the wheel stopped spinning, then fell upon it again, but more respectfully.

Soon he could feel the nose of the ship come reeling around in response to his effort with the jury rudder.

A series of muffled whistling sounds puzzled him, until he decided someone was trying to get his attention over the mechanical speaking tube which connected the jury steering position with the bridge. Doc wedged a knee against the wheel, raised the speaking-tube lid with his thumb, and asked, "Is there something that doesn't suit you fellows?"

"A chom eedyot rech?" a voice screamed from the tube.

"Do you speak English?" asked Doc.

"*Dah.* Yoo wan' speak him?"

"Listen, you son of a sea dog," warned Doc, putting his major effort into sounding as hard-boiled as possible, "I'm going to run this scow straight into the nearest iceberg. How do you like that?" He added hastily, "The first one of you who comes fooling around here is going to get his head shot off, too."

This must not have sounded very impressive coming from the speaking tube, because the response was a derisive noise made with tongue and lips.

At length, the engines stopped. When Doc looked out on deck, he saw no one, but the ship had attained a position favorable for launching the lifeboat, so he straightened the rudder. The vessel lost headway. Doc heard sounds indicating the lifeboat was being lowered.

Drawing back into the dreary niche which contained the jury steering mechanism, he looked closely to ascertain whether there was some method of locking the rudder. He could find none. However, he noticed with satisfaction that the cubbyhole was equipped with a lamp for extreme emergencies—an old-fashioned sailing-ship type of kerosene lamp suspended in gimbals.

From the vicinity of the lifeboat came the sound of a light machine gun, as if a large metal woodpecker had started operating on the ship hull.

Doc removed the kerosene lamp from its gimbals and dashed it against the floor. Kerosene splattered floor and walls. Doc applied the flame from his cigarette lighter. The kerosene caught fire and burned more rapidly than he expected.

Slapping at a smoking spot on his fur outer garment, the bronze man scrambled out on deck.

From over the side of the ship, came the sound of a boat being rowed.

Plunging forward, Doc pitched in the general direction of the sound. He had trouble with the slippery deck, almost upsetting twice.

Rounding the deck house, he discerned three figures leaping toward him. Flames licking from the niche containing the steering mechanism gave enough light to disclose them. They were crewmen armed with rifles.

Doc went into reverse. He withdrew behind the deck house, barely in time.

Fascinated, he watched bullets chip clouds of ice off the deck. His own gun ready, he waited for the enemy to appear. But they had halted cautiously.

Silence came. The guns were silent. The ship sat motionless on a rolling sea.

"Ahoy the deck!" called Dryden.

The lifeboat had moved under the stern. Doc said, "It's about time!" Fear had raised his voice pitch noticeably.

"You all right?" asked Dryden.

"I'm fine," said Doc, not sounding it. "Throw up a rope."

There was the noise of struggling with an icy line. "Damn this thing!" Dryden cursed bitterly. The frozen rope was defying him. "You may have to jump overboard. We can pick you up."

"Not if it can be avoided," said Doc. "If I had a choice, I'd sooner be shot than frozen to death." He watched closely for enemies. "Go ahead, take your time." He was angry about the delay. "Any time before Christmas will do—"

The line came snaking up and fell across the taffrail. In great haste, Doc made the end fast.

Calling, "Look out below," Doc slid down the ice-covered rope like a dropped rock. He landed in the lifeboat with stunning force. He lay dazed a moment from the impact. His strong legs had taken the brunt of it, but the pitching of the craft had caught him off-guard.

Breckenridge seized an oar. "Let's go!" he bellowed. "Heave-ho!"

Above them on the ship, they could hear shouting and men running. A heavy voice started bawling, *"Agon! Agon!"* They had found the blazing kerosene. Nina Kirkegaard, Breckenridge, and Dryden threw their weight onto oars. The lifeboat climbed a long hill of hissing, green-blue, ice-cold water.

Doc endeavored to sit erect. The motion of the lifeboat pitched him over sidewise. He felt of his right calf.

"What's the matter with you?" asked Dryden.

"Don't worry about me," Doc snapped, angry that he had landed so awkwardly. "Just row this boat away from here."

"Did they shoot you?" demanded Breckenridge.

Doc crawled toward the engine housing. "They certainly tried." A waterproof canvas cover enclosed the engine box. "Let's get the engine going."

"I hope you know how to start the thing," said Dryden. "None of us do."

Doc didn't answer. He loosened the cover, peered into

the engine housing, but it was too dark to distinguish much. He thrust an arm inside, exploring with cold-numbed fingers.

"You want a flashlight?" Dryden asked.

"No," said Doc. "They'd see the light."

"They can see us anyway," said Dryden. The ship stern seemed to loom alarmingly close. Sheets of flame were spurting from the steering-gear compartment, making the aft section of the vessel light up with blood-red flashes.

A light machine gun fired a burst. It made a deep-throated bawling noise, the rapidity of fire so great that individual reports were not distinguishable. The bullets did not strike near enough to be heard.

"Good God!" Dryden gasped. "Get that engine going!"

"That sounded like a Mauser machine pistol, the one they call an M1932." Doc seemed undisturbed by the gun's enormous rate of fire. "After about the third shot, nobody can hold one of those things on a target."

Breckenridge was not relieved. "A Mauser is a damned good gun," he pointed out.

"Try holding the M1932 model on a target sometime," grunted Doc Savage, not looking away from his labors.

Dryden rowed in a frenzy, watched the ship. "What's keeping them from shooting us to pieces?"

"I think the flames must be blinding them," said Nina Kirkegaard.

"What'd you set on fire?" Breckenridge asked.

"Some kerosene from a lamp," explained Doc.

"Will the ship burn?"

"I doubt it," said Doc. "The best we can hope for is they won't be able to steer the ship for ten or fifteen minutes."

The lifeboat crawled laboriously to the crest of one mountainous sea after another, staggering over the top, racing downward with surfboard speed. There were alarming possibilities for capsizing. It seemed darker. From somewhere ahead of them came dull booming noises.

"How you coming with the engine?" Dryden asked.

Doc struggled to turn a petcock with cold-stiffened fingers. "I think I have it figured out." He braced himself, seizing the engine crank with both hands. The engine back-fired loudly. Doc eyed the ship for a time. "Guess they didn't hear the backfire," he said with relief. "We must be farther away than it looks." He spun the crank vigorously. "Get going, you stubborn Norwegian piece of junk!" he said to the engine. The engine began running smoothly.

Nina Kirkegaard seized the tiller. "Thank goodness!"

"The engine seems to understand your language," Dryden grunted.

"Force is universal," said Doc dryly. "Thank God."

They watched the *Norge Pike* anxiously for flashes of gunfire. They could see sailors pouring the contents of fire extinguishers onto the kerosene blaze. There was very little fog, Doc realized with alarm. "It's lucky I panicked them into disabling their searchlight last night," he remarked. "That could have given us trouble."

"Maybe they've got another one," worried Dryden.

"They have," said Nina flatly.

Doc opened the engine throttle wider. "We're not out of the woods, then."

He listened to the booming noises from ahead. They became louder for a time, then subsided somewhat.

Dryden, eyeing Nina Kirkegaard, asked, "Aren't you frightened the least bit?"

Nina replied coolly, "I haven't had time to notice."

Breckenridge said, "We were sure lucky to get off that ship safe and unharmed."

Dryden snorted derisively. "You call this safe? Adrift in a lifeboat in an Arctic storm?"

It was fortunate the lifeboat was well-designed, Doc Savage thought. He could not claim a gale of wind was blowing, but neither was it calm. He noticed the excellent behavior of the little boat. It was a double-ended design, having about the same shape aft as forward, and such seas as overtook them did not have much tendency to make the craft yaw. Occasionally the wind picked the crest off a wave and dashed it into the craft, but otherwise they did not ship much water.

"Are all five cases safe aboard?" Doc called out.

"Yes," Dryden said.

"What do you have in those boxes?" wondered Nina Kirkegaard. "Or is it a big secret?"

"You guessed it," Dryden said aridly. "It's a big secret."

"Poltov was certainly curious about them," Nina pointed out. She tried a wheedling tone. "Aren't you going to tell me what is in the boxes?"

"No," said Doc flatly. "He's not." The booming sounds were again louder ahead. "Anyone curious about that noise?" he asked.

They listened.

"It's surf!" said Breckenridge excitedly. "Land! Land is close!"

Nina Kirkegaard said, "I don't think so. The sound isn't regular enough for surf. It is more like . . ." She listened. "More like stones bumping together."

"Not stones," said Doc Savage. "Ice cakes."

"You mean ice—" said Dryden.

"Floe ice," Doc explained. "A lot of cakes pushed together and shoved against the coast by the wind." He visualized what the pack ice might be like. "Probably some rough walking," he added.

Suddenly the seas, which climbed darkly about them, became brilliantly frosted. A single enormous whisker, an incandescent white rod of a thing, twitched nervously from the *Norge Pike*. The beam of a searchlight. Doc held his breath. But the light passed on, without disclosing them.

"Whew! That was close!" Dryden had snatched up a submachine gun.

Doc Savage twisted around. He waited for the searchlight beam to make a second sweep. When the light did come, it bejeweled the sea all about them.

"Look yonder!" Doc pointed ahead of the bow.

Not more than a quarter of a mile ahead, the sea was

tearing itself to pieces against a broken-toothed wall of granitic ice. The floes, spray-scrubbed, were the same blue as U.S. Air Force uniforms.

"Great Scott!" said Breckenridge.

"A bit impressive, I would say," said Dryden.

"Beautiful!" said Nina Kirkegaard. "Horrible, but beautiful, too."

"Somebody," said Doc, "had better figure out how we're going to climb onto that ice shelf with all these boxes."

The white rod of light passed on with magical speed. The darkness now seemed blue-black. Doc heard a click. He knew Dryden had inserted a fresh box magazine into his submachine gun. Doc said, "You keep fooling with that chattergun in the dark, you're liable to accidentally shoot one of us, or worse yet, blow the bottom out of this boat."

"I wonder if I could hit that searchlight from here." Dryden pondered.

"Don't try it," warned Doc. "Your muzzle flame would set us up for them like clay pigeons."

With complete unexpectedness, a blinding glare of light slapped against them. Shot sound came from the ship. Short ugly *glug*s! nearby indicated where the bullets hit.

"They spotted us anyway," Doc added tightly. By misfortune, the searchlight had impaled the lifeboat while it was on the crest of a wave. "You better try potting it, after all," Doc told Dryden.

The lifeboat traveled fast, the engine laboring. It made a diving descent into a wave trough, clawed up the following slope.

Dryden stood, submachine gun to shoulder, waiting for a glimpse of the *Norge Pike*.

When the lifeboat reached the top, the wave broke, jolted the boat badly. Dryden lost his balance. The boat plunged down a hissing slope of icy seawater. Dryden fell heavily into the bottom of the boat.

"Damn it, did you lose the gun?" Doc demanded.

"If you're gonna steer this thing, keep it steady!" Dryden was under the impression Doc Savage was handling the tiller. "No, I didn't lose anything," he grumbled.

"I'd like to see you steer any better!" said Nina Kirkegaard angrily.

The ice-pack edge was now very close. The sea burst against the ice, exploded into spray, in some places surged over the ice. The effect was that of an enormous beast with bluish fangs, gargling water.

Nina suddenly put the helm hard to starboard. Dryden, in the act of arising, fell again. He asked, "What the devil?"

Now the lifeboat traveled longer on the crest of a wave. Bullets whistled past, pursued by shot sound from the ship. Miraculously, they were unhit.

"A lead," said Nina Kirkegaard. She sounded surprisingly composed.

"A what?" said Dryden.

"She means there seems to be a crack in the ice pack just ahead," Doc Savage explained. He looked backward. The *Norge Pike* had gotten a way on. It headed toward them, gathering speed. The fire in the auxiliary steering cubicle appeared extinguished.

Dryden's submachine gun clattered. His fire had no effect on the searchlight.

The lifeboat twisted into the opening in the pack ice. It shot forward on water that was suddenly smoother.

Doc said, "Lady Luck is sure with us."

Breckenridge inquired, "They could have run us down in a few minutes, couldn't they?" His voice exploded shrilly.

Nina Kirkegaard's laughter was brittle, like a crone's. "You think we are safe now? You are foolish." She threw out an arm. "Look!"

Doc peered fearfully at the walls of ice on either side. The walls were composed of huge cakes which ground together under the pressure of sea and wind. He turned his flashlight on the ice. Before his eyes, a cake the size of a locomotive burst into fragments under the pressure. He extinguished the light, repressing a shuddery thrill of danger.

"I hope this crack doesn't take a notion to close up," he said fervently.

"You think there's a chance it will?" Breckenridge gasped.

"Definitely," Doc said calmly. "The only question is, when?"

The lifeboat charged along the open lead. Twice it struck floating ice with alarming jolts. The water became smooth, except that it heaved slowly, like a monster breathing. The lead angled slightly so that the lights of the ship, should they appear at the mouth of the lead, could not be seen.

"Hold it!" Doc reduced the throttle. "How about over there!" He decided to risk using his flashlight again. The flash beam traveled over a ledge. "Looks as if we could unload the stuff there. Is everyone game?"

"I suppose we'll have to take to the ice sometime." Dryden's left side was becoming caked with rime where cold spray had splashed him.

Doc hurriedly removed a device from his pack. He strapped it to his left foot, the metal spikes pointing downward, then fastened another to his right boot. "Crampons," he explained. "For walking on ice."

When the lifeboat grated against the ledge, Doc sprang to the pack ice. The boat painter was in his hand. He wrestled the craft close to the ice and managed to hold it while the others passed the boxes to the ice.

"Drag the gadget back into the ice a ways," he suggested. "I think we better cache it and stow the lifeboat elsewhere."

"What's the idea of that?" asked Dryden.

Doc helped Nina Kirkegaard climb back into the lifeboat. "You want to run those Russians a footrace with you packing a couple of those boxes for a handicap?" he asked Dryden.

Losing his footing on the ice, Dryden fell heavily. "You got any more of them whatcha-callems to go on your feet?" Picking himself up, Dryden crawled into the boat. Breckenridge shoved off, sprang aboard.

Doc said, "I have a pair for each of us, and some spares." He handed the tiller over to Nina Kirkegaard. "For heaven's sake, keep track of where we left those boxes," he warned. He passed out the crampons.

The dark mass of the ship pushing behind it, the searchlight beam suddenly came into view. It advanced down the lead in the ice pack.

"The stupid idiots!" Nina's cry shook with rage. "They've run the ship into the lead! They'll wreck her!"

"Be a piece of luck for us if they do," commented Doc.

Nina Kirkegaard cursed Doc in Norwegian. "It's half my ship they're trying to sink!" she said. Doc looked at her in astonishment. He had never heard Norwegian spoken so feelingly.

A small swarm of bullets passed overhead. They had been discovered. The *Norge Pike* accelerated, traveling at dangerous speed in the narrow channel in the ice pack.

Doc said, "They've spotted us. That's enough to draw them away from the boxes." He gestured at the ice. "Let's go ashore."

Nina Kirkegaard, angry with Doc and the others, deliberately drove the lifeboat into the ice. The crash piled Breckenridge into the bow. Dryden fell also; his gun emitted a stuttering bawl that deafened them. Doc retained his balance. They scrambled onto the ice floe.

"Shoot a hole in the bottom of the lifeboat," Doc said. "Sink it. They'll think the boxes went down with it."

Dryden hesitated. Doc Savage used his own gun to blast a ragged rent in the lifeboat planking. It promptly started filling with water. "That should trick them into thinking the boxes are lost," he said confidently. Doc eyed the approaching ship angrily, shading his eyes against the searchlight glare.

"Let's take a couple of potshots at them before we light out," he suggested.

"Good idea." Dryden stamped his crampon spikes into the ice. "I can hit something now, I bet you."

Nina Kirkegaard tried to snatch Doc's submachine gun. "You're all crazy! You'll sink my ship!" Doc waved his gun in the air to keep it from the Norwegian blonde's clutch. While he was doing this, Dryden fired a burst. Guttering flame played on the slots in the compensator on the end of Dryden's gun barrel. About fifteen shots came from his gun. Two thirds of a box magazineful, Doc thought with alarm.

"You must think we're carrying an ammunition factory!" Doc said hotly.

"Hah!" said Dryden. "That's a lot different than trying to hit something from a pitching boat."

Doc decided not to fire any shots himself. "These peashooters can't do any damage to a ship," he said. "Let's take to our heels before they get closer."

The searchlight beam suddenly pointed at the sky, remained fixed there. Low-flying clouds impaled their dark bellies on the white rod of light, slowly squirmed free, and fled.

The *Norge Pike* veered sharply to the port. It did not slacken speed. It crashed into the wall of the ice crevasse. The pack ice made shotgun sounds under the impact as cracks opened. The bow climbed tiredly onto the ice. Steel plates gave way with startled shrieking sounds. Swinging slowly, the stern struck the opposite side of the ice lead and lodged. Amazingly, the lead began closing. It crushed the ship slowly, the way a hand would wad a cigarette package.

"What on earth?" Doc was stunned. "What did you aim at, Dryden?"

Dryden slapped his thigh delightedly. "I fixed 'em, didn't I?" he chortled.

"That you did. But what did you aim—?"

Doc reached hastily for Nina Kirkegaard's arm. He missed, and her swing landed on Dryden's jaw. He sprawled on the ice.

"Sink my ship, will he!" Nina was furious. Buckling

hull plates on the *Norge Pike* sounded like hounds baying in the distance.

"You should be glad Dryden stopped them," Doc Savage pointed out.

"I should be glad!" Nina cried. "Do you know what my half of that ship was worth?" Her eyes were too hot for tears to form.

"Dryden saved our necks," Doc pointed out.

"A million and a quarter kroner!" said Nina Kirkegaard. "This I should laugh about?"

With a coughing sound, the deck house of the ship split. Sheets of flame lunged up at the clouds. A cargo hatch sailed upward, twisting slowly like a wind-blown leaf.

"I remember seeing iron drums in the cargo," said Breckenridge. "Aviation gasoline, do you suppose?" The amount of flames increased, became bluish, roaring like a blowtorch.

Dryden sat up. Nina would have kicked him had Doc not intervened. "A million and a quarter kroner! Gone!" Her eyes glittered in the firelight. She tried to reach Dryden.

Doc Savage restrained her. "You didn't lose anything," he said reassuringly.

"How do you figure that?" she asked.

"Poltov had already stolen your half of the ship," explained Doc. "You had nothing to lose."

"I would have taken it away from him," said Nina Kirkegaard.

"Maybe," said Doc. "Maybe not."

Breckenridge leveled an arm. "Good God, look!" An animallike ball of flame traveled over the forecastle of the ship, dropped to the ice pack, and scampered about. Screams came out of the fiery ball. "Ugh!" said Breckenridge.

Dryden blew out a long breath. "You know who I hope that was?"

"I think you wasted your wish," Doc told him.

"Why?"

"I don't think she would burn," said Doc. "I think she could walk through fire, like the devil, and laugh through it all."

"Yeah, you're probably right," said Dryden, disappointment coloring his tone.

"Who are you talking about?" demanded Nina.

"An old acquaintance of ours," offered Doc. He tried to put Anna Gryahznyi out of his mind. He tore his mud-brown eyes from the blazing ship and fixed Nina Kirkegaard. "Your half of the ship was really worth one million two hundred fifty thousand kroner?" he asked.

"You bet," she said. "Maybe more."

"Insurance?"

"Yes, there was coverage."

Doc looked at her irritably. "It's lucky the ship hit the ice and got crushed," he said. "That'll be covered in your insurance. If I know insurance companies, it would be a hot day before they paid off on Poltov stealing your ship. Those policies all have a clause in there about you warranting them free of responsibility in the event of strikes, riots, capture, seizure, arrest, restraint, or consequences of any warlike operation."

"You really think I could get by and collect insurance?" demanded Nina Kirkegaard excitedly.

"Probably."

"For God's sake," said Dryden. "How long do we stand around here while you two figure out how to chisel an insurance company?" He watched some men scrambling off the burning ship. "We should latch onto our boxes and get the hell out of here," he added.

"Let's go," said Doc.

"I couldn't help it if the ice caught my ship, could I?" said Nina Kirkegaard, as if trying to convince herself.

Their lifeboat had disappeared below the surface. The stern section of the *Norge Pike* was slowly doing likewise. Smoke and steam boiled over the vicinity.

"Ice is a normal risk. The insurance policy says so." Nina was becoming more cheerful. "That's why they charged me extra premiums."

They worked their way across the ice. Progress was a matter of crawling precariously up the faces of jagged cakes and sliding, or falling, down the other side. A deposit of several inches of snow did not make the going less treacherous.

"Hey!" Nina grabbed Doc's arm. "When Poltov seized the ship, wouldn't that be piracy?"

"At least," said Doc.

"Piracy! But I'm not insured against piracy, am I?"

Doc considered. "Probably not."

"My God!" Nina breathed. "We've got to forget to tell the insurance company about Poltov grabbing the ship. That's what we've got to do." Her fingers took repeated bites at Doc's arm. "You keep mum about the piracy angle, you hear?"

Doc recalled that he had been surprised to discover that Nina Kirkegaard owned a bar in Bergen. He thought it would be no surprise now to find she owned a lion's share of Norway. She was able to keep her mind on a dollar. Which was fortunate. In her agitation, she had all but forgotten the aluminum boxes containing the Moonwinx radio transmitter.

"Have you noticed," said Breckenridge. "The ship got wrecked right next to where we left the boxes."

Alarm seized Doc. He gestured the others back, saying, "You wait here while I scout ahead."

"Be careful when you look over that ice ridge," Dryden warned. "You stand a good chance of getting shot between the eyes."

Doc took some time to work his way silently to the crest of an ice ridge which overlooked the spot where they had left the packing-cases containing the UHF radio transmitter for reflecting signals off the surface of the moon.

He returned to his companions much more rapidly.

"We're in a spot!" His voice was metallic with concern. "They've found the boxes and taken possession of them."

XIX

JOURNEY INTO MYSTERY

Snow, falling gently in large flakes like butterfly wings, made the whole world seem quiet. Doc Savage found himself wishing a wolf would howl. He distrusted the silence very much. It gave a deceitful air of peace to his surroundings, which he regarded as anything but peaceful. A voice interrupted his thoughts.

"They really put out silence in gobs around here, don't they?" muttered Dryden uneasily.

He was buried to his neck in a snowdrift and, except for his eyes, his head was shrouded in a white parka hood. Anyone standing a few feet away would have had difficulty seeing him.

"If you like it still," allowed Doc, "you can't beat this."

By pulling his brow downward, the bronze man could see that his eyebrows were thick with frost. He imagined it must be around twenty degrees below zero. "I think it must be warming up," he said, wondering if the extreme weather would cause his Banner disguise to come apart. Then he remembered it had stood up well enough to the rough Russian wilderness he had struggled through before returning to New York City, just prior to embarking upon the Moonwinx mission.

Dryden's eyes jerked sidewise inside the hood, looked at Doc. He did not say anything. The two men were silent for quite a while. They were supposed to be sleeping, but neither was sleepy. The snow, unhurried by any wind, continued to fall soundlessly.

"Do you suppose Breck and Miss Kirkegaard are okay?" asked Dryden.

"Let's hope so."

"Aren't they due back?"

"Not for a while yet," said Doc quietly.

"I hope nothing happens to them," said Dryden.

"What is likely to happen to Breckenridge," offered Doc, "is that he is apt to find himself promising to buy Miss Kirkegaard a new steamship."

Dryden chuckled. "That will give her three. I heard you telling her the U.S. government would probably buy her a new ship."

"I had to tell her something to get some peace of mind." Doc squirmed to a more comfortable position in the snow. "She claims she should have a new ship from the insurance company and a new ship from Uncle Sam. Maybe if Breckenridge promises her one too, that will shut her up." Doc closed his eyes. He was tired of looking at the limitless monotony of the tundra. "Miss Kirkegaard can keep her mind on a dollar," he reminded.

"You gotta give her credit," said Dryden. "This trouble we're having doesn't seem to faze her."

"She's durable," agreed Doc. "Let's hope that's all there is to her."

"Meaning?"

"How's your self-control?" Doc was watching Dryden thoughtfully.

"Eh?" Dryden's eyes narrowed suspiciously.

"Could I ask you a question without you getting mad?" Doc asked.

Dryden snorted. "Since when have you been stopped by a little thing like ruffling a man's feathers?"

"True. But I would like an answer."

"Well, ask your damn question, then." Dryden was very suspicious now. "What is it?"

Doc scrutinized him. "You won't blow up?"

"How'n hell do I know?" Impatience made Dryden's eyes flare like a struck match.

"Mad already," said Doc, unconcerned. "I'll put that down to nerves." He prepared to defend himself, if necessary, from the hot-tempered Special Security chief's wrath.

"Have you ever actually had a good look at Anna Gryahznyi in full daylight?" the bronze man asked.

Dryden froze.

Hastily, Doc added, "Seen her under good light, I mean. It could be incandescent light, daylight, candlelight, firelight. Any kind of light. But have you ever seen her clearly, ever?"

Dryden was starkly silent.

"Come," said Doc. "I asked a simple question."

Dryden cleared his throat. "What are you getting at?" His voice sounded as if it were squeezed between weights.

"Have you?"

"Seen Anna Gryahznyi's actual face? Well, not really. . . ."

Doc frowned, making his artificial face bunch up like a bulldog's. "I understood—"

"It was in the dark I met her," said Dryden, thick-voiced. He emitted a rumbling, throat-clearing sound, as if dredging up some poison lodged deep in his soul. "I was the only one of our network to emerge alive."

"I understand it was not your fault, what happened to your agents in Moscow," Doc said sympathetically.

"I don't want to talk about it!" Dryden exploded.

Doc Savage recalled his own brushes with the Red Widow. "Both times I met her, it was in the dark," he said. He fingered his swollen earlobe thoughtfully. "And neither time was I absolutely certain it was actually her," he continued. "I still am not. Such an experience leaves very little chance for certainty, I would say." He paused. "Where was it you crossed her trail?"

"Moscow," Dryden said shortly.

Doc nodded, his eyes reflective. "I first heard of her in Moscow, as a matter of fact. Before the war. When the Russians were on our side and so was she. Her man-breaking reputation scared me even then."

"What are you leading up to?" Dryden demanded hoarsely.

"I've been thinking of that absent earlobe." Doc lost

himself in speculation for a moment. "So, neither one of us has seen her face."

"For all I know," Dryden admitted, "she may be uglier than a mud fence in February."

"I wonder." Doc said.

"Wonder what?"

"What put Anna on Banner's trail in the first place?"

Both men fell silent. They were silent a long while.

Doc Savage opened his eyes and sat up and looked at a low rise in the tundra about a quarter of a mile distant. He did not see Nina Kirkegaard and Breckenridge, although he knew they were on the small hummock keeping watch on the camp of Poltov and his crew. He hoped they were all right, but Dryden was right about their being due back.

"Better lie low," Doc warned, noting Dryden beginning to stir.

"Why?" Dryden sounded alarmed. "You see something?"

"No. But Breck and the girl aren't moving around any. That may mean Poltov has stationed a lookout where he could see us, and they've spotted him."

"Poltov hasn't been posting a lookout for the last three days," Dryden said. "He feels safe."

"I bet his face doesn't feel so good," Doc said. His legs ached.

They had been ploughing through snow and swamp brambles and thickets of dwarf birch for five days. The dwarf birch grew in sprawled postures close to the ground and made travel difficult. The snow was often hip deep.

"Are you hungry?" asked Dryden, suddenly.

"I could eat a stallion," Doc admitted. "And the hoofs for desert."

"When are you going to dig us up a reindeer steak dinner?" Dryden licked his lips hungrily. "I thought you knew this country, and where to find food in it."

Doc grinned. "I'll wager we have our reindeer steak before Miss Kirkegaard gets her three free steamships." Doc worried that a Charley horse was coming on his leg.

"When we get out of this tundra, we'll come across some game." He fell to watching the hummock for Peter Breckenridge and Nina Kirkegaard.

"When will that be?" Dryden wondered.

"Before long, I hope." Doc wished Dryden would stop talking about food. Dryden did not feel very weak, evidently, judging from the way he was complaining. They had been subsisting on U.S. Army K rations, so there was some justification for complaint, Doc felt.

Dryden swore gloomily. "Damn a place where it never gets dark and it never gets daylight," he said feelingly.

"And never gets warm," Doc added dryly.

"Yeah," said Dryden. "Lord, what a country."

"That's tundra for you."

"You can have it."

"No, let the Russians have it," said Doc. "Believe it or not, this entire swamp never thaws out. In summer, the thermometer gets to ninety and the mosquitoes are big as sparrows and thick as taxes. But any old time you can kick a toe down in the mud and hit ice."

"You weren't planning to spend next summer here?" Dryden said, scowling. They were silent for a while. Their eyes watched the distant hummock, worried about Breckenridge and Nina Kirkegaard. There had been no shots or other sounds of violence. The intense cold made Doc's eyeballs feel chilled. It was the mud-brown contact lenses, he knew. He daren't remove them as long as Nina Kirkegaard was with them. *Women,* he thought wryly, *invariably complicate things.*

What *was* keeping Breckenridge and the blonde?

Doc wondered if Breckenridge and Nina were able to see Poltov's camp clearly from the hummock. He wondered if Breckenridge was getting a glimpse of Anna Gryahznyi. An identifying glimpse, that is. Since the ship sinking, which had marooned everyone on the Arctic coast of Russia, they had done no close-range reconnoitering of Poltov's gang of survivors. They had not identified a woman. But a woman would be dressed like a man for traveling of this kind, so this did not mean the Red Widow had not survived the sinking. Doc did not imagine for a minute that she had not survived. If anybody survived the catastrophe, it would be Anna Gryahznyi. Doc thought of her as perpetual, like some forms of virus.

At least, he reflected, they were sure Poltov's gang was dragging or carrying the five aluminum cases of radio equipment with them. And there was no indication that the cases had been opened. Doc felt sure they had not been opened. He knew how the Communist system worked. If Poltov should open the cases, and later some higher-ranking Red got the notion that the contents of the cases were not as important as they should be, then Poltov stood certain to be accused of rifling or losing the more vital contents. Poltov was not stupid. Besides, the boxes were boobytrapped to explode if opened the wrong way.

"Doc," said Dryden. "I mean, Banner."

"Yes," Doc told him. "I know what you're thinking about."

"The hell you do!" Dryden's words were startled puffs of steam. "What, since you are extra-sensory, am I thinking of?"

"Care to bet I don't know?" Doc asked.

"I'm just inquiring."

"You're thinking about Anna Gryahznyi," said Doc. He watched the breath steam stop rising from the hole in the snow which Dryden was using for breathing. "I know your innermost thoughts," Doc added, with a trace of humor.

"You blankety-blank know-it-all!" Dryden said pointedly. Presently, he resumed breathing.

"I assume you are referring to Banner," Doc said dryly. "I wonder if she's alive and with them. That's what you were thinking, wasn't it? Do you figure she's really too mean to die? I sometimes do. But like you, I almost hope she drowned. I don't think she did." Doc hesitated, grinned, and added, "Of course, that's assuming it was Anna Gryahznyi who was the mysterious fourteenth crewman."

"Who else would it have been?" Dryden snorted.

"Turn the question around. Who else might be Anna?"

Dryden did not have to think about that one long.

"Nina?" he demanded.

"Have you had the opportunity to examine her left ear?" Doc asked.

"No. Have you?"

"No," Doc admitted glumly. "She wears her hair in the most frustrating arrangement I have ever seen."

"You don't really think . . . ?" Dryden swallowed.

"I don't know. And don't tell me it hasn't crossed your mind."

Dryden was impressed. "Say, you're pretty good at reading people's minds."

"I manage to get by," said Doc dryly.

"I hope to God you are as good as you think you are at reading Russian minds," said Dryden.

Doc looked at him. "What do you mean by that?"

"I mean the Russky damn well better not open those cases and screw up that tricky Moonwinx radio transmitter; like you say, they won't. If they do, we've had a hell of a lot of exercise for nothing."

"They won't," Doc Savage said confidently.

"You better be right."

"Don't you worry," said Doc. "When there is a big to-do about something, a party man gets foxy as anything. Those cases will be sealed and untampered with when the top Soviet brass get them. That way, nobody can be accused of pilfering the contents. You notice how carefully they are packing those cases? Taking pains not to drop or jar them? They're actually doing a better job than we could. We're being very clever to let them pack those cases to civilization for us."

"I hope to God you know what you're doing," said Dryden.

Doc felt some irritation. "In what way?"

"You keep saying we should wait and the Russkies will get near the Urals, then we will grab the radio transmitter away from them." Dryden's voice had a peevish ring. "Let 'em be packhorses for us, you keep saying. Okay. By

God, they better not come to a town you didn't happen to know about, and get away from us with our radio."

Doc frowned. The frown drew his frosty eyebrows down. They reminded him of ermines. "The way you fret now, what would it be like if you had to pack a couple of hundred pounds of moon-bouncer radio gear on your back?" he wondered.

Dryden became more angry. "So now you've made a rule against worrying? When did that happen?" The steam of Dryden's breath rose straight up from the snow in spurts like thrown blades. "The hell with you and your rules," he said.

Doc started to sit up. He changed his mind, grinned, and said, "Okay, the hell with me and my rules." He was amused. Sometimes, he enjoyed being Banner. He could be freer with his opinions. Like now.

"You've run every damn thing since we left New York!" Dryden snorted with rage. "And you've run it into the ground, if you ask me."

"Into the snow, you mean," said Doc without rancor. "I don't see any actual ground around here."

Dryden fell silent. When he spoke, he asked sheepishly, "What's the matter with me? My damn nerves giving way?"

"You've got a touch of *singa-maluk-machuk*, I'd venture," said Doc.

"What's that?"

"An Eskimo disease."

Dryden blinked. "You're a doctor. Any cure for it?"

Doc said, "A dunking in a nice frigid river swimming with ice cakes," Doc said, making up his facts. "At least, that's how the Eskimos treat it."

Dryden got the hint. He hurriedly changed the subject, asking, "What's keeping Breck and Miss Kirkegaard?"

"I don't know," Doc admitted.

Dryden began swearing. He cursed Breckenridge roundly. Dryden said, "Do you suppose that son of a gun is snuggling up to her in the snow over on that hill?"

Doc sat up. The abruptness of his erecting caused the

snow to explode about him. Doc eyed the hummock suspiciously. "No," he said. "Breckenridge is the quiet type. He wouldn't."

Dryden's eyes blazed with fury. "A lot you know about Breckenridge!"

"You mean—" said Doc, surprised.

"Yes, he sure would try." Dryden had sat up also. "It's too damn cold for him to do much more than play spin the bottle," he added. "That's one consolation."

Doc cursed Breckenridge himself. "You may feel consoled," he said, "but if you were alone in a snowdrift with that little blonde, your logic might not sound so convincing."

Dryden sprang to his feet. "Damn it, let's look into this!"

Doc also leaped erect. "They are really overdue now."

They charged through the deep drifts, throwing up snow like tugboats making waves.

Before they reached the hummock, two figures appeared: Nina Kirkegaard and Peter Breckenridge. Stooping low, they came running.

Breckenridge drew near. "Keep down!" he warned.

Nina followed close behind him. "Poltov's men are breaking camp," she said, breathlessly. "They're resuming their march."

"We were worried about you," Doc said tightly. He examined them narrowly.

"Yes, why didn't you two come back when you were supposed to?" demanded Dryden.

"Are we overdue?" said Breckenridge, seemingly contrite. "We didn't notice. Sorry."

Breckenridge did not look sorry. His face was ruddy, animated. He did not look like a man who had been crouching for two hours in the snowy tundra at twenty below zero watching an outnumbering force of enemies who would kill him on sight. Breckenridge did not have the strained look of a man relentlessly stalking the aforementioned force with the desperate purpose of recovering a fabulous radio transmitter which might well be responsible for the future of mankind. This was the true situation, too, Doc reflected, and it was enough to scare any man who let himself become serious and think about it. It frightened Doc when he thought of it. That was why he was not thinking about it any more than he had to. He did not need anything to help him be frightened and determinedly serious about their predicament, and their future, not to mention the consequences to the world if they failed.

The bronze man saw that Dryden looked determined and serious, and he felt he was wearing the same expression himself. He felt that he and Dryden were wearing appropriate expressions. But not Breckenridge. Clearly, Breckenridge's expression was that of a man who had just been in a snowdrift with blond Nina Kirkegaard.

"This fooling around has got to come to an end," said Doc.

"Damn right!" said Dryden. He was surreptitiously eyeing the curves Nina Kirkegaard made inside her sealskin suit.

"Beginning right now, we're going to travel full speed in a half circle," Doc directed, ignoring his aching leg muscles. "We're going to get in front of Poltov's outfit, and lay an ambush."

Nina Kirkegaard looked bright-eyed. "Action, eh?" she asked. "About time!"

Breckenridge asked, "What kind of ambush?" He wore a startled look.

"We're going to take those five boxes away from Poltov and associates," answered Doc Savage.

"Oh," said Breckenridge, the look fading into sullen concern.

"That will be nice," said Nina Kirkegaard sarcastically. "Then we can all look forward to running away through the snow, carrying the boxes, all five hundred pounds of them, while Poltov chases us."

Doc said curtly, "Don't worry about that."

Nina Kirkegaard intended to worry. "If Poltov does catch you boys—and I don't see what will prevent him—

who is going to buy me a new steamship?" she wanted to know.

Doc prepared to set out through the snow. On second thought, he gestured for Breckenridge to go ahead and break the trail.

"I'm not afraid of defeated men catching me," said Doc ominously. "And believe me, if this ambush works, that's all that will be left to chase us."

Breckenridge, without an argument, set out breaking trail. Ordinarily he would have objected violently to this strenuous work, Doc knew.

Doc felt outrage welling up inside him. There *had* been monkey business in the snowdrift! If his growing suspicions about Nina turned out to be true—and he was by no means certain they would—it would mean Breckenridge's loyalties would be divided.

As they trudged along, Doc kept his eyes constantly on Nina Kirkegaard's lithe figure. He was wondering if he should ask her how her cabaret had acquired the name, Useful Widow, and whether that pointed question might force a premature climax, and someone's sudden death.

XX

TUNDRA TURMOIL

Some seven hours later, they reached the first scattered trees of what was obviously an extended forest. "Good God, I can hardly believe it," Dryden said, embracing the nearest tree rapturously. "I was beginning to think the world had turned entirely to snow and ice." He raised his voice to recite, " 'I think that I shall never see, A poem lovely as a tree—' "

Nina Kirkegaard regarded him with amusement. "You're taking it big, aren't you?" Her face, ruddy from exertion behind her frost-rimmed parka hood, was the color of an apple surrounded by whipped cream.

"Take a break, but keep your eyes open,'" Doc Savage directed.

The brittleness in Doc's voice jarred their pleasure at reaching the timbered country.

"And don't go wandering off," Doc added, "before I get back."

He floundered away through the snow. He limped. His leg muscles howled with weariness at each step. The snow stood a foot deeper in the forest. Doc fervently wished he was back in New York. He wished he could find a warm cozy fire behind the next tree. He wished most of all that Anna Gryahznyi was far from this place.

Breckenridge looked after Doc's departing figure. "What's eating on old Blood and Violence?" he asked. "He's crankier than a widow bear," Breckenridge added. Breckenridge showed less fatigue than any of them.

"Pipe down," said Dryden curtly, eyeing Nina.

"Say, now. . ." Breckenridge began.

"You talk too much!" Dryden was more abrupt than Doc had been.

"Say, what's eating *both* you guys?" asked Breckenridge, plainly befuddled.

Nina Kirkegaard selected a snowdrift and began making a hole sufficiently large to accommodate herself. "You boys go ahead and bite each other," she said. "I'm going to rest my weary bones. And I *do* mean weary."

Dryden waited ominously. If Breckenridge snuggled down into the snow near Nina, Dryden intended to walk across the same drift and accidentally step on Breckenridge's face. But Breckenridge wandered away a short distance and began to cut small boughs off the evergreen trees with his pocketknife. Dryden frowned. Breckenridge was constructing a lean-to shelter. For Miss Kirkegaard, probably. That meant he would be unable to scrutinize her as carefully as he would like. The thought that she might be the Red Widow was paralyzing in its implications.

"Why don't you put up a neon sign advertising the fact we have been here?" complained Dryden.

Breckenridge looked startled. "Say, maybe we shouldn't leave too many traces, at that."

Dryden walked away. He knew he was tired. He was afraid that if he lay down in the snow to rest, he would suddenly become so stiff he could never rise again. Still, he had to rest sometime.

Snow whined like puppies under Dryden's boot soles. Cold, he thought. Colder than hell. He walked toward a nearby ridge, which was the direction Doc Savage had taken, at the same time wondering what the bronze man had in mind.

Did Savage know what he was doing? Well, if he didn't, they were too far out on the limb to retreat. Dryden was glad Doc had the responsibility for the management of this thing.

What am I glad about? he thought suddenly. *If Savage has bollixed this up as bad as it looks like he has, and we all get killed and, on top of that, lose the moon-bouncing radio gizmo to the damned Reds, then I'll be as dead as anybody.*

Why had Savage gone toward the ridge? Better, he should have climbed a tree and from its vantage searched the tundra for Poltov's approaching group. Better he should be figuring out how to ambush the Poltov party.

Dryden shivered. He was horrified to recall he had thought it sensible to let the Russians pack the radio gear from the Arctic coast shipwreck scene to the neighborhood of the nearest civilization, and then to figure they could take the radio apparatus away from them. The whole idea was crazy, Dryden now felt. He wondered how he could have been so sheep-headed as to let Doc lead him into such a risk-fraught thing.

Dryden came upon the bronze man unexpectedly. Doc stood behind a tree near the ridge crest, peering over the top at something beyond.

"Pssst!" hissed Dryden. He was wary about startling

Doc, not wishing to be accidentally shot as a skulker. "You see something?"

Doc Savage said, "Come here and take a look." The bronze man sounded satisfied with himself. "Right where I calculated it was. A fair guiding job, if I do say so myself."

Dryden hurried forward. "The hell!" He stared with surprise. A few miles away, there were mountains. "Say, what are they?" Snow was smeared on the craggy mountains like barber's lather on an ugly man's face.

"Nenets," Doc replied.

"Oh!" Dryden showed disappointment. "I hoped they were the Ural Mountains."

"They are," Doc said. "The foothills of the Urals, anyway." He did not seem to be peering at the mountains. His interest lay in a small valley immediately before them.

Dryden caught movement against the backdrop of spruce trees. "Hey! There's something down there! It's moving." Dryden became elated. "Say, it's an elk of some kind." He grasped his submachine gun excitedly. "I could go for an elk steak."

Doc eyed him with disdain. "Don't be a complete fool."

"Oh, I know this Tommy gun wouldn't hit that elk from here," said Dryden. "But is there a law against sneaking close enough to potshoot the critter?"

"The Nenets," said Doc casually, "probably wouldn't like it."

Dryden scratched the end of his nose thoughtfully. "The who?"

"Nenets." Doc pointed at the valley floor. "If you'll stop watering your mouth at that reindeer—which is what it is, incidentally—and look at a spot by the bend of that creek, or what would be a creek if it wasn't frozen, you'll see—"

Dryden stiffened. "Yipe!" His eyes grew wide with alarm. "Who the hell are those guys?"

Wind straight from the cold, pale-blue mountains picked up and twisted little spirals of snow as it sped across the valley.

Doc suggested, "Don't jump around too much. I don't think they've seen us." He continued to watch two huts in the valley. They were shapeless huts that could have been mistaken for piles of brush. They resembled the dwellings beavers would build, but were larger. There were reindeer grazing in pens. A number of dogs skulked about. "You want to watch out for those dogs," Doc cautioned. "They like nothing better than to eat up a stranger."

Dryden ceased to move, knowing motion might attract notice. "What are Nenets?" he asked huskily.

Doc wished he had binoculars. "They're a Russian version of Eskimo," he told Dryden. "They trap furs, raise reindeer, and carve ivory for a living. They lead what you would call a rugged life. But you should see some of the carving work they do on mammoth ivory."

Dryden pondered for a moment. "You needn't be so smart."

Doc looked at him. "What do you mean?"

"I'm not that unschooled." Dryden was insulted. "I know a mammoth is a hairy elephant that became extinct twenty thousand years or so ago. Nobody is trapping any mammoths for ivory these days."

Doc became amused. "They lived back in the Pleistocene age."

"What's that?"

"It's a period of history," explained Doc. "Mammoths must have been thick as fleas around here up into the glacial age. A lot of them sank in this tundra mud in the summer, became frozen, and it preserved them like a deep-freeze. Now and then, they find one so well preserved they can eat the flesh."

Dryden was impressed. "I bet it makes gamy eating." He did not know whether or not to believe the mammoth story. "So that's where the ivory comes from that they carve." He looked at Doc suspiciously. "You ever eat one?"

"No!" Doc grimaced. "I'd never get that hungry."

They continued to watch the Nenet camp. With great care, Dryden sank until he was flattened in the snow beside Doc Savage. Apparently, no one noticed them. Pale smoke arose from a hole in one of the huts like a thread of dirty yarn being yanked out of the hut by the wind. Hunger tortured Dryden as he imagined food cooking. "I wouldn't mind trying one of them prehistoric mammoth steaks," he related.

"I'll ask them to serve you one," said Doc dryly.

"You're not—!" Dryden's face grew pale except where the cold kept apple-red spots in his cheeks. He swallowed several times, as he tried to push the words out. "You're not going down there?"

"Why not?"

"But they're Russians. . . ."

"About like an Alaskan Eskimo in an igloo is a Yankee," Doc said confidently. "They're Russians, but they hardly know it. I doubt if they ever heard of that great enemy of the people's republic, the U.S.A."

Dryden shook his head. "I don't see why we have to pay them a call."

"We need to swap them out of a couple of reindeer," Doc said. "Unless you want to pack five hundred pounds of boxed Moonwinx into those mountains on your back?"

"Not particularly," said Dryden.

The cold wind quickened itself for a moment and howled faintly in the trees. It was very cold indeed, Dryden reflected. Now and then, a bough creaked from the movement in the cold. Dryden watched his breath steam. He thought it was almost like a campfire and he wished there was a steak broiling on it.

"You know," he said abruptly. "I've been thinking about that wild theory of yours."

"Theory?"

"That Nina may be . . ." Dryden swallowed, went on. "Be the Red Widow. It won't wash. It just doesn't hold water."

"I didn't actually come out and say that I believed—"

Dryden cut him off vehemently, as if trying to convince himself. "If Nina was the Red Widow, who came aboard at Tromso? And why was Poltov so anxious to get the new passenger's identity out of Nina, and at knife point, at that? The Anna we know would have reduced that scut of a Russian to quivering jelly before letting herself get hog-tied to a chair." He snorted derisively. "Nina is Anna Gryahznyi? What a laugh!"

"When I first ran roughshod through Scandinavia as Banner," Doc said, "I must have encountered Anna, or someone connected with her, and aroused her interest. Otherwise, why would she have been stalking Banner through New York? There is no reason to suspect her of penetrating my imposture."

"You didn't meet Nina that first time, though."

"No, but I did hook up with Poltov, who is Nina's partner."

"I'd sooner believe Poltov is Anna than Nina is," Dryden scoffed. "Say, you don't suppose Anna could be a man, or could successfully disguise herself as a man, do you?"

Doc frowned darkly. "I'll admit as theories go, neither of those strike one as particularly plausible," he admitted sheepishly. "And I'd rather it not be true, myself. But we cannot afford any slip-ups, and there are aspects of Nina's behavior that do not entirely add up."

"Give me one good reason to believe it," Dryden challenged.

Doc said, "Notice that she hasn't asked about our mission, or even what is in the aluminum boxes, since we beached."

"She's too busy trying to survive to worry about things that don't concern her," Dryden scoffed.

"There may be women in this world who lack the customary bump of feminine curiosity," Doc allowed, "but I have yet to encounter one."

Dryden had no immediate response to that. After a while, he said in a small voice, "Nina could be in *league* with Anna, though."

Later a bird, a variety of partridge, arose from some nearby trees with a startling buzz of wings. Both men eyed the bird. It was the first winged thing they had seen in days.

"Wasn't that some kind of quail?" Dryden's mouth worked with hunger. "They're good eating!"

"They can be." Doc stiffened. His eyes were not on the partridge, which had become a receding dot in the dull, lead-hued sky. "They sit in the snow until you almost step on . . ." His voice trailed away.

"Something scare that bird?" Dryden was showing signs of alarm himself.

"Don't move!" Doc's voice had turned urgent. "And whatever you do, don't shoot off that gun!"

"What . . . ?"

XXI

KILL A RED WIDOW

To Special Security Chief Arthur Dryden's profound amazement, Doc Savage spoke out loudly in a language which Dryden did not understand. The tongue was full of oogle sounds and grunts. Doc addressed his speech to a nearby clump of trees.

"What . . . ?" Dryden said, his voice dull with shock.

"Don't wave that gun at anything," Doc said urgently.

A figure clad in furs emerged warily from a brush thicket, then. The fur garments swathed the newcomer completely. The presence of a long-barreled, old-fashioned rifle proved the stranger was no animal.

"Nenet," said Doc. He spoke again in the odd language, as loudly as before. "I am informing this man we are his friends," Doc explained.

Dryden kept motionless, asked, "How do you know *he's* a friend?"

Doc ignored him.

Three additional figures appeared. It shocked Dryden to realize they moved in the snow almost without sound.

Doc Savage, speaking earnestly, sounding as friendly as he could, addressed the Nenets. They listened impassively, holding their rifles. Their brownish faces were framed by bristling parka fur, looked like the visages of snub-nosed minks.

Dryden eyed their guns. The rifles were 7.62 millimeter Moisins, a design of the year 1900. The czar had equipped his army with such relics, Dryden reflected, noticing the old barleycorn front sights and the rear signs calibrated in paces, not meters. They could kill a man as quickly as a Garand, though.

Doc completed his speech. After a silence, one of the Nenets responded. He did not sound hostile. The native finished by gesturing toward the camp.

"Good." Doc passed a hand across his forehead to gather sweat coming up through his disguise. "I told them we are lost, and they invited us to stay for dinner," he told Dryden. "Act grateful and hungry."

Dryden sighed with relief. "That'll take no acting."

Sanitary conditions inside the huts were awful. Doc clamped his teeth together, endeavored not to breathe. There were gnawed bones in a corner, some of them not entirely cleaned of flesh. Remains of a stew in a kettle had been set aside and the contents had cooled and congealed. Doc saw Dryden staring at the kettle in horror. One of the ingredients of the stew in the kettle had been a rabbit, and no one had troubled to remove the fur from the animal before cooking it. Doc, who knew Nenet cooking technique, did not assume the entrails had been extracted either.

Doc realized a Nenet was staring at him. Something seemed familiar about the Nenet. "Well, I'll be damned if it's not my old buddy, Reindeer-Sits-Down," exclaimed Doc, falling into the style of Banner once more. He put this into the Nenet language.

Reindeer-Sits-Down did not change a single expression on his tobacco-colored face. However, he came over and gravely gave Doc's nose a rub with his own nose.

Doc's pleasure at meeting an old acquaintance was

tempered somewhat by the way Reindeer-Sits-Down stank. It was Nenet custom to bathe infrequently, he recalled.

"For crying out loud!" Dryden's jaw had dropped like a steam shovel. "You know this guy?"

"Yes," Doc low-voiced in English. In Nenet, Doc inquired as to Reindeer-Sits-Down's health and was informed it was good. "This fellow and I operated a crosscut saw between us in a Russian labor camp," Doc told Dryden.

"What's he doing here?" Dryden demanded suspiciously.

"I don't think he liked lumberjacking any better than I did." Doc put the question to the Nenet. A slight glitter came into Reindeer-Sits-Down's eyes. He said he preferred to be with his people. Doc passed the information to Dryden, adding, "That means he bugged out of that lumber camp."

"You think we might be safe with them?" Dryden asked.

Doc shook his head carefully. "I wouldn't venture to guess. It depends on who else is here."

Reindeer-Sits-Down suddenly became talkative. He told Doc how many fish he had caught the previous summer and how many furs he had taken. Doc knew he was exaggerating. Doc told about a two-year trip he had taken into Siberia, and how amazingly strong he had found the big Siberian girls to be. This was a lie, too, but it got the first sign of emotion out of the Nenet—a single explosive giggle. Reindeer-Sits-Down then stalked out of the hut, returning shortly leading a very fat Nenet girl by the hand.

Doc recalled the Nenet girl. Her name was Noalska, and she had been one of the prettiest girls in the camp, which wasn't saying a lot. Doc eyed her in alarmed respect.

Reindeer-Sits-Down introduced her as his wife. Then he giggled louder. Noalska giggled. The giggling turned to uncontrollable whoops of laughter, and the Nenet husband and wife fell to the floor and flopped with mirth. Other Nenets joined in the howling glee. So did Doc.

Puzzled, Dryden demanded, "Is everybody nuts?"

Laughing had brought tears to Doc's eyes. He frowned

at Dryden between spasms. "You had better join in, be one of the folks," he said warningly in English.

Dryden managed a few unenthusiastic giggles. He stopped abruptly, facing the door. "Wasn't that Breckenridge's voice?" he asked.

They went outdoors. Peter Breckenridge and Nina Kirkegaard were being herded into camp by two Nenets with rifles.

"Thank heavens!" Breckenridge exploded in relief, when he spied Doc and Dryden. "I was afraid we were in hostile hands. Or are we?"

A frown warping his unlovely features, Doc asked, "How did they catch you?" when they came within speaking distance.

Obviously not proud of himself, Breckenridge said, "They sneaked up on us. Just all of a sudden, there they were!"

"You were out in the open timber!"

"I know, but . . ."

"How could you let them sneak up on you?" Doc demanded angrily.

Breckenridge flushed guiltily. "I must have been thinking about something else," he said. He flushed a deep scarlet.

"I see." Doc eyed Nina Kirkegaard. "And you?"

"I was thinking about something else, too," she said. Her expression was as placid as that of any of the Nenets.

"Damn you!" Dryden glared at Breckenridge. "I bet I know what was going on that you didn't hear anything. Maybe it has something to do with that lipstick on your parka trim."

"Boys have kissed girls before," said Doc hastily.

Dryden was positively purple-colored. "He must've been setting an endurance record . . ."

"I think we should see about something to eat," said Doc loudly to everyone. He grasped Dryden's arm. "You were the hungry one. Let's see what the cupboard offers."

He led the infuriated Dryden toward the creek, added, "You're making an ass out of yourself."

"That juvenile so-and-so crawled into that snowdrift with her!" Dryden shook with fury. He glowered at Doc. "The next time you go prowling, take him with you and leave *me* with her!"

"I don't recall asking you to come with me the last time," Doc pointed out reasonably.

Reindeer-Sits-Down joined them as they tramped along. Grinning, the Nenet said they would prepare a feast. Along with his Moisin, he carried an ax, and he led the way to the creek, which was covered with approximately a foot of ice.

Selecting a spot, the Nenet began chopping at the ice.

"Are we going fishing?" Dryden wanted to know.

"He's opening the refrigerator," explained Doc.

Dryden looked dubious. He watched the huts where they had left Nina Kirkegaard and Breckenridge.

Presently, Reindeer-Sits-Down rested from his ice-chopping. Doc offered to spell him, but the Nenet shook his head, then turned slowly until he had faced all directions around the horizon.

"Two men of our camp are not of our people," the Nenet said unexpectedly. He watched Doc. "You understand my language well enough to know what I say?" he asked.

"I think so," Doc said. His tongue, suddenly thick, wanted to stick to the roof of his mouth.

"It could be a worthwhile thing for you to know," the Nenet added.

"I agree." Doc wondered if making contact with the Nenets had been a good idea after all. He could have avoided doing so. But his group required food and pack reindeer. "Which are the two party stooges?" he asked.

"The ones who brought in your friends," the Nenet said.

Doc tried to remember the Nenet word for thanks, but could not do so. He gave the Nenet a package of cigarettes he carried as a Banneresque prop, from which none had been smoked. The Nenet was pleased. He separated one of the cigarettes in the middle and inserted a half in each nostril.

Dryden stared. "Whew! That the way they smoke?"

"They get smoking confused with the snuff habit, it would seem," Doc explained. He looked toward the camp. "You had better brace for some bad news."

Dryden looked apprehensive. "More? Don't you ever have anything else?"

"Our friend here thinks the two who brought in Breckenridge and Miss Kirkegaard may be state police agents," Doc told Dryden.

"That right?" Dryden licked his lips anxiously. "How sure is he?"

"I imagine he is positive," Doc said, looking about warily. "These fellows are addicted to understatement."

Dryden ran alarmed fingers along the hood of his parka. "What are we going to do?"

Doc watched the Nenet chop at the creek ice. "Nothing until we eat. It would be bad strategy to risk death on an empty stomach."

Water suddenly arose to fill the hole the Nenet had chopped. The water was the pale green of diluted mint gin. The Nenet enlarged the hole, water flying about.

With disgust, Dryden watched the Nenet drag a haunch of reindeer into view. It had been held impaled on a sharpened stick beneath the surface. It was in a ripe condition. The hair slipped freely on the area from which the skin had not been removed.

"Good God!" Dryden became green around the jowls. "Do we eat that? Why, it's half rotten."

Doc was as horrified as Dryden, but he pretended unconcern. "A little aging adds to the palatability of reindeer beef," he said.

Dryden looked at him with a revolted expression that transfigured his face.

"The process accomplishes the dissolution of the connective tissue by the work of enzymes," the bronze man added.

Dryden got a whiff of reindeer and lapsed into silence.

The Nenet was smacking his lips over the reindeer haunch. It was obviously quite a morsel, in his opinion.

"I think I'll pass up the banquet," Dryden said when he could safely speak.

They followed the Reindeer-Sits-Down back to the huts, keeping on the upwind side of the fellow's burden.

Wind rushing steadily from the mountains refilled footprints with snow as rapidly as they were made. The sky had the color of a schoolroom blackboard. Sleeping dogs were tufts in the snow, a little hair protruding. Catching whiffs of the meat, though, the dogs came up out of the snow like cannonballs.

The Nenet hurled the reindeer haunch into a hut, seized a club, and belabored the dogs. Doc seized a club, too. He used it to ward off snapping canine jaws, thus protecting his shins. The dogs fled.

Breckenridge burst out of the hut into which the meat had been pitched. "Whew! What did you throw in there?" he demanded. He had been shaving, but the left side of his face was still blue-black with beard.

"Where is Miss Kirkegaard?" Dryden asked suspiciously.

"Over there." Breckenridge indicated another hut. "Sleeping. She said she was tired." He became angry also. "Why the hell don't you keep track of her yourself?" he asked.

Doc retained his club in case the dogs should attack again. He peered into the hut which Breckenridge had pointed out. Nina Kirkegaard was there, apparently asleep. So were several snoring Nenets, men and women. He retreated, thinking that the odor in the sleeping-hut might well overwhelm a man.

"What became of the two Nenets who brought you and the girl in?" Doc demanded.

"I can't imagine." Breckenridge was still scowling at Dryden.

He grew concerned. "They didn't wander off someplace?" asked Doc.

Breckenridge shrugged. "Why should I know?"

Reindeer-Sits-Down approached, looked expressionlessly into Doc Savage's face, and informed him the two natives suspected of being state police had left the camp immediately after the meat-seeking expedition had departed for the creek.

"I don't like this." Doc hunted for the tracks of the pair in the snow. "Which way did they go?"

Dryden, his eyes shiny with alarm, said, "Ask your pal here. Does he know if they've got a radio transmitter cached around here somewhere? If so, those two have slipped off to ask Moscow if we're legitimate."

The Nenet pointed southward, saying the pair had gone that direction, according to another Nenet.

"Come on." Doc plunged off through the snow. "There is no time to lose." He had a peace-making thought, halted. "Dryden, you stay and guard Miss Kirkegaard."

Breckenridge did not welcome this order. "What's going on here? Why do I have to leave—"

"The Nenets figure those two strangers are Moscow agents," Doc told him. "Do you want to stand here and argue over a girl while they inform the Kremlin of three suspicious characters who just happen to be us?"

Breckenridge jammed his fists against his hips. He looked very angry, the half of his face that was not shaven managing to look much more enraged than the other half. He addressed Doc in a heated tone. "Every damn idea you've had since we left New York has gotten us deeper in trouble," he complained. "If you want those two guys chased, chase them by yourself!"

Doc turned to Dryden. "Then we'll have to push on ourselves," he started to say.

Dryden was not sympathetic. "The devil with you!" he snapped. "I'm not slogging through any more snow right now on your whims." Dryden was not going to leave the vicinity of Nina Kirkegaard if Breckenridge remained behind, that much was clear.

Doc knew he should be angry. He was. But he was more disgusted. He said, "Then the only solution is for the pair of you to go hunt the Nenets and I will remain—"

"Like hell!" Dryden snarled.

"The rough stuff is your job," Breckenridge added.

Doc Savage saw he would have to hunt the two Russian agents himself, if they were to be hunted.

"I'm on my way then," he said tightly. He noted the dislike with which Dryden and Breckenridge were eyeing each other. Doc added, "I hope I get back in time to view the battle you two are going to have if you don't acquire some sense."

He took possession of Dryden's submachine gun and started off.

"You could leave me your revolver, you know," Dryden called after him in a sour voice.

Without speaking, Doc extracted the sightless pistol from his clothing and tossed it back to Dryden, who caught it clumsily between two mittened hands.

No thanks were offered.

Cold gave the snow the hard quality of sand underfoot. Doc loosened his parka at the waist and tucked his submachine gun under it next to his body so that the action would be kept warm. The gun felt so cold through his chain-mesh undergarment that he grimaced.

"You coming along?" Doc asked Reindeer-Sits-Down.

The Nenet trudged along beside Doc. When they had put the camp behind them, the Nenet asked in his language, "What they want fight about?"

"Woman trouble," said Doc, unhappily.

Reindeer-Sits-Down looked puzzled. Doc remembered the Nenets used the wife-sharing arrangement common to the Eskimos. A visitor was welcome to borrow an Eskimo's mate. Doc said, "You wouldn't understand. White-man-crazy-in-the-head stuff."

That satisfied the Nenet.

The voices of Dryden and Breckenridge, lifted in bitter argument, reached them. The sound was pushed away by a gust of wind carrying pelleted snow.

"I feel like I could climb into a snowdrift and sleep for a week," said Doc, surprised at his own diminished stamina. Nervous tension could sap a man's reserves faster than sun or cold.

The Nenet speculatively regarded the snow. He swung abruptly to their left.

Unable to distinguish the footprints of the two Russians, Doc asked, "You think they went this way?"

The Nenet slogged ahead through the snow. "Yes." They mounted the ridge, heading now toward the tundra, and presently there was a spot where the tracks of two men showed clearly in the snow. Reindeer-Sits-Down seemed puzzled. "I do not understand why they take this direction," he said.

Doc caught up with him. "Any reason why they shouldn't go this way?" He had difficulty keeping up with the Nenet, another symptom of his flagging energies.

"They have never done so before, when they left camp together," declared the Nenet. "There is nothing on the tundra. No game. Nothing." The Nenet's eyes were as black as soot. "Could they have gone to meet the men who were following you?"

Doc was so startled by this sudden revelation, he tripped over a snow-concealed log. He ended up half buried in snow.

"Who told you someone was following us?" he demanded. Annoyed with his carelessness, he rubbed snow off his face, out of his eyes. He was dumbfounded.

The Nenet shrugged. "Nobody tell. I just know."

Doc sprang erect. "Listen, friend—" Realizing he was using English in his excitement, Doc reverted to the Nenet tongue. "Don't give me forked words, friend. One does not merely know such a thing. Tell me, how did you find out?"

The Nenet's eyes glinted. "I see others." His teeth shone in his brown face like bone dice on an army blanket. "All of yesterday, I scout your party and the other party which is behind you. This I do not tell you." His eyes were wary over the shining teeth. He explained his silence by adding, "Flies do not find their way into a closed mouth."

"Your whole camp know we were hurrying to get here ahead of the other outfit?" Doc asked.

"No," said the Nenet. "I tell nobody."

"Did the two Russian agents know about this?" demanded Doc.

"No."

Doc pressed. "Are you sure?"

"They did not hear it from me." The Nenet was emphatic. "What they find out for themselves, I could not tell you."

They approached the ridge. The tundra would lie beyond, flat and cold and hairy with stunted swamp shrubs all the way to the Arctic coast. Doc was impressed with nature's harshness. He asked guardedly, "You figure the two Russians are meeting Paul Poltov's outfit, don't you?"

The Nenet blinked both eyes at once. "Poltov? Is he the Poltov who smuggles on the coast?"

"The same. You know him?"

The Nenet said, "I am friends to some who know him." His eyes shone with hate.

"Answer my question about the two Russians, please," Doc said sharply.

"I think they meet," admitted the Nenet. "I think they already meet!" His voice was no longer placid. "I think we got big trouble right now." He sounded as if he had stones in his mouth. "I think we must hurry like hell."

Doc nodded. "Let's get going, then." He wondered how the two Moscow agents had been tipped off to meet Poltov's crew. He thought about Anna Gryahznyi, who must be near. It was not a comforting thing to contemplate.

"I wonder how those two Moscow agents found out Poltov was coming." Doc wondered aloud.

In silence, they pushed on.

It was surprisingly hard for Doc Savage to keep up with Reindeer-Sits-Down. The stubby Nenet seemed to float over the snow with ease. The air Doc inhaled was so cold it felt as if he were breathing flames. He hoped his shaky feeling was due to rage, and not a growing fatigue.

The Nenet plunged through a heavy snowdrift, stamping a path for the bronze man. Doc was silently grateful for the Nenet's assistance.

They labored through soft whiteness that felt like quicksand to Doc's tired legs. Evergreens grew thickly on the ridge, their boughs laden with snow, which they dumped on Doc whenever he nudged them.

"Ah!" The Nenet came to a stop, nostrils dilating. "We are too late!" He looked like an angry beaver standing on point.

They had come upon a freshly churned trail in the snow.

"How many passed here?" asked Doc.

The Nenet moved a short distance along the trail. He indicated, holding up fingers, that the party had numbered nine.

"Then the two Moscow agents have joined them." Doc eyed the marks in the snow. "There were only seven survivors in Poltov's party," he announced. He could distinguish separate footprints, but no other identifying marks.

Doc felt a surge of excitement.

"They've ditched the boxes," he said. He pointed at the trail. "No toboggan marks. They're not dragging anything." He set off in the direction from which the trail-making party had come.

The Nenet overtook him. "They did not go this direction!" Reindeer-Sits-Down sounded disgusted.

Doc said, "I know it." He found easier going on the trail that had been broken. "They hid the Moonwinx gadget somewhere. I intend to find it," he said confidently.

"But they go to attack the camp—"

"I know that too," Doc said. "But the gadget comes first." His chest hurt from gulping icy air and his legs were rubbery. "After all the trouble I've had getting the equipment this far, I'm taking no chances," he added grimly.

They covered some distance in laboring silence. Then the Nenet halted, and Doc asked, "You hear something?"

The Nenet pointed at an innocent-looking stretch of snow, said, "If you hunt something, maybe it is there."

Doc watched the wind carry small corkscrews of snowflakes across the smooth white surface. He saw nothing to indicate a hiding place, but he knew the Nenet was better skilled at reading sign than he. "Let's hope you are right!" Doc waded into the snowdrift and soon barked his shin on a hard object. Instead of crying out, he grinned.

"We couldn't have done better with a divining rod!" he told Reindeer-Sits-Down.

Doc raked the snow away from the equipment cases. All five boxes were there. Their aluminum protective covering had not been broken.

"This is it." Doc was excited. "Give me a hand. We'll hide them elsewhere."

The Nenet eyed the cases with apprehension. "There is talk of a blast that burns with the fire of many hells in the sky. . . ."

"No cause for alarm." Doc looked at the Nenet in amazement. "Have you seen the Russians test one of their atom bombs? This fire in the sky, did you see it yourself?"

The Nenet shook his head. "No. It is talk I hear."

"Remind me to run that talk down to its source," Doc said dryly. "Let's get these boxes cached."

They transferred the cases approximately a hundred yards along the trail and placed them in another drift. They leveled the drift with a bough. The wind, Doc saw, would soon smooth out the snow, masking the hiding place.

"Remember this place," Doc warned. "If I become incapacitated, you'll have to show the boxes to my friends, Dryden and Breckenridge."

"And if you all get killed?" The Nenet was calm.

"Don't try to open them," Doc warned. "Build a whopping fire, throw them in, and get away from there," Doc added, his eye on the Nenet's imperturbable face. "Don't get greedy and try to open them, either. There's poison gas inside the cases to overcome anyone who tampers with them. And they'll blow up from protective explosive charges."

The Nenet was impressed. "I understand."

The boughs of trees around them bent under burdens of snow like the tired arms of old green men. The flakes powdered their clothing. The sky had turned the color of ancient zinc. It was impossible to hear anything but the faint sound of the wind tuning up like a tired orchestra in the trees. The cold gnawed at their lips like tiny frozen teeth.

Doc asked, "The other Nenets expect trouble?"

"Yes," the Nenet said. "They will be ready."

"Will they fight?"

"Fight?" Reindeer-Sits-Down spat. "They will fight." His teeth glistened in the eerie light.

The trail topped the ridge and led downward toward the huts beside the creek. The wind lost its vigor. The cold had a static quality and was embedded in silence.

"Too quiet," Doc breathed. His whisper was alarmed.

"I think they take their time putting an ambush around the camp," the Nenet muttered.

"Let's hope the camp isn't caught napping," Doc said tightly.

"Yes," said the Nenet.

"Dryden and Breckenridge will be scrapping over the girl," Doc predicted. "Chances are they won't notice anything until they start getting shot at."

"My people watch," said the Nenet. His lips, drawn thin, looked like a knife slit in a leather shoe.

A partridge went buzzing up out of the snow. It was far away and sounded, wings beating, like a low note from a distant bassoon. Doc concluded that someone had frightened the bird into flight.

"Yonder," Doc pointed. "Isn't that the two from Moscow?"

The two Red agents were slogging through the snow toward the huts. Grunting, Reindeer-Sits-Down swung his rifle to his shoulder. His breath stopped steaming around his lips as he held his air, aimed.

Doc eyed the old Moisin rifle dubiously. "I hope your musket shoots straighter than I think it will," he said.

"Good gun."

"Aim for the legs."

The Moisin made an astonishing report, kicked the Nenet back half a pace. Powdered snow sprang in a cloud from the surface about them. Evergreen boughs nearby dumped their snow like startled men dropping their burdens. There was fire, smoke, and an odd acrid odor.

"What in heaven's name are you shooting in that thing?" Doc could not see the camp for the cloud of snow and smoke.

The Nenet worked the rifle bolt. "Load own ammunition," he said. "Powder hard to steal from People's Army. Sometimes have to mix in some TNT."

The hills rattled with echoes as if it had thundered. Presently, Doc saw that the Moscow agents were down. He was amazed. He had not dreamed one shot would drop both of the enemy, but apparently it had.

"Good gun." The Nenet grinned, pleased.

Doc dropped to all fours in the snow and hurriedly crawled. "Better duck," he said. He endeavored to travel below the surface of the snow, like a gopher.

Bullets reached their neighborhood, as Doc expected they would. They sounded like angry bumblebees, in a fantastic hurry, butting into the tree boughs. The Nenet hastily joined Doc. They got behind an evergreen that resembled a stupendous Christmas tree ornamented with angel food cakes.

The Nenet struggled angrily with his rifle, which was jammed, the brass cartridge case split and blackened in the breech. He dug at the mutilated brass with a large hunting knife.

Doc Savage listened carefully to the noise of shooting. He discounted the multiplying effect of the echoes, and concluded that most of the shooting was not being done at them.

"Sounds as if the battle is dying down." Doc, taking a chance, stood up for a better look. "There's Poltov!"

The bronze man raised his submachine gun and it banged out three well-spaced shots. He had pushed the weapon's fire-control lever to single position. It had no more loudness, compared to the blast of the Nenet's musket, than the snapping of a cap pistol.

"Poltov's gang is rushing your camp," he told the Nenet. Doc looked around. He did not think he had hit anyone. He hoped not. He was firing for effect. To force his enemies to flatten to the ground or seek shelter, to discourage but not kill. They were some three hundred yards from the camp, which was about the limit of the Thompson's accurate range, anyway.

"Ah!" The Nenet had cleared the breech mechanism of his piece. He jammed in another hand-loaded cartridge.

Poltov's force was rushing the huts. Doc counted them. He made out seven figures. They were not charging openly, but bushwhacking from tree to tree.

"I guess it's safe to do some charging ourselves," Doc Savage decided. He did not think it likely that any of Poltov's men were at their back. "Hold your fire so they won't spot us," Doc urged. He explained, "That cannon of yours makes more smoke than a volcano."

Reindeer-Sits-Down grunted agreement.

There was plenty of noise. But not as many bullets were arriving in their general vicinity.

The Nenets in the huts, and Dryden and Breckenridge, were not showing themselves. But puffs of snowflakes, dusted up by the muzzle blasts from guns, showed there was sporadic firing from the huts.

Poltov's men pressed forward doggedly, recklessly. Doc tried to figure out why they were being so foolhardy.

He saw Poltov gesture, then take small metal objects from a sack. Poltov hurled the objects to his men, using his bandaged hands awkwardly. There was a bandage on Poltov's face, but it must have been obstructing his vision, because he wrenched it away angrily; it hung about his neck like a bloodstained necktie.

"Grenades!" Doc was horror-struck. "That's why they're taking such chances to get close." He made a mouth funnel with his hands. "Dryden! Watch for hand grenades!" he yelled. "Stop them where they are! Don't let them get close!" He did not see Dryden anywhere.

Poltov came to his feet, cursing loudly, and rushed toward the huts. His men followed.

Breckenridge stepped from one of the huts, aimed deliberately, and dropped two of Poltov's group with his first blast. Several Nenets joined him.

Doc sprinted for the fight, mentally damning the high, obstructive snow.

The Nenet, Reindeer-Sits-Down, passed him, running in the snow with the agility of his namesake.

The dogs of the Nenet camp, their normal ferocity frightened out of them, were bolting for the timber. Five reindeer, confined in a pole corral, suddenly cleared the bars with spectacular leaps and left the vicinity.

A thrown grenade fell short, blossomed into a scarlet heart in a white flower of snow that was some fifty feet in diameter. Concussion made shock waves and noise disturbed the air, inflicting pain and violent pressure on their own eardrums.

Doc Savage set his gun on full automatic and dropped the grenade-thrower through the simple but brutal expedient of riddling both his legs. The cold had scraped the lining from Doc's throat and was working on his lungs. He felt like a violin string drawn to the snapping point.

The Nenets staged a foolish charge. Breckenridge was vainly screaming at them—in English which they would not understand—to use some sense and stay under cover.

Where was Dryden? Doc wondered. Had he been killed?

The Nenets, Doc Savage saw, were not so foolhardy after all. They were diving into the deep snow, burrowing about, changing their positions, springing up to fire, and then ducking back into the snow to reload.

Soon, Poltov's men began doing the same thing.

The new tactics gave the fight a character that was weird and leisurely. A man, Nenet or Poltovist, would spring erect and peer about at the snow surface. Spying movements, he would fire, or heave a grenade, then dive out of sight into the snow.

Doc, crawling into the snow himself, neared the huts. The odor of cordite assailed him.

Unexpectedly, Arthur Dryden came out of a hut. Doc Savage eyed him with alarm, because Dryden acted dazed. Dryden stumbled along, seemed dulled, peered about vacantly. He did not offer to contribute to the raging fight. He clutched the side of his head. Strings of blood were crawling down his fingers like escaping worms.

It was from the hut where Nina Kirkegaard had been sleeping that Dryden had come, Doc realized suddenly.

Dryden stumbled over an animated hump in the snow. The latter proved to be one of Poltov's men, and the fellow sprang up and struck Dryden in the face. Dryden's gun flew away. He and the Poltov aide became locked in combat. When Doc concluded that neither combatant was armed with more than fists and teeth, he let them go at it.

A figure heaved from the snow, staggered toward the hut from which Dryden had come.

Poltov! Doc realized. He swung his gun around and brought his finger back against the trigger so hard that it ached. Nothing happened. The gun did not fire. Frozen, probably. Doc bumped it savagely with his palm. Evidently, the trigger had locked back, because when the frozen mechanism released, the gun went into cyclic fire of about seven hundred rounds per minute.

Taken by surprise, Doc struggled to control the bawling operation. It was about equal to subduing a speeding motorcycle with his arms. The prospect of inadvertently killing someone made his blood run cold as the bronze man fought to unjam the trigger with element-numbed fingers.

The dilemma soon solved itself—the magazine ran out.

Doc saw that he had expended more than half a box of cartridges without hitting friend or foe. He realized he had not been contributing his share to this fight. Less even than

Dryden, who was at least belaboring a Russian with his fists.

Poltov had reached the hut from which Dryden had emerged in a dazed condition. His heavy face was intent. Beard growth made it darkly apish. He dived into the hut.

Doc lunged for the hut himself. Additional ammunition for the submachine gun was inside his parka, but his working fingers were too cold-stiffened to hold the cartridges. He went into the hut with the gun useless for anything but clubbing.

Poltov stood over Nina Kirkegaard. In fluttering lemon-yellow light from two blubber lamps, Nina Kirkegaard's face was pale, composed, unbelievably serene. She lay on the floor on her back, lying on and partially covered by a large wolfskin robe. Her mouth was too red.

Outside, a man gave a gurgling scream. But Poltov was oblivious to the fate of his crewman.

"Darling!" Poltov said thickly. "Oh, darling! Darling!"

When Nina Kirkegaard did not respond, Paul Poltov swung slowly and saw Doc. "Now I kill you," he snarled. His nose, which Doc had smashed on the ship, had not healed. It bled red yarns over his mouth, chin, pooled and matted in his coat collar.

"Back!" Doc's voice was shaking. The animal quality of Poltov's brassy features was ferocious, inhuman. The bronze man thrust his empty gun out menacingly. "I said, keep back!"

Outside, Breckenridge screamed, "Banner! Banner! Where are you?"

"In here." Doc prepared to club with his gun. "With Poltov."

Paul Poltov came forward doggedly. His eyes and his teeth were the same shade of oyster-gray. From somewhere on his person, a wicked icicle of a knife jumped into one hand.

Doc decided not to fool with the man. Too much was at stake. He just swung his submachine gun back and smashed the butt plate between Poltov's eyes. Poltov's head was driven back, but he kept coming. Doc stepped back and repeated the action, this time aiming for the wrist behind the knife.

Poltov threw up his other hand and caught the blow between elbow and wrist, and it broke his arm. Poltov hardly blinked. Knife held low, he lunged for the bronze man. Retreating, Doc swung the gun again and again.

Poltov kicked clumsily, but then he had a piece of luck. He caught Doc in the stomach with an inexpertly thrown knife. The tip of the heavy bone-handled blade sank through Doc's thick clothing, to protrude like a bloated thorn.

Doc felt paralysis all through his midriff, numbness in his arms. Trying to fade back out of striking range, his legs would not function, and he fell.

With a lung-ripping cry, Poltov crashed down upon him, took him in a bear hug, but there was no strength in Poltov's clasp. He held Doc gently, as he would have embraced a child.

Presently, even that little strength was gone. . . .

Someone asked, "Did you get him?"

It was Breckenridge. Doc struggled and rolled Poltov's form off him. The knife hilt still jutted from his midriff.

Breckenridge gawked wordlessly as Doc extracted it. There was a little blood on the mangled tip, but not much.

"My bulletproof undergarment will turn most bullets," Doc explained, "but a sharp knife can sometimes get through the chain mesh." He tossed the blade aside. "That one wasn't as fine as it might have been."

Breckenridge indicated Poltov. "Dead?"

Doc Savage knelt and examined the Russian briefly. "Yes, he's dead," he said with surprise, a note of horror in his voice.

"You killed him?"

Doc Savage shook his head in the negative. "From his color, I'd say his heart burst from exertion." He eyed

Breckenridge warily. A flicker of a veiled look came over his face. "But I was too late to stop him," he added.

"What do you mean 'too late'?" Breckenridge glanced around the hut. His puzzled eyes fell on Nina Kirkegaard at that moment. They went wide as coins. "Oh, Lord!" He sank beside her. "She's dead! Shot!" Breckenridge's voice became a tremulous wail.

Doc got to his feet. "I'm afraid so."

Breckenridge whimpered and buried his face in his hands. "I—she said she loved me," he moaned. "And I loved her."

"I'm sorry," Doc said gravely. Moving quickly now, the bronze man covered Nina Kirkegaard's body with the fur robe. He noticed a small revolver which had been lying on a corner of the robe. After a wary glance at Breckenridge, Doc pocketed the gun. Breckenridge still had his hands over his face.

"Who . . . ?" Breckenridge moaned, refusing to uncover his face. "Did Poltov . . . ?"

"I was too late," Doc said, letting the statement speak for itself.

Breckenridge was kicking Poltov's corpse in a frenzy of hate when Doc slipped out of the hut.

He found Dryden lying on the Russian he had been fighting.

"Any life in that one you're using for a mattress?" Doc asked calmly.

"I don't think so." Dryden sounded spent. "I just haven't got the strength left to climb off him." His breathing was a series of hoarse moans.

Doc said, "Here, let me give you a hand."

The Nenets were circulating cautiously, kicking the snow away from bodies, looking for any of Poltov's men who still lived. They were finding none.

Doc drew Dryden behind a hut.

"I picked up your gun for you." Doc handed Dryden the small revolver he had found beside Nina Kirkegaard's body. It was the one the bronze man had carried as Banner. He added quickly, "Put it in your pocket, quick!"

Dryden obeyed numbly.

Doc asked, "Did anybody see you shoot her?" He watched Dryden's head shake slowly. He said quickly, "Good. I led Breckenridge to think Poltov was responsible. He's satisfied with that."

XXII

THE MOON WINKED BACK

There were six white crosses made of wood showing above the snow in the graveyard beside the long-abandoned Russian church. The church was made of logs and most of the chinking was still in place, but the roof shakes were bad in spots. Snow sifted through, and angry breaths of cold wind. Special Security Chief Arthur Dryden was holding Peter Breckenridge aloft on his shoulders while the latter fitted scrap-wood patches under the holes, contriving a repair which would not be apparent from the outside. They worked in silence. The chill odor of disuse, of religious emotions crushed and long dead, filled the place.

Both men started nervously when Doc Savage came climbing down a makeshift ladder from the enclosed steeple.

Doc eyed the ladder distrustfully. "We should find a better ladder, or somebody will break a leg," he said. He added, "You wouldn't want to break a leg in a godforsaken place like this, I assure you."

Dryden saw that the bronze man was quietly pleased.

"Hey, boy!" Dryden became excited himself, forgot to grip Breckenridge's ankles firmly as the latter balanced on his shoulders.

"Hey!" Dryden called. "You get through? You get the

gizmo to work?" Breckenridge awkwardly waved his arm for balance.

"Oh, sure." Doc pretended to be calm. "I was just talking to Cedar Rapids, Iowa. That's where they have the other transmitter set up."

"How did they come through?" Breckenridge demanded. Abruptly, he was windmilling his arms. "Watch out, I'm gonna fall!" he warned Dryden.

Doc lunged, caught Breckenridge before he crashed to the floor.

"I wouldn't call the reception broadcast quality," Doc said, setting the man on his feet. "We understood each other, however." Doc saw with relief that Breckenridge was unhurt by his tumble.

"You two care to listen to Cedar Rapids coming in via the moon?" he asked casually. Pride made his flake-gold eyes shine. He had removed the mud-brown Banner contacts. A little of the natural bronze of his hair peeped through the shaggy, disordered mop atop his head.

They ascended the ladder to the steeple attic where Doc had set up the complicated apparatus, including the trumpetlike UHF antenna. From a small loudspeaker came hillbilly music, a cowboy singer.

"What the hell!" Dryden was indignant about the music. "Did we go to all this trouble to tune in *that*?" He snorted loudly, then asked in an awed tone, "Is that coming off the moon?"

"It is," Doc said simply. "They are going to keep their transmitter on the air steadily and pipe us broadcast programs so we can keep tabs on propagation conditions between us and the moon." He couldn't hold his grin.

"Oh." Dryden blinked. "Well, tell 'em to transmit something befitting the occasion. Something classical."

Doc shook his head stubbornly. "This is classical enough for me." He picked up a microphone. "I'll show you how it works." Into the mike, he said, "Testing, one, two . . . Say, fellow, is Bill Veeck still trying to move the Browns out of St. Louis?"

The music stopped. A voice said, *"Affirmative on Veeck. Receive you three and eight."* The music resumed.

Grins went around the group like flashlights winking on.

Their telescope had a magnification power of one hundred and twenty, and no one had thought to pack a tripod with it. A tripod, or some other means of holding the scope absolutely steady, was a necessity. It was Dryden's suggestion that they pilfer a small headstone from one of the graves in the churchyard and wire the telescope to this, and they did so. Doc Savage tried out the resulting arrangement.

"Perfect," he decided. "Steady as a rock."

The abandoned church was situated on a high knob affording an extensive view of mountains and valleys. The telescope brought a paved road remarkably close to Doc's canny eye. Ragged laborers working with shovels were keeping the road clear of snow. Day and night, in eternal effort, they dug away at the snow. The shovelers, mostly women, wore white.

The road disappeared into the mouth of a tunnel in the mountain. The tunnel was in the center of a mat of barbed wire freckled with sentry boxes, all painted white for purposes of camouflage.

Doc asked Dryden, "I'd say we're close enough to that road for our Geiger counter to show action if they move an atom bomb, don't you?"

"Sure," said Dryden.

"I guess we're all set, then." Doc rubbed his jaw dubiously with a forefinger. His rubber chin piece was coming loose. "Who wants first watch?"

Breckenridge was eager, excited. "I'll watch first."

Doc grinned at him.

"I'm glad to see such enthusiasm," he said. "You could be stuck here for decades, you know."

"I'll take that yawl of mine to the Caribbean yet," Breckenridge vowed. "Right, Chief?"

Dryden nodded. "Something will work itself out.

Maybe the Reds will catch some sense. Maybe not. But we'll work out a way to swap agents in and out of this station. We'll fetch you out of here, Breck. Somehow."

Dryden and Doc Savage climbed into the steeple attic. Doc declined Dryden's offer of a cigarette.

Dryden grunted, said, "I guess I oughta quit smoking. Breck, too. Somebody might stick his head in downstairs and smell the tobacco sometime." He applied the flame of his cigarette lighter to his cigarette.

"Breckenridge," Doc said in a normal tone. "Can you hear me, Breck?"

Breckenridge, below watching the Soviet atomic storehouse through the telescope, evidently could not hear.

Dryden said, "If you want Breck, why not just raise your voice and—"

"I don't want him," Doc explained. "I just wanted to make sure he couldn't overhear us." Doc eyed Dryden thoughtfully. "Did you get rid of that revolver of yours?" He added pointedly, "The one you used to assassinate Nina Kirkegaard?"

"Lord!" Dryden was frightened. "Keep that quiet! If Breckenridge ever dreamed . . ."

The drifting cigarette smoke smarted Doc's eyes. He batted it away. "That's why I would hide that revolver, if I were you."

Dryden experienced a spell of violent coughing.

"By the way," Doc asked after it had subsided, "where is it?"

"In Poltov's pocket," Dryden said. "I put it there before we buried him."

"That was smart," Doc said.

"It was the best I could think of."

Dryden carefully snuffed out the cigarette to save until his lungs recovered from all the cold air they had breathed.

"When you going to tell Breckenridge about it?" Doc asked.

Dryden shuddered. "Never!"

"Breck is, as they say, a smart customer." Doc grew

speculative. "It might tone him down to find out his sweetheart, Nina Kirkegaard, was really Anna Gryahznyi, the one-woman reign of terror."

Apprehensively, Dryden seized Doc's arm. "God, don't tell him!" he gasped. "Breck would murder us both if he knew. He was practically in love with her."

"I didn't cause her death," Doc pointed out. "Not that I mourn her passing, either."

"You won't tell Breck?" Dryden was frantic. "For all I know, he'd desert his post just to make me look bad."

Doc eyed Dryden speculatively.

"I'll make you a deal," said Doc. "You tell me how you caught on she was Anna Gryahznyi, and I'll neglect to breathe a word about her demise to anyone."

Dryden nodded a hurried agreement. "You remember when you went off with that Reindeer-what-was-his-name, that Nenet? Well, Breck and I had a row over the girl. Breck was pretty nasty. He wanted me to know she was his. Meaning he'd already won her over." Dryden's face became red. "He waxed poetic about what he called her 'rare beauty.' To tell the truth, he came across as pretty asinine. Said even her flaws were exquisite. Breck went into some details. . . ." Dryden eyed the floor.

"Well?" asked Doc.

"One of the details was that missing earlobe," said Dryden. His neck turned scarlet. "That was why I insisted on hanging back that last time. I got to thinking about that wild theory of yours, and not trusting anyone. So I thought I'd find a way to run my fingers through Nina's—I mean Anna's—hair. I didn't fall for her, but I couldn't tell you that without Breck and the girl overhearing. Breck spilled the beans before I could see for myself."

"Breckenridge is no gentleman," said Doc. "A gentleman would never mention such personal matters. Luckily for all of us, he is no gentleman."

"When Breck spilled those particular beans," Dryden went on, "I knew what I had to do. I slipped into the hut when no one was looking. I caught her asleep. But not for long. She went at me like a tigress. Look."

Dryden removed his parka hood to expose an ear. It was red and rapidly swelling. Doc recalled that Dryden was bleeding from the head when he had emerged from the hut.

"She did this to the U.S. agents she killed in Moscow," Dryden explained. "She does this to all her intended victims. Like earmarking a steer for slaughter, I guess. I didn't give her a chance to add me to her list of victims."

Feeling his own still-hard earlobe, Doc Savage shuddered at the memory of that last encounter in the dark with the deadly Red Widow.

"There are a few things I still don't get," Dryden said quietly. "Such as who *did* come aboard the *Norge Pike* at Tromso?"

"Poltov seemed to believe it was Anna Gryahznyi," Doc said. "Working back from that one fact, we can assume he never knew his partner, Nina, was the notorious Anna. Poltov probably received instructions from Moscow that she was going to join his crew en route. A ringer may have come aboard at Tromso, to steer suspicions away from Nina. One of the reasons that there are no known photos or records of Anna Gryahznyi is that she sometimes operated under other identities, ones carefully built up over a period of years."

"So Nina Kirkegaard was just a cover, eh?"

"Possibly." Doc's flake-gold eyes were distant. "Perhaps Nina was the real Anna, and Anna Gryahznyi was the fictitious identity. We may never know."

"I hadn't thought of that," Dryden said, letting a pent breath escape his lungs. "Why do you think she strung along with us the way she did?"

"Simple. To see where we went, and what we were up to. That time she ambushed me in the cabin, she was no doubt looking for documents when she searched me. Not finding any, it made more sense to let us go on believing we were the bellwethers—when all along she was prodding us like sheep to the slaughter pen."

"I guess this goes a little ways toward getting you off

the hook," Dryden remarked. "At least as far as that Kremlin death sentence goes."

"More than a little," Doc told him. "Before I left New York, Dwight Wilcox promised me he would raise a diplomatic ruckus with the Soviet over that slight matter. When the first Moonwinx transmission was answered a few minutes ago, Wilcox was at the other end. He had succeeded."

Dryden grabbed Doc's arm excitedly. "They lifted it?"

Doc shook his head. "Officially, they deny there is any such death order. But Wilcox painted a picture for them of such dire diplomatic consequences should I fall victim to any assassination attempt that they went to great and circuitous lengths to assure him that no Red agents had any such orders."

"Can you trust that?"

"According to Wilcox, the indirect assurances came just after I left New York. It would explain why Anna Gryahznyi returned to Bergen, and her Nina identity."

"It would at that," Dryden said effusively. "Congratulations."

"Save them," Doc said.

"Why?"

"The new Kremlin attitude won't save any of us from a firing squad if we're captured as spies while in Soviet territory."

Both men were thoughtful for a time. It was a sobering item to contemplate.

"Say," said Dryden, suddenly. "When exactly did *you* find out Nina was Anna Gryahznyi?"

"Just now," said Doc.

Later, Doc Savage slipped out for some fresh air.

The bronze man looked up at the full moon overhead. It was like a bowl of ice, blue and white and faintly transparent. The man in the moon peered down wisely. It seemed to wink at him. He winked back.

Somehow, Doc knew that they would make the submarine rendezvous all right. With the demise of Anna

Gryahznyi, a great weight had been lifted from his shoulders.

More importantly, a terrible Sword of Damocles had been lifted from the shoulders of the free world.

Thanks to Moonwinx.

AFTERWORD

At the end of 1944, Lester Dent penned a Doc Savage novel entitled *Flight Into Fear*. His editor at that time happily accepted the story, but she rejected the title. The novel was published as *King Joe Cay*.

When *King Joe Cay* appeared the following summer, Dent, apparently miffed by the title change, submitted a *new* Doc Savage story called *Flight Into Fear*. Once again, the story was retitled for publication in *Doc Savage* magazine. This time, it was called *Terror and the Lonely Widow*.

Lester Dent obviously thought *Flight Into Fear* made for a great Doc Savage title, but he got the message, and submitted no more Docs under that name. So how does it happen that the 60th anniversary of the Man of Bronze is being celebrated by a previously unpublished Doc adventure written by Lester Dent and entitled *Flight Into Fear*?

The story behind this new Lester Dent Doc Savage novel is a fascinating, if convoluted, one.

Lester Dent's writing career spanned some thirty years, 1929 to 1959, and is roughly divisible into three ten-year phases. The 1930s, in which he was exclusively a pulp magazine writer, the 1940s, in which he attempted to expand beyond the pulps while continuing to write his Doc novels, and the 1950s, the final decade of his life—the post-Doc Savage period—in which he was a gentleman-farmer, businessman, and occasional writer.

Each decade, it seemed, held its professional disappointments. But the 1940s ended on a doubly bitter note for the writer from La Plata, Missouri. The cancellation of *Doc Savage* in 1949 and the simultaneous unraveling of his fledgling career as a hardcover mystery novelist left Dent without a regular income or steady markets for his storytelling skills. And while he was relentlessly writing formulaic stories aimed at such slick magazine markets as *Liberty, Colliers's* and *The Saturday Evening Post*, sales were scanty.

Fortunately, Dent was prepared for this market drought. In 1948, seeing Doc winding down, Dent launched Airviews, an aerial photography service which supported him during the transitional post-Doc Savage period.

Then his father died in June, 1950, forcing Dent to undertake a responsibility he never wanted to assume: running the family farm. Although he put off dealing with it for over a year, Dent, who had grown up on farms and ranches, found himself immersed in the kind of work-a-day farm chores he thought he had put behind himself forever. Yet he was determined not to let the family farm swallow him at the expense of his goals.

Through his long-time New York agent, Willis Kingsley Wing, Dent plunged back into novel writing early in 1951. He cast his eye on two markets, the slicks and the hardcover book publishers. As for the pulps, they were shambling old dinosaurs in the new television age, and represented a dead end for a working writer.

Dent's first effort was a breakout mainstream novel, *Time Has Four Faces*, which focused on the schemes of a willful young woman bent on corrupting twin brothers. Houghton Mifflin saw in the proposed book a major novel by a unique voice, and quickly put Dent under contract to complete it.

By a happy stroke of coincidence, Dent was simultaneously contacted by Fawcett's Gold Medal line, which had been showcasing such former pulp colleagues as John D. MacDonald, Steve Fisher, Bruno Fischer, and his former Doc ghost, Ryerson Johnson, and asked to join their growing stable of paperback original writers.

For Fawcett, Dent penned an unusual—for him—book called *Cry at Dusk*. Not quite a mystery, but with adventurous overtones, it represented a departure for Dent—especially inasmuch as the Fawcett formula called for liberal doses of sex. He self-mockingly called the effort a "boudoir chiller."

Sex scenes were not Dent's forte. Fawcett kept shipping the novel back with instructions to add more sex. Grudgingly, Dent complied and Fawcett, satisfied with the result and eager to make Lester Dent a star in the exploding paperback field, requested a followup.

Dent proposed a story about a cynical knockabout named Dwight Banner, who becomes involved in Balkan political intrigues, and overthrows a corrupt dictator only to become a tyrant himself. Fawcett passed on the proposal, so Dent retooled his protagonist for a story set against the backdrop of the Korean War and heightened East-West tensions, which he called *Death Sentence*. Electrified by his powerful opening chapters, Fawcett contracted Dent to complete the book.

Meanwhile, Dent was having trouble with *Time Has Four Faces*. He missed his first delivery date—the first deadline he had muffed in two decades of writing, he admitted ruefully. Unfortunately, Dent was never to finish it. The unexpected death of his mother in August, 1952, knocked the motivation out of the prolific powerhouse as no event before had. He was in the midst of writing his second Fawcett novel, now called *Kill a Red Lady*, when it happened.

Unlike *Cry at Dusk*, this was a story more to Dent's personal taste, a Cold War suspense book that harkened back to *The Red Spider*, a 1948 Doc Savage which was buried by the final Doc editor. It was exactly the kind of thing he would have been writing for *Doc Savage* had the magazine still been going in 1952.

Concerned about Fawcett's reputation with other writers for requesting automatic rewrites, Dent sent the draft he had just completed to his editor, in case there were problems.

There were. Fawcett shot the story back to him with a long list of suggestions for revision. Dent normally balked at rewriting his books, but he buckled down to do the job. Fawcett had huge hopes for *Kill a Red Lady*, and for Dent's future with them.

Finally, in the spring of 1953, it was done.

Dent's rewrite was greeted with great displeasure. It was not entirely Dent's fault. In the intervening months, Fawcett had come under sharp criticism over the sexual explicitness of their Gold Medal line. Dent, preoccupied with his personal grief, and out of touch with his editor, had been unwittingly writing to now-abandoned guidelines.

By mutual agreement, Dent and his editor decided too much work would be needed to make the book suitable to the new publishing realities. Indeed, it would virtually have to be started from scratch. The project was shelved. For reasons of his own, Dent never attempted to market the manuscript again.

After he and Fawcett parted company over *Kill a Red Lady*, Dent, unused to rejections and still grieving, lost interest in writing for some time. He returned the *Time Has Four Faces* advance, effectively abandoning that book, as well.

But in 1956, his writing ambitions stirred anew. Two more novels were written, but only one sold. He returned to work fitfully on *Time Has Four Faces*, in which Houghton Mifflin remained keenly interested. But Dent never managed to finish it.

The highlight of Dent's third decade of writing—if not the culmination of his entire career—was the publication of "Savage Challenge" in *The Saturday Evening Post* a scant year before he passed away in 1959. Making the *Post* had been a cherished dream of Dent's going back to his earliest Doc Savage days.

Although Lester Dent's final writing years were difficult ones, he continued to write to the very end. Upon his death, a notebook was found beside his hospital bed. In it he had begun to write, in longhand, a new *Post* story, "The Day of Crow Tails." In his own way, Lester Dent died with his boots on.

The events surrounding *Kill a Red Lady* all took place long before my involvement with Doc Savage. Dent was finishing the book about the time I was being born, in fact.

I first became aware of the existence of *Kill a Red*

Lady during a 1978 research foray of the Lester Dent manuscripts. So when Bantam Books asked me to write a second group of Doc Savage novels, I naturally thought of that story and obtained a copy of the manuscript from the Lester Dent Collection housed in the Western Historical Manuscript Collection of the University of Missouri at Columbia. All of Dent's manuscripts and papers had been donated to that respository by Norma Dent in 1986.

I had a dim awareness of the plot and wondered if it was convertible into a new Doc Savage novel. Up to that point, I'd written Docs from complete outlines, unfinished plots, and novel fragments. The thought of having a finished novel to work from was a tremendous opportunity to create a new Doc Savage novel that was something more than a pastiche.

Kill a Red Lady did not disappoint me. Unlike much of his later writing, it had the trademark Dent combination of vivid, hardboiled style and quirky humor. While it was hopelessly dated on its own terms, that very quality made it perfect for Doc Savage.

The novel, of course, had its rough spots. The obligatory sex scenes would all have to go. The rest was very comfortably in the mold of the later Doc novels, and as I read along, I realized that the specific motivation of Dent's original hero, Banner, could be grafted onto Doc simply by making this a direct followup to the events of *The Red Spider*, in which Doc exposed the truth behind the Soviet Union's fledgling atomic bomb program, and embarrassed the Kremlin.

Make no mistake, a great deal of rewriting, pruning, and editing proved necessary. But I tried to do it with an eye to preserving as much of the original as feasible. In the end, the finished book is probably close to ninety percent the way Dent originally wrote it. I added only two new chapters. One of my own, and one taken from an earlier Dent draft of the story. Both were necessary to firmly establish the protagonist as Doc Savage. (I leave it to Doc Savage scholars out there to figure out which chapters those are.)

I did make a point of taking out all references to the Korean War and other topical 1952–53 events, so that the story fits into the Doc Savage chronology after *The Red Spider* but before the final Doc novel *Up From Earth's Center*. I prefer to let Doc's recorded adventures end where Dent ended them, and not drag the Man of Bronze into the cynical 1950s.

One amusing, and ultimately fortunate, result of there being so many extant drafts of *Kill a Red Lady* was my discovery—months after I'd finished my rewrite of the original manuscript—that I had *not* been working from the actual final draft as I had believed.

A comparison of the two showed me that the draft I had used did not greatly differ from the true final draft, and where it did, I was inclined to favor the earlier text. In essence, I went with the pure Dent draft of the story and not the obligatory Fawcett-directed rewrite.

All I needed, in the end, was a suitable title.

Kill a Red Lady seemed an inappropriate title for a Doc novel, inasmuch as the bronze man is pledged never to kill. So a new title was in order. Dent's earlier working title, *Death Sentence*, was perfect—except that I had already penned a Destroyer novel under that title. True, there was a certain odd appeal to having authored—or in this case co-authored—two separate novels called *Death Sentence* under two different bylines, but I decided to spare possible future bibliographers the resultant migraines.

So what to call it? The earliest working title, *My Banner Is Blood*, definitely didn't work. I brainstormed, made a list of titles, but none quite appealed to me.

Then I recalled Dent's misadventures with the title *Flight Into Fear*. Perfect!

And here it is: A largely Lester Dent Doc Savage novel rescued from obscurity and carrying a title which I'm sure he would have heartily approved. What could be more fitting for the 60th anniversary of the greatest adventure hero of all time?

—WILL MURRAY

Continue the all-new series written by Will Murray, writing as Kenneth Robeson, with an adventure story based on an unpublished outline by Lester Dent.

THE WHISTLING WRAITH

The disappearance of a Balkan king from a limousine en route to the White House brings Doc Savage to Washington D.C., where he becomes embroiled in a mystery so gargantuan it baffles even the brilliant Man of Bronze!

Here is the exciting first-chapter preview from THE WHISTLING WRAITH.

The King of Merida vanished before the eyes of the entire world.

In truth, there were perhaps less than three hundred witnesses to the king's actual vanishment, but one of them happened to be a newsreel cameraman, and the inexplicable event wound up being repeated in movie theaters all over the world in subsequent weeks. So, there was more truth in the statement than falsehood, technically.

The king—his royal name was Egil Goz the First—had come to Washington, District of Columbia, for one of those elegant soirees known as a state dinner. The king was to dine with the President of the United States and other dignitaries. His homespun steak and baked potato dinner was never consumed.

King Goz's motorcade pulled up to the White House at a little past five in the afternoon. The machine was heavy, its sides armor-plated, glass bulletproofed, and tonneau windows curtained to protect His Highness from the stares of commoners. The king had enemies. Particularly in a neighboring state.

The official car was driven by a liveried chauffeur. When the car pulled up, a footman in a uniform more appropriate to an opera than a state affair stepped smartly from the front seat where he had been riding beside the chauffeur, and opened the back door.

The footman stood with his back ramrod straight, his head thrown back and his eyes looking—seemingly—at nothing, while he waited for King Goz to step forth, resplendent in his bemedaled official uniform. Although King Goz had started out on the road of life as a war chieftain, he was a thoroughly modern king. No regal robes or showy crowns for him.

King Goz did not step out. Minutes crawled past. Overeager newshounds wasted flashbulbs. The lone newsreel cameraman cursed to himself as he wasted expensive film. The President of the United States looked at his watch with polite interest.

Finally, the footman was forced to unbend his military posture and look inside the limousine tonneau.

He gave a squeak in his native tongue and suddenly there was pandemonium.

King Goz could not be found!

Excitement boiled around the limousine. The seat cushions were thrown about. The floorboards examined. Dignified aides suffered the indignity of getting down on hand and knee to look under the chassis. They even checked the trunk, even though witnesses—and there were many—clearly recollected the king entering the limousine outside Blair House, where visiting dignitaries enjoyed American hospitality.

When questioned by District of Columbia police, the other passengers of the limousine—the chauffeur and the befuddled footman—insisted that at no time did the limousine stop to deposit a passenger. Of this, they were quite certain, even vociferous.

One, however, did recall stopping at a light. This was the stiff-faced chauffeur.

"Notice anything suspicious?" a cop inquired.

The chauffeur considered this a moment. Then he remarked in a remarkably unaccented voice, "I do recall a whistling."

"Whistling?"

"Yes, it was rather a melancholy air."

The footman, too, suddenly recalled hearing the whistling. He could not tell from whence it had originated. But he, too, remembered a whistled refrain that was infinitely sad in its strains.

The police next asked for an official photograph, with the idea of manufacturing missing posters for telephotoing purposes.

They received an unpleasant surprise. There were no photographs of King Goz. The point was pressed and a member of the king's anxious retinue remembered a solitary snapshot, which was speedily dispatched to Washington by air mail.

It proved to have been taken when King Goz was a mere lad—a beardless mountain youth dressed in flowing native clothes. It was quite a handsome photograph, showing that the future monarch possessed a certain warrior flair even then.

Unfortunately, it was useless for the purpose required.

That was on Tuesday.

Doc Savage arrived in Washington the following Thursday to look into the matter.

His arrival was quiet. This was necessary, because everybody, almost, knew who Doc Savage was.

It did not stay quiet for long.

Doc Savage arrived by passenger plane at the Washington airport. Normally, Clark Savage, Jr.—to use his given name—seldom resorted to public conveyance. By repute, he owned a fleet of airplanes, and was an expert pilot. The fact that he himself had designed the fleet—which consisted of bronze-painted marvels of aeronautical engineering instantly recognizable to anyone familiar with his reputation—probably had something to do with his choice. Doc Savage was the stuff that newspaper copy was made out of.

Doc Savage was spotted by an eagle-eyed newshawk as he deplaned. The airport was awash in reporters. Some had staked out the place in hope of ambushing arriving dignitaries come to the nation's capital to gather first-hand accounts of the inexplicable regal vanishment. Others were themselves just arriving. The disappearance of King Goz was hot copy.

"Is *that* who I think it is?" gulped a surprised scribe.

"Is who?"

"The tall chap coming down the air stairs."

The other man emitted a bleat of surprise. "I'll be!" he said with the enthusiasm of a man who smells a story. "The Man of Mystery himself."

A third individual joined them, and asked, "Who?"

"The lad they claim is a human scientific product," the first scribe explained. "The man who was trained from the cradle by the great scientists of the world until he was greater than any of them—a kind of superman. And he was trained so as to be a kind of modern knight in an armor of science to go around the world helping people and righting wrongs."

The second observer whistled. "So *that's* the fellow they claim is probably the most remarkable living human being," he muttered.

"Yeah," said the first. "Blazes! I thought he'd be an old guy. He's ten years younger'n I am, bet you."

"Who are you talking about?" asked the exasperated third journalist.

"Doc Savage."

"Oh." The befuddled scribe had heard of Doc Savage.

Presently, the object of their attention entered the terminal building.

He was a tall man bundled in a tan gabardine coat, who towered over his fellow passengers. A gray hat was pulled low, the snap brim throwing a shadow over his face, in an attempt to mask the distinctiveness of his features. It was a futile gesture.

Even bundled up as he was, the amazing nature of his muscular development was evident. The sinews stood in great bars under the fine-textured skin of his neck. Huge cables sprang out in his hands as he walked along. They indicated fabulous physical strength.

Long exposure to tropical sun, coupled with the use of a solar health radiator which he himself had perfected and which had all the beneficial qualities of natural sunlight, had given Doc Savage's skin a bronze hue which caused him frequently to be called the Man of Bronze.

This distinctive bronze coloration all but shouted his identity.

The scribes plucked copy pencils and note pads from about their persons and made a beeline for the big bronze man.

They were blocked by a sudden wall of men.

"One side, pal," invited the first newspaperman in an indignant voice. "We're the Fourth Estate."

The blocking wall of men did not move. They were polite, but very firm about their not moving. They looked tough. Not in the gangster manner, but tough nevertheless.

"Please step away," one invited in a no-nonsense tone

of voice. But for his crisp suitcoat, he might have been a Marine.

"Press, see?" the anxious scribe insisted. Press cards in hatbands were indicated with stabbing fingers.

One of the blocking men removed his billfold and offered it open, for the belligerent newshound to see.

He got a gander at an ornate badge, stepped back and croaked, "G-men!"

Thereafter, the press contingent became as polite as the human wall of what were obviously government agents. They made room as the agents approached the big bronze fellow and, after exchanging low words, surrounded him protectively.

Doc Savage was efficiently escorted from the building.

A few newspapermen were so bold as to shout questions to the departing bronze man. No answers were forthcoming. No one seemed surprised.

"Well, for the love of Mike!" said one of the press men. "Doc Savage is working with the Feds on this thing."

"So what are we waiting for? Let's hotfoot it after them."

The reporters charged through the busy terminal to the taxi line outside. They spilled out, heads turned every which way. One spied the big bronze man ducking into a nondescript sedan in a line of nondescript sedans.

"There!"

They rushed the column of machines.

One of the federal men, seeing them approach, flashed his badge and growled, "Any man found to interfere with Uncle Sam's business will find his pants clapped in the local pokey."

That seemed to settle that. The reporters, wearing disappointed faces, watched the line of sedans bear the mystery man, Doc Savage, away.

The scribes then found a bar and began swapping yarns about Doc Savage, hoping to bring to light something new and unpublished which they could give their city editors in lieu of the story they had not gotten.

Doc Savage, their talk disclosed, was quite a remarkable fellow, being something, in fact, of a combination of mental wizard, physical superman, and inventive genius. Concocting wild stories about Doc Savage's fabulous feats, it developed, was a favorite passtime with the tabloid quota of the gathering.

Doc Savage, they all agreed, was a strange fellow who went to the far corners of the world on the rather thankless business of helping other people out of trouble, righting wrongs, aiding the oppressed, and punishing evildoers. It might have been noted that several reporters did not believe this muddlesome matter of the missing king of Merida was really Doc Savage's business at all. The king was hardly oppressed. In fact, he was something of a benign tyrant, having been elected president in a popular vote and, after a suitable interval, declaring himself king. But all present admitted Doc Savage was a man of mystery, and anything was possible where he was concerned.

One thing was noteworthy about the confab. No one spoke deprecatingly of Doc Savage. They all seemed to agree that he was a personage of great ability.

One person who was an avid listener was a woman, or girl—if girls are still girls in their early twenties.

She was a little mouse of a girl. She wore a mousey coat, a mousey hat and her stringy hair was remindful of a rodent that had been washed until all the color had leached out of its fur. She had followed them out of the airport terminal and been privy to their reaction to the unexpected arrival of Doc Savage. No one had paid her any mind, and now she was listening intently.

A reporter was yarning enthusiastically now. "I heard that this Doc Savage was once offered the crown of a Balkan country, not far from Merida, but turned it down cold. And there was a princess gonna be thrown in with the deal, too."

"Imagine! Jilting a princess!"

"How thrilling—if true," the girl murmured. She was noticed then. Not many looked at her twice. She was that plain. But reporters are afflicted by an innate curiosity, and noticing the press card affixed to the lapel of her spring coat, asked after her identity.

Her name, she said, was Barbara Bland. With the Denver *Globe*. Everyone had heard of the *Globe*. No one had heard of her.

The conversation veered back to the subject at hand. Some one remembered that a magazine had just published an extensive article on Doc Savage and one of the journalists went to fetch a copy off a news stand.

The magazine—it was of the sensational true-crime variety—rapidly became dog-eared as it was passed around, reporters taking turns reading the most interesting portions aloud. More than one scribbled notes for later use.

After the young woman reporter had absorbed her fill of the topic at hand, she slipped away and found a telephone booth, where she fed a nickel into the slot and whispered a number to the answering operator.

She continued to whisper after she had reached her party. Her manner was clipped. She might have been dictating copy to a rewrite man on the other end.

"Doc Savage has just arrived." She paused while that sunk in. "Federal agents met him at the airport and took him away. There is no doubt but why he is in town."

The voice on the other end of the line was firm, cultured and masculine.

"If anyone can find the king," said the voice, "it is this man, Savage. He may represent the opportunity we have been waiting for. Attempt to learn all that can be learned."

"Understood," the girl said, and terminated the connection.

On her way out the door, she passed the reporters. They were still engaged in the swapping of yarns about Doc Savage. If anything, their talk was wilder than it had been.

The girl reporter, Barbara Bland, gave a tiny snort of disbelief as she walked by. It was plain she took the reportorial tall tales with a very large grain of sodium.

The Federal agents who had taken charge of Doc Savage were respectful. He might have been their superior. In a way, he was. Doc Savage held an honorary rank of special agent with the Justice Department's Bureau of Investigation, in return for certain assistances rendered in the past.

They first took him to the scene of the disappearance—or rather to the spot where it had been discovered, in front of the White House door.

From there, the bronze man backtracked to the intersection where the eerie whistling had been heard, according to the chauffeur and footman. It was an open intersection, literally around the corner from the White House. The circuitous route the kingly motorcade had taken was evidently for purposes of making a dramatic entrance and impressing the cameras. The king could have walked to his assignation in less time than it took to be driven.

At the intersection, there were no objects or buildings which might have produced a whistling sound, whether mechanically or through the action of wind. There was not even a whistle-blowing traffic cop stationed at any corner.

If the bronze man made any discoveries, he gave no outward indication.

"Take me to the king's limousine," he requested.

The vehicle was garaged in the Department of Justice Building. It was a short walk from Blair House to the Justice Building—virtually everything in official Washington is within walking distance of everything else—but they drove, anyway.

There, the bronze man examined the machine. The hood and boot had been thrown up and the doors all lay open. Additionally, fenders had been removed for inspection of the wheels and chassis.

After a cursory examination of these cavities, the bronze man fell to investigating the tonneau into which the King of Merida had stepped, not to be seen again. He lifted cushions, pried up the floor coverings and conducted what appeared to be a very thorough search.

He rolled the windows up and down, examining the thick, bulletproof glass. There was a glass partition between tonneau and driver's compartment. This, he cranked up and down as well. The speaking tube came in for scrutiny, too.

The Federal men watched in silence. Their orders

were not to interfere with the bronze man who was Doc Savage. This had come from the Director himself.

When he was finished in the back, Doc Savage fell to examining the driver's compartment. He was not at this long when an unexpected sound permeated the garage confines.

It was a trill, low and melodious. Tuneless, it roved the scale, sounding in the confines of the garage like the sound of a small breeze in a chill Arctic ice pack. It hardly seemed to be a product of human vocal cords, but there was no other possible source. The Federal agents found themselves looking at one another doubtfully as if suspecting one of their number to be the author of the elusive sound.

Doc Savage suddenly emerged from his study, and the sound trailed off. Only then did it occur to the agents that the strange bronze man might have been responsible for the nebulous tremolo.

Doc straightened, holding something between metallic thumb and forefinger.

An agent was so bold as to ask, "Have you found something, Mr. Savage?"

"Hairs."

"Eh?"

"Red hairs."

The agents exchanged blank looks. The royal car had been examined for fingerprints, blood, and other forensic clues. No one had thought to look for hairs, or if they happened upon any, would have attached great importance to them. Hairs fall out of perfectly healthy heads all the time.

But the mysterious bronze man evidently thought the hairs he discovered had significance. The G-men looked at the hairs. They were short and thick and definitely reddish. Almost like copper wire.

"Must belong to the chauffeur," said an agent promptly. "He was a redhead, by reports."

Doc reached into his coat and from somewhere produced a metal phial with a screw cap. He unscrewed the cap and let the metallic red hairs drop into the phial. Recapping it, he stowed it back on his person.

Then Doc Savage said, "There were numerous press

photographers and a newsreel cameraman present when the king's limousine stopped before the White House."

"There were," an agent admitted.

"I would like to see these," Doc said.

"All of them?" gulped the agent.

"All."

It was not as difficult an undertaking as the Federal agents expected. They had already on file several sample photographs and when none proved illuminating, further requests were abandoned. It was assumed that the king had disappeared en route to the state dinner and no clues were to be found among the photographic record any more than a photograph of a patch of sky where lightning had appeared a day before would reveal any trace of the flash.

Too, the name of Doc Savage opened many doors. The photos began arriving at the Department of Justice Building, along with requests for interviews. The photographs were accepted. The interview requests were not.

A few magazines and newspapers, hearing of this lack of reciprocity, made noises about withholding their photos.

The editors in question received personal telephone calls from no less than the Director of the Bureau of Investigation of the Department of Justice. The photographs were sheepishly surrendered.

In a projection room in the Justice Department, Doc Savage was studying the photographs. Oddly enough, he had not removed his hat and his fine-textured features were not readily visible to onlookers. A person familiar with the bronze man's methods would have found this behavior uncharacteristic. Doc Savage seldom wore a hat.

"The newsreel is here," announced a government clerk.

The bronze man left off his examination. The reel was loaded and the room darkened.

They watched intently.

The so-called raw footage was brief. Ragged. It depicted the king's limousine arriving, the chauffeur and footman visible through the windscreen. The film darkened and brightened again, this time showing a different angle.

The footman emerged from the ostentatious machine,

went to the rear door and threw it open. The footage dwelt on the open door for what seemed an interminable interval until the footman, impatient, bent and looked within.

The rest was chaos. Milling reporters and police. A shot of the waiting president and other dignitaries. It was difficult to imagine how the footage had been spliced into anything coherent, but it had, and was already packing in theater-goers around the civilized world.

After the lights had come on again, Doc Savage stood up and said, "I think the chauffeur might help clear up the mystery."

"Don't you want to see the film again, Mr. Savage?"

"Not necessary," replied Doc.

They went to the dignified hostelry where the chauffeur—and the rest of the king's retinue—were ensconced and asked for him. The Merida party had long since departed the official hospitality of Blair House, to await the results of the official investigation.

There they were met by a stern-faced white-haired man in an ostentatious crimson uniform who carried about him a very dignified air. The medals on his chest were many.

"I am General Graul Frontenac," he said by way of introduction. Even his voice had a stiffness.

"This is Doc Savage," one of the G-Men said, indicating the bronze giant.

The general was burdened by the stiff-backed carriage of the European military man to whom soldiering is a point of family honor.

At the mention of the name Doc Savage, he lost some of his stiff-necked bearing.

He was wearing a monocle in one eye and it popped out, saved from extinction only by a long black cord anchored to his gold uniform braid, which was profuse. The general clamped the monocle back into his eye and employed it to give Doc Savage a thorough going over. He was very bold in the manner in which he did this.

"The Director personally asked that Mr. Savage enter the investigation," one of the Federal men said, hoping to dispel the awkwardness of the moment.

General Frontenac clicked his heels together and executed a stiff bow.

"I am honored to meet the great *Domnule* Savage," he purred.

If the bronze man was impressed by this morsel of flattery, he did not acknowledge it. Instead, he said, "We would like to question the chauffeur who was driving the limousine on the night the king vanished."

"But he has already been questioned thoroughly."

"We would like to question him further, please."

Behind the monocle, the weaker eye of General Frontenac of Merida swam blearily.

"As you wish," he said, snapping his fingers at two courtiers who rushed ahead to pave the way. "Let us go to him now."

They were led to a suite elsewhere on the same floor. The courtiers had thrown open the door and stood waiting impassively.

They entered. The room was unoccupied. General Frontenac pointed his monocle at the two trembling courtiers.

"Where is he?" he snapped.

"W-we do not k-know, General," one stammered.

"W-we have not seen him today," the other gulped.

Red-faced, General Frontenac demanded of the courtiers, "When was he last seen?"

The courtiers looked blank. Neither, it turned out, could recall when he last laid eyes on the missing chauffeur to the missing king.

"Find him!" General Frontenac thundered, his face crimsoning until it threatened to rival the blood hue of his sumptuous uniform.

The chauffeur was nowhere to be found. It was not surprising. In the land from which the chauffeur had come, men had lost their heads for less offense than misplacing a head of state.

"Ce plictistor! How vexing!" said General Frontenac, after a complete search had turned up no trace of the man. "This is very strange." He turned his monocled eye in the bronze man's direction. "Tell me, Savage, do you suppose

the strange fate that befell our glorious monarch might have taken the chauffeur, as well?"

The bronze man did not answer. Indeed, he seemed to not have heard the question. His eyes were questing about the chauffeur's room. It was quite lavish.

He turned abruptly, and said, "The footman, if you do not mind."

Again, General Frontenac snapped his fingers and courtiers rushed ahead to, presumably, announce them.

Why they would have to be announced to a flunky of the low status of a footman no one thought to ask. Or if they did, the question was never put forth.

The courtiers came rushing back, white-faced and winded. They talked over one another in a violent effort to be the first to break the news.

Finally, the plainly exasperated general demanded of one, simultaneously hushing the other with a curt chop of his hand, "*Cum?* What is it? Speak!"

"The footman," gasped the courtier who had been given leave to speak, "is dead."

"Dead?"

"Murdered."

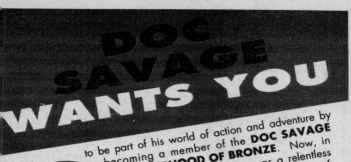

THE LEGENDARY MAN OF BRONZE—IN A
THRILLING NEW ADVENTURE SERIES!

DOC SAVAGE

❏ **PYTHON ISLE, Kenneth Robeson**
29357-5 $4.50/$5.50 in Canada
After more than forty years, Doc is back in an all-new novel based
on an unpublished outline by Doc Savage's original creator. A
mysteriously vanished aviator returns and a mysterious woman
in a battered plane with plates of pure gold embroil Doc Savage
in a raging battle for control of the lost secret of Python Isle.

❏ **ESCAPE FROM LOKI, Philip José Farmer**
29093-2 $4.50/$5.50 in Canada
A brilliant supervillain has the ultimate secret weapon to assure
victory for the Kaiser or obliterate all of mankind! Hugo Award
winner Philip José Farmer, superstar of speculative fiction and
author of biographical studies of Doc Savage, now adds to the
legend of the Man of Bronze in this adventure of Doc's early days.

❏ **WHITE EYES, Kenneth Robeson**
29561-6 $4.99/$5.99 in Canada
An insidious wave of dead bodies turn up around the city. Doc
Savage soon discovers that the mysterious plague is the result
of a scheme to unite all of New York's criminal elements and
seize the fabled Mayan wealth of the Man of Bronze.

❏ **THE FRIGHTENED FISH, Kenneth Robeson**
29748-1 $4.50/$5.50 in Canada
The World is about to lurch into the next global war, and Doc
Savage must defeat his most loathsome adversary yet, someone trained by the same teacher, possessing the same genius;
someone he has fought before.

INDIANA ── JONES

Bold adventurer, swashbuckling explorer, Indy unravels the mysteries of the past at a time when dreams could still come true. Now, in an all-new series by Rob MacGregor, officially licensed from Lucasfilm, we will learn what shaped Indiana Jones into the hero he is today!

❑ **INDIANA JONES AND THE PERIL AT DELPHI**
28931-4 $4.99/$5.99 in Canada
Indy descends into the bottomless pit of the serpent god of the Order of Pythia. Will Indy find the source of Pythia's powers—or be sacrificed at their altar?

❑ **INDIANA JONES AND THE DANCE OF THE GIANTS**
29035-5 $4.99/$5.99 in Canada
Indy takes off on an action-packed chase from the peril-filled caves of Scotland to the savage dance of the giants at Stonehenge—where Merlin's secret will finally be revealed.

❑ **INDIANA JONES AND THE SEVEN VEILS**
29334-6 $4.99/$5.99 in Canada
With his trusty bullwhip in hand, Indy sets out for the wilds of the Amazon to track a lost city and a mythical red-headed race who may be the descendants of ancient Celtic Druids.

❑ **INDIANA JONES AND THE GENESIS DELUGE**
29502-0 $4.99/$5.99 in Canada
Indy sets out for Istanbul and Mount Ararat, fabled location of Noah's Ark, when various forces try to bar him from finding a certain 950-year-old boat-builder...
